'The very personification of SF [Arthur C. Clarke] writes always with lucidity and candour, often with grace, sometimes with a cold, sharp evocativeness that has produced some of the most memorable images in SF'

The Encyclopedia of Science Fiction

'The most popular English SF writer in the world'

David G. Hartwell

'One of the colossi of SF'   John Clute

'More than any other SF author, Clarke has been faithful to a boyhood vision of science as a saviour of mankind, and of mankind as a race of potential gods destined for the stars. If Stapledon has successors, Clarke is the foremost . . . [*Rendezvous With Rama* is] memorable and at times magical . . . it is Clarke's ability to evoke in us a true sense of wonder at unfolding marvels which enlivens the work'

Brian W. Aldiss

D1628462

Also by Arthur C. Clarke

RENDEVOUS WITH RAMA

Arthur C. Clarke

The right of Arthur C. Clarke to be identified as the
author of this work has been asserted by him in accordance
with the Copyright, Designs and Patents Act 1988.

This edition published in Great Britain in 2006 by
Gollancz
An imprint of the Orion Publishing Group
Carmelite House, 50 Victoria Embankment,
London, EC4Y 0DZ
An Hachette Livre UK company

23 25 27 29 30 28 26 24 22

A CIP catalogue record for this book
is available from the British Library

ISBN 978 0 57507 733 1

Printed and bound in Great Britain by Clays Ltd, Elcograf S.p.A.

The Orion Publishing Group's policy is to use papers that
are natural, renewable and recyclable products and made
from wood grown in sustainable forests. The logging and
manufacturing processes are expected to conform to the
environmental regulations of the country of origin.

www.orionbooks.co.uk

to Sri Lanka
where I climbed
the Stairway of the Gods

1
Spaceguard

Sooner or later, it was bound to happen. On 30 June 1908, Moscow escaped destruction by three hours and four thousand kilometres – a margin invisibly small by the standards of the universe. Again, on 12 February 1947, yet another Russian city had a still narrower escape, when the second great meteorite of the twentieth century detonated less than four hundred kilometres from Vladivostok, with an explosion rivalling that of the newly invented uranium bomb.

In those days, there was nothing that men could do to protect themselves against the last random shots in the cosmic bombardment that had once scarred the face of the Moon. The meteorites of 1908 and 1947 had struck uninhabited wilderness; but by the end of the twenty-first century, there was no region left on Earth that could be safely used for celestial target practice. The human race had spread from pole to pole. And so, inevitably ...

At 09.46 GMT on the morning of 11 September, in the exceptionally beautiful summer of the year 2077, most of the inhabitants of Europe saw a dazzling fireball appear in the eastern sky. Within seconds it was brighter than the sun, and as it moved across the heavens – at first in utter silence – it left behind it a churning column of dust and smoke.

Somewhere above Austria it began to disintegrate, producing a series of concussions so violent that more than a million people had their hearing permanently damaged. They were the lucky ones.

Moving at fifty kilometres a second, a thousand tons of rock and metal impacted on the plains of northern Italy, destroying in a few flaming moments the labour of centuries. The cities of Padua and Verona were wiped from the face of the earth; and the last glories of Venice sank forever beneath the sea as the waters of the Adriatic came thundering landwards after the hammer-blow from space.

Six hundred thousand people died, and the total damage was more than a trillion dollars. But the loss to art, to history, to science – to the whole human race, for the rest of time – was beyond all computation. It was as if a great war had been fought and lost in a single morning; and few could draw much pleasure from the fact that, as the dust of destruction slowly settled, for months the whole world witnessed the most splendid dawns and sunsets since Krakatoa.

After the initial shock, mankind reacted with a determination and a unity that no earlier age could have shown. Such a disaster, it was realised, might not occur again for a thousand years – but it might occur tomorrow. And the next time, the consequences could be even worse.

Very well; *there would be no next time*.

A hundred years earlier a much poorer world, with far feebler resources, had squandered its wealth attempting to destroy weapons launched, suicidally, by mankind against itself. The effort had never been successful, but the skills acquired then had not been forgotten. Now they could be used for a far nobler purpose, and on an infinitely vaster stage. No meteorite large enough to cause catastrophe would ever again be allowed to breach the defences of Earth.

So began Project SPACEGUARD. Fifty years later – and in a way that none of its designers could ever have anticipated – it justified its existence.

2
Intruder

By the year 2130, the Mars-based radars were discovering new asteroids at the rate of a dozen a day. The SPACEGUARD computers automatically calculated their orbits, and stored away the information in their enormous memories, so that every few months any interested astronomer could have a look at the accumulated statistics. These were now quite impressive.

It had taken more than a hundred and twenty years to collect the first thousand asteroids, since the discovery of Ceres, largest of these tiny worlds, on the very first day of the nineteenth century. Hundreds had been found and lost and found again; they existed in such swarms that one exasperated astronomer had christened them 'vermin of the skies'. He would have been appalled to know that SPACEGUARD was now keeping track of half a million.

Only the five giants – Ceres, Pallas, Juno, Eunomia and Vesta – were more than two hundred kilometres in diameter; the vast majority were merely oversized boulders that would fit into a small park. Almost all moved in orbits that lay beyond Mars; only the few that came far enough sunwards to be a possible danger to Earth were the concern of SPACEGUARD. And not one in a thousand of these, during the entire future history of the solar system, would pass within a million kilometres of Earth.

The object first catalogued as 31/439, according to the year and the order of its discovery, was detected while still outside the orbit of Jupiter. There was nothing unusual about its location;

many asteroids went beyond Saturn before turning once more towards their distant master, the sun. And Thule II, most far-ranging of all, travelled so close to Uranus that it might well have been a lost moon of that planet.

But a first radar contact at such a distance was unprecedented; clearly, 31/439 must be of exceptional size. From the strength of the echo, the computers deduced a diameter of at least forty kilometres; such a giant had not been discovered for a hundred years. That it had been overlooked for so long seemed incredible.

Then the orbit was calculated, and the mystery was resolved – to be replaced by a greater one. 31/439 was not travelling on a normal asteroidal path, along an ellipse which it retraced with clockwork precision every few years. It was a lonely wanderer between the stars, making its first and last visit to the solar system – for it was moving so swiftly that the gravitational field of the sun could never capture it. It would flash inwards past the orbits of Jupiter, Mars, Earth, Venus and Mercury, gaining speed as it did so, until it rounded the sun and headed out once again into the unkown.

It was at this point that the computers started flashing their 'Hi there! We have something interesting' sign, and for the first time 31/439 came to the attention of human beings. There was a brief flurry of excitement at SPACEGUARD Headquarters, and the interstellar vagabond was quickly dignified by a name instead of a mere number. Long ago, the astronomers had exhausted Greek and Roman mythology; now they were working through the Hindu pantheon. And so 31/439 was christened Rama.

For a few days, the news media made a fuss of the visitor, but they were badly handicapped by the sparsity of information. Only two facts were known about Rama – its unusual orbit, and its approximate size. Even this was merely an educated guess, based upon the strength of the radar echo. Through the telescope, Rama still appeared as a faint, fifteenth magnitude star – much too small to show a visible disc. But as it plunged in towards the heart of the solar system, it would grow brighter and larger, month by month; before it vanished forever, the orbiting observatories would be able to gather more precise information about its shape and size. There was plenty of time, and perhaps during the next few years some spaceship on its ordinary business might be routed close enough to get good photographs. An actual rendezvous was most unlikely; the energy cost would be far too great to permit physical contact with an object cutting across the orbits of the planets at more than a hundred thousand kilometres an hour.

So the world soon forgot about Rama; but the astronomers did not. Their excitement grew with the passing months, as the new asteroid presented them with more and more puzzles.

First of all, there was the problem of Rama's light curve. It didn't have one.

All known asteroids, without exception, showed a slow variation in their brilliance, waxing and waning within a period of a few hours. It had been recognised for more than two centuries that this was an inevitable result of their spin, and their irregular shape. As they toppled end over end along their orbits the reflecting surfaces they presented to the sun were continually changing, and their brightness varied accordingly.

Rama showed no such changes. Either it was not spinning at all or it was perfectly symmetrical. Both explanations seemed equally unlikely.

There the matter rested for several months, because none of the big orbiting telescopes could be spared from their regular job of peering into the remote depths of the universe. Space astronomy was an expensive hobby, and time on a large instrument could easily cost a thousand dollars a minute. Dr William Stenton would never have been able to grab the Farside two-hundred-metre reflector for a full quarter of an hour, if a more important programme had not been temporarily derailed by the failure of a fifty cent capacitor. One astronomer's bad luck was his good fortune.

Bill Stenton did not know what he had caught until the next day, when he was able to get computer time to process his results. Even when they were finally flashed on his display screen, it took him several minutes to understand what they meant.

The sunlight reflected from Rama was not, after all, absolutely constant in its intensity. There was a very small variation – hard to detect, but quite unmistakable, and extremely regular. Like all the other asteroids, Rama was indeed spinning. But whereas the normal 'day' for an asteroid was several hours, Rama's was only four *minutes*.

Dr Stenton did some quick calculations, and found it hard to believe the results. At its equator, this tiny world must be spinning at more than a thousand kilometres an hour; it would be rather unhealthy to attempt a landing anywhere except at the poles. The centrifugal force at Rama's equator must be powerful enough to flick any loose objects away from it at an acceleration of almost one gravity. Rama was a rolling stone that could never have gathered any cosmic moss; it was surprising that such a body had managed to hold itself together, and had not long ago shattered into a million fragments.

An object forty kilometres across, with a rotation period of only four minutes – where did that fit into the astronomical scheme of things? Dr Stenton was a somewhat imaginative man, a little too prone to jump to conclusions. He now jumped to one which gave him a very uncomfortable few minutes indeed.

The only specimen of the celestial zoo that fitted this description was a collapsed star. Perhaps Rama was a dead sun – a madly spinning sphere of neutronium, every cubic centimetre weighing billions of tons ...

At this point, there flashed briefly through Dr Stenton's horrified mind the memory of that timeless classic, H. G. Wells' *The Star*. He had first read it as a very small boy, and it had helped to spark his interest in astronomy. Across more than two centuries of time, it had lost none of its magic and terror. He would never forget the images of hurricanes and tidal waves, of cities sliding into the sea, as the other visitor from the stars smashed into Jupiter and then fell sunwards past the Earth. True, the star that old Wells described was not cold, but incandescent, and wrought much of its destruction by heat. That scarcely mattered; even if Rama was a cold body, reflecting only the light of the sun, it could kill by gravity as easily as by fire.

Any stellar mass intruding into the solar system would completely distort the orbits of the planets. The Earth had only to move a few million kilometres sunwards – or starwards – for the delicate balance of climate to be destroyed. The Antarctic icecap could melt and flood all low-lying land; or the oceans could freeze and the whole world be locked in an eternal winter. Just a nudge in either direction would be enough ...

Then Dr Stenton relaxed and breathed a sigh of relief. This was all nonsense; he should be ashamed of himself.

Rama could not possibly be made of condensed matter. No star-sized mass could penetrate so deeply into the solar system without producing disturbances which would have betrayed it long ago. The orbits of all the planets would have been affected; that, after all, was how Neptune, Pluto and Persephone had been discovered. No, it was utterly impossible for an object as massive as a dead sun to sneak up unobserved.

In a way, it was a pity. An encounter with a dark star would have been quite exciting.

While it lasted ...

3
Rama and Sita

The extraordinary meeting of the Space Advisory Council was brief and stormy. Even in the twenty-second century, no way had yet been discovered of keeping elderly and conservative scientists from occupying crucial administrative positions. Indeed, it was doubted if the problem ever would be solved.

To make matters worse, the current Chairman of the SAC was Professor (Emeritus) Olaf Davidson, the distinguished astrophysicist. Professor Davidson was not very much interested in objects smaller than galaxies, and never bothered to conceal his prejudices. And though he had to admit that ninety per cent of his science was now based upon observations from space-borne instruments, he was not at all happy about it. No less than three times during his distinguished career, satellites specially launched to prove one of his pet theories had done precisely the opposite.

The question before the Council was straightforward enough. There was no doubt that Rama was an unusual object – but was it an important one? In a few months it would be gone forever, so there was little time in which to act. Opportunities missed now would never recur.

At rather a horrifying cost, a space-probe soon to be launched from Mars to beyond Neptune could be modified and sent on a high-speed trajectory to meet Rama. There was no hope of a rendezvous; it would be the fastest fly-by on record, for the two bodies would pass each other at two hundred thousand kilometres an hour. Rama would be observed intensively for only a few minutes – and in real closeup for less than a second. But with the right instrumentation, that would be long enough to settle many questions.

Although Professor Davidson took a very jaundiced view of the Neptune probe, it had already been approved and he saw no point in sending more good money after bad. He spoke eloquently on the follies of asteroid-chasing, and the urgent need for a new high-resolution interferometer on the Moon to prove the newly-revived Big Bang theory of creation, once and for all.

That was a grave tactical error, because the three most ardent supporters of the Modified Steady State Theory were also members of the Council. They secretly agreed with Professor Davidson that asteroid-chasing was a waste of money; nevertheless ...

He lost by one vote.

Three months later the space-probe, rechristened Sita, was launched from Phobos, the inner moon of Mars. The flight time was seven weeks, and the instrument was switched to full power only five minutes before interception. Simultaneously, a cluster of camera pods was released, to sail past Rama so that it could be photographed from all sides.

The first images, from ten thousand kilometres away, brought to a halt the activities of all mankind. On a billion television screens, there appeared a tiny, featureless cylinder, growing rapidly second by second. By the time it had doubled its size, no one could pretend any longer that Rama was a natural object.

Its body was a cylinder so geometrically perfect that it might have been turned on a lathe – one with centres fifty kilometres apart. The two ends were quite flat, apart from some small structures at the centre of one face, and were twenty kilometres across; from a distance, when there was no sense of scale, Rama looked almost comically like an ordinary domestic boiler.

Rama grew until it filled the screen. Its surface was a dull, drab grey, as colourless as the Moon, and completely devoid of markings except at one point. Halfway along the cylinder there was a kilometre-wide stain or smear, as if something had once hit and splattered, ages ago.

There was no sign that the impact had done the slightest damage to Rama's spinning walls; but this mark had produced the slight fluctuation in brightness that had led to Stenton's discovery.

The images from the other cameras added nothing new. However, the trajectories their pods traced through Rama's minute gravitational field gave one other vital piece of information – the mass of the cylinder.

It was far too light to be a solid body. To nobody's great surprise, it was clear that Rama must be hollow.

The long-hoped-for, long-feared encounter had come at last. Mankind was about to receive its first visitor from the stars.

4
Rendezvous

Commander Norton remembered those first TV transmissions, which he had replayed so many times, during the final minutes of the rendezvous. But there was one thing no electronic image could possibly convey – and that was Rama's overwhelming size.

He had never received such an impression when landing on a natural body like the Moon or Mars. Those were worlds, and one expected them to be big. Yet he had also landed on Jupiter VIII, which was slightly larger than Rama – and that had seemed quite a small object.

It was very easy to resolve the paradox. His judgement was wholly altered by the fact that this was an artifact, millions of times heavier than anything that Man had ever put into space. The mass of Rama was at least ten million million tons; to any spaceman, that was not only an awe-inspiring, but a terrifying thought. No wonder that he sometimes felt a sense of insignificance, and even depression, as that cylinder of sculptured, ageless metal filled more and more of the sky.

There was also a sense of danger here, that was wholly novel to his experience. In every earlier landing he had known what to expect; there was always the possibility of accident, but never of surprise. With Rama, surprise was the only certainty.

Now *Endeavour* was hovering less than a thousand metres above the North Pole of the cylinder, at the very centre of the slowly turning disc. This end has been chosen because it was the one in sunlight; as Rama rotated, the shadows of the short enigmatic structures near the axis swept steadily across the metal plain. The northern face of Rama was a gigantic sundial, measuring out the swift passage of its four-minute day.

Landing a five-thousand-ton spaceship at the centre of a spinning disc was the least of Commander Norton's worries. It was no different from docking at the axis of a large space-station; *Endeavour*'s lateral jets had already given her a matching spin, and he could trust Lieutenant Joe Calvert to put her down as gently as a snowflake, with or without the aid of the nav computer.

'In three minutes,' said Joe, without taking his eyes from the display, 'we'll know if it's made of anti-matter.'

Norton grinned, as he recalled some of the more hair-raising theories about Rama's origin. If that unlikely speculation was true, in a few seconds there would be the biggest bang since the solar system was formed. The total annihilation of ten thousand tons would, briefly, provide the planets with a second sun.

Yet the mission profile had allowed even for this remote contingency; *Endeavour* had squirted Rama with one of her jets from a safe thousand kilometres away. Nothing whatsoever had happened when the expanding cloud of vapour arrived on target – and a matter-anti-matter reaction involving even a few milligrams would have produced an awesome firework display.

Norton, like all space commanders, was a cautious man. He had looked long and hard at the northern face of Rama, choosing the point of touchdown. After much thought, he had decided to avoid the obvious spot – the exact centre, on the axis itself. A clearly marked circular disc, a hundred metres in diameter, was centred on the Pole, and Norton had a strong suspicion that this must be the outer seal of an enormous airlock. The creatures who had built this hollow world must have had some way of taking their ships inside. This was the logical place for the main entrance, and Norton thought it might be unwise to block the front door with his own vessel.

But this decision generated other problems. If *Endeavour* touched down even a few metres from the axis, Rama's rapid spin would start her sliding away from the pole. At first, the centrifugal force would be very weak, but it would be continuous and inexorable. Commander Norton did not relish the thought of his ship slithering across the polar plain, gaining speed minute by minute until it was slung off into space at a thousand kilometres an hour when it reached the edge of the disc.

It was possible that Rama's minute gravitational field – about one thousandth of Earth's – might prevent this from happening. It would hold *Endeavour* against the plain with a force of several tons, and if the surface was sufficiently rough the ship might stay near the Pole. But Commander Norton had no intention of balancing an unknown frictional force against a quite certain centrifugal one.

Fortunately, Rama's designers had provided an answer. Equally spaced around the polar axis were three low, pill-box shaped structures, about ten metres in diameter. If *Endeavour* touched down between any two of these, the centrifugal drift would fetch her up against them and she would be held firmly in place, like a ship glued against a quayside by the incoming waves.

'Contact in fifteen seconds,' said Joe. As he tensed himself above the duplicate controls, which he hoped he would not have to touch, Commander Norton became acutely aware of all that had come to focus on this instant of time. This, surely, was the most momentous landing since the first touchdown on the Moon, a century and a half ago.

The grey pill-boxes drifted slowly upwards outside the control port. There was the last hiss of a reaction jet, and a barely perceptible jar.

In the weeks that had passed, Commander Norton had often

wondered what he would say at this moment. But now that it was upon him, History chose his words, and he spoke almost automatically, barely aware of the echo from the past:

'Rama Base. *Endeavour* has landed.'

As recently as a month ago, he would never have believed it possible. The ship had been on a routine mission, checking and emplacing asteroid warning beacons, when the order had come. *Endeavour* was the only spacecraft in the solar system which could possibly make a rendezvous with the intruder before it whipped round the sun and hurled itself back towards the stars. Even so, it had been necessary to rob three other ships of the Solar Survey, which were now drifting helplessly until tankers could refuel them. Norton feared that it would be a long time before the skippers of *Calypso, Beagle* and *Challenger* would speak to him again.

Even with all this extra propellant, it had been a long hard chase; Rama was already inside the orbit of Venus when *Endeavour* caught up with her. No other ship could ever do so; this privilege was unique, and not a moment of the weeks ahead was to be wasted. A thousand scientists on Earth would have cheerfully mortgaged their souls for this opportunity; now they could only watch over the TV circuits, biting their lips and thinking how much better *they* could do the job. They were probably right, but there was no alternative. The inexorable laws of celestial mechanics had decreed that *Endeavour* was the first, and the last, of all Man's ships that would ever make contact with Rama.

The advice he was continually receiving from Earth did little to alleviate Norton's responsibility. If split-second decisions had to be made, no one could help him; the radio time-lag to Mission Control was already ten minutes, and increasing. He often envied the great navigators of the past, before the days of electronic communications, who could interpret their sealed orders without continual monitoring from headquarters. Why *they* made mistakes, no one ever knew.

Yet at the same time, he was glad that some decisions could be delegated to Earth. Now that *Endeavour*'s orbit had coalesced with Rama's they were heading sunwards like a single body; in forty days they would reach perihelion, and pass within twenty million kilometres of the sun. That was far too close for comfort; long before then, *Endeavour* would have to use her remaining fuel to nudge herself into a safer orbit. They would have perhaps three weeks of exploring time, before they parted from Rama forever.

After that, the problem would be Earth's. *Endeavour* would be virtually helpless, speeding on an orbit which could make her the first ship to reach the stars – in approximately fifty thousand years. There was no need to worry, Mission Control had promised. Somehow, regardless of cost, *Endeavour* would be refuelled – even if it proved necessary to send tankers after her, and abandon them in space once they had transferred every gramme of propellant. Rama was a prize worth any risk, short of a suicide mission.

And, of course, it might even come to that. Commander Norton had no illusions on this score. For the first time in a hundred years an element of total uncertainty had entered human affairs. Uncertainty was one thing that neither scientists nor politicians could tolerate. If that was the price of resolving it, *Endeavour* and her crew would be expendable.

5
First EVA

Rama was as silent as a tomb – which, perhaps, it was. No radio signals, on any frequency; no vibrations that the seismographs could pick up, apart from the micro-tremors undoubtedly caused by the sun's increasing heat; no electrical currents; no radioactivity. It was almost ominously quiet; one might have expected that even an asteroid would be noisier.

What did we expect? Norton asked himself. A committee of welcome? He was not sure whether to be disappointed or relieved. The initiative, at any rate, appeared up to him.

His orders were to wait for twenty-four hours, then to go out and explore. Nobody slept much that first day; even the crew members not on duty spent their time monitoring the ineffectually probing instruments, or simply looking out of the observation ports at the starkly geometrical landscape. Is this world alive? they asked themselves, over and over again. Is it dead? Or is it merely sleeping?

On the first EVA, Norton took only one companion – Lieut-Commander Karl Mercer, his tough and resourceful life-support officer. He had no intention of getting out of sight of the ship, and if there was any trouble it was unlikely that a larger party would be safe. As a precaution, however, he had two more crew members, already suited up, standing by in the airlock.

The few grammes of weight that Rama's combined gravitational and centrifugal fields gave them were neither help nor hindrance; they had to rely entirely on their jets. As soon as possible, Norton told himself, he would string a cat's-cradle of guide ropes between the ship and the pill-boxes, so that they could move around without wasting propellants.

The nearest pill-box was only ten metres from the airlock, and Norton's first concern was to check that the contact had caused no damage to the ship. *Endeavour*'s hull was resting against the curving wall with a thrust of several tons, but the pressure was evenly distributed. Reassured, he began to drift around the circular structure, trying to determine its purpose.

Norton had travelled only a few metres when he came across an interruption in the smooth, apparently metallic wall. At first, he thought it was some peculiar decoration, for it seemed to serve no useful function. Six radial grooves, or slots, were deeply recessed in the metal, and lying in them were six crossed bars like the spokes of a rimless wheel, with a small hub at the centre. But there was no way in which the wheel could be turned, as it was embedded in the wall.

Then he noticed, with growing excitement, that there were deeper recesses at the ends of the spokes, nicely shaped to accept a clutching hand (claw? tentacle?). If one stood *so*, bracing against the wall, and pulled on the spoke so ...

Smooth as silk, the wheel slid out of the wall. To his utter astonishment – for he had been virtually certain that any moving parts would have become vacuum-welded ages ago – Norton found himself holding a spoked wheel. He might have been the captain of some old wind-jammer standing at the helm of his ship.

He was glad that his helmet sunshade did not allow Mercer to read his expression.

He was startled, but also angry with himself; perhaps he had already make his first mistake. Were alarms now sounding inside Rama, and had his thoughtless action already triggered some implacable mechanism?

But *Endeavour* reported no change; its sensors still detected nothing but faint thermal crepitations and his own movements.

'Well, Skipper – are you going to turn it?'

Norton thought once more of his instructions. 'Use your own discretion, but proceed with caution.' If he checked every single move with Mission Control, he would never get anywhere.

'What's your diagnosis, Karl?' he asked Mercer.

'It's obviously a manual control for an airlock – probably an emergency back-up system in case of power failure. I can't imagine *any* technology, however advanced, that wouldn't take such precautions.'

'And it would be fail-safe,' Norton told himself. 'It could only be operated if there was no possible danger to the system …'

He grasped two opposing spokes of the windlass, braced his feet against the ground, and tested the wheel. It did not budge.

'Give me a hand,' he asked Mercer. Each took a spoke; exerting their utmost strength, they were unable to produce the slightest movement.

Of course, there was no reason to suppose that clocks and corkscrews on Rama turned in the same direction as they did on Earth …

'Let's try the other way,' suggested Mercer.

This time, there was no resistance. The wheel rotated almost effortlessly through a full circle. Then, very smoothly, it took up the load.

Half a metre away, the curving wall of the pill-box started to move, like a slowly opening clamshell. A few particles of dust, driven by wisps of escaping air, streamed outwards like dazzling diamonds as the brilliant sunlight caught them.

The road to Rama lay open.

6
Committee

It had been a serious mistake, Dr Bose often thought, to put the United Planets Headquarters on the Moon. Inevitably, Earth tended to dominate the proceedings – as it dominated the landscape beyond the dome. If they *had* to build here, perhaps they should have gone to the Farside, where that hypnotic disc never shed its rays ...

But, of course, it was much too late to change, and in any case there was no real alternative. Whether the colonies liked it or not, Earth would be the cultural and economic overlord of the solar system for centuries to come.

Dr Bose had been born on Earth, and had not emigrated to Mars until he was thirty, so he felt that he could view the political situation fairly dispassionately. He knew now that he would never return to his home planet, even though it was only five hours away by shuttle. At 115, he was in perfect health, but he could not face the reconditioning needed to accustom him to three times the gravity he had enjoyed for most of his life. He was exiled forever from the world of his birth; not being a sentimental man, this had never depressed him unduly.

What did depress him sometimes was the need for dealing, year after year, with the same familiar faces. The marvels of medicine were all very well, and certainly he had no desire to put back the clock – but there were men around this conference table with whom he had worked for more than half a century. He knew exactly what they would say and how they would vote

19

on any given subject. He wished that, some day, one of them would do something totally unexpected – even something quite crazy.

And probably they felt exactly the same way about him ...

The Rama Committee was still manageably small, though doubtless that would soon be rectified. His six colleagues – the UP representatives for Mercury, Earth, Luna, Ganymede, Titan and Triton – were all present in the flesh. They had to be; electronic diplomacy was not possible over solar system distances. Some elder statesmen, accustomed to the instantaneous communications which Earth had long taken for granted, had never reconciled themselves to the fact that radio waves took minutes, or even hours, to journey across the gulfs between the planets. 'Can't you scientists do something about it?' they had been heard to complain bitterly, when told that face-to-face conversation was impossible between Earth and any of its remoter children. Only the Moon had that barely acceptable one-and-a-half-second delay – with all the political and psychological consequences which it implied. Because of this fact of astronomical life, the Moon – and *only* the Moon – would always be a suburb of Earth.

Also present in person were three of the specialists who had been co-opted to the Committee. Professor Davidson, the astronomer, was an old acquaintance; today, he did not seem his usual irascible self. Dr Bose knew nothing of the infighting that had preceded the launch of the first probe to Rama, but the Professor's colleagues had not let him forget it.

Dr Thelma Price was familiar through her numerous television appearances, though she had first made her reputation fifty years ago during the archaeological explosion that had followed the draining of that vast marine museum, the Mediterranean.

Dr Bose could still recall the excitement of that time, when the lost treasures of the Greeks, Romans and a dozen other civilizations were restored to the light of day. That was one of the few occasions when he was sorry to be living on Mars.

The exobiologist, Carlisle Perera, was another obvious choice; so was Dennis Solomons, the science historian. Dr Bose was slightly less happy about the presence of Conrad Taylor, the celebrated anthropologist, who had made his reputation by uniquely combining scholarship and eroticism in his study of puberty rites in late twentieth-century Beverley Hills.

No one, however, could possibly have disputed the right of Sir Lewis Sands to be on the Committee. A man whose knowledge was matched only by his urbanity, Sir Lewis was reputed to lose his composure only when called the Arnold Toynbee of his age.

The great historian was not present in person; he stubbornly refused to leave Earth, even for so momentous a meeting as this. His stereo image, indistinguishable from reality, apparently occupied the chair to Dr Bose's right; as if to complete the illusion, someone had placed a glass of water in front of him. Dr Bose considered that this sort of technological *tour de force* was an unnecessary gimmick, but it was surprising how many undeniably great men were childishly delighted to be in two places at once. Sometimes this electronic miracle produced comic disasters; he had been at one diplomatic reception where somebody had tried to walk through a stereogram – and discovered, too late, that it was the real person. And it was even funnier to watch projections trying to shake hands ...

His Excellency the Ambassador for Mars to the United Planets called his wandering thoughts to order, cleared his throat, and said: 'Gentlemen, the Committee is now in session. I think I am correct in saying that this is a gathering of unique talents, assembled to deal with a unique situation. The directive that the Secretary-General has given us is to evaluate that situation, and to advise Commander Norton when necessary.'

This was a miracle of over-simplification, and everyone knew it. Unless there was a real emergency, the Committee might never be in direct contact with Commander Norton – if, indeed, he ever heard of its existence. For the Committee was a temporary creation of the United Planets' Science Organisation, reporting through its Director to the Secretary-General. It was true that the Space Survey was part of the UP – but on the *Operations*, not the Science side. In theory, this should not make much difference; there was no reason why the Rama Committee – or anyone else for that matter – should not call up Commander Norton and offer helpful advice.

But Deep Space Communications are expensive. *Endeavour* could be contacted only through PLANETCOM, which was an autonomous corporation, famous for the strictness and efficiency of its accounting. It took a long time to establish a line of credit with PLANETCOM; somewhere, someone was working on this; but at the moment, PLANETCOM's hard-hearted computers did not recognize the existence of the Rama Committee.

'This Commander Norton,' said Sir Robert Mackay, the Ambassador for Earth. 'He has a tremendous responsibility. What sort of person is he?'

'I can answer that,' said Professor Davidson, his fingers flying over the keyboard of his memory pad. He frowned at the screenful of information, and started to make an instant synopsis.

'William Tsien Norton, Born 2077, Brisbane, Oceana. Educated Sydney, Bombay, Houston. Then five years at Astrograd, specialising in propulsion. Commissioned 2102. Rose through usual ranks – Lieutenant on the Third Persephone expedition, distinguished himself during fifteenth attempt to establish base on Venus ... um ... um ... exemplary record ... dual citizenship, Earth and Mars ... wife and one child in Brisbane, wife and *two* in Port Lowell, with option on third ...'

'Wife?' asked Taylor innocently.

'No, child of course,' snapped the Professor, before he caught the grin on the other's face. Mild laughter rippled round the table, though the overcrowded terrestrials looked more envious than amused. After a century of determined effort, Earth had still failed to get its population below the target of one billion ...

'... appointed commanding officer Solar Survey Research Vessel *Endeavour*. First voyage to retrograde satellites of Jupiter ... um, that was a tricky one ... on asteroid mission when ordered to prepare for this operation ... managed to beat deadline ...'

The Professor cleared the display and looked up at his colleagues.

'I think we were extremely lucky, considering that he was the only man available at such short notice. We might have had the usual run-of-the-mill captain.' He sounded as if he was referring to the typical peg-legged scourge of the spaceways, pistol in one hand and cutlass in the other.

'The record only proves that he's competent,' objected the Ambassador from Mercury (population: 112,500 but growing). 'How will he react in a wholly novel situation like this?'

On Earth, Sir Lewis Sands cleared his throat. A second and a half later, he did so on the Moon.

'Not exactly a novel situation,' he reminded the Hermian, 'even though it's three centuries since it last occurred. If Rama is dead, or unoccupied – and so far all the evidence suggests that it is – Norton is in the position of an archaeologist discovering the ruins of an extinct culture.' He bowed politely to Dr Price, who nodded in agreement. 'Obvious examples are Schliemann at Troy or Mouhot at Angkor Vat. The danger is minimal, though of course accident can never be completely ruled out.'

'But what about the booby-traps and trigger mechanisms these Pandora people have been talking about?' asked Dr Price.

'Pandora?' asked the Hermian Ambassador quickly. 'What's that?'

'It's a crackpot movement,' explained Sir Robert, with as much embarrassment as a diplomat was ever likely to show, 'which is convinced that Rama is a grave potential danger. A box that shouldn't be opened, you know.' He doubted if the

Hermian *did* know: classical studies were not encouraged on Mercury.

'Pandora – paranoia,' snorted Conrad Taylor. 'Oh, of course, such things are *conceivable*, but why should any intelligent race went to play childish tricks?'

'Well, even ruling out such unpleasantness,' Sir Robert continued, 'we still have the much more ominous possibility of an active, inhabited Rama. Then the situation is one of an encounter between two cultures – at very different technological levels. Pizzaro and the Incas. Peary and the Japanese. Europe and Africa. Almost invariably, the consequences have been disastrous – for one or both parties. I'm not making any recommendations: I'm merely pointing out precedents.'

'Thank you, Sir Robert,' replied Dr Bose. It was a mild nuisance, he thought, having two 'Sirs' on one small committee; in these latter days knighthood was an honour which few Englishmen escaped. 'I'm sure we've all thought of these alarming possibilities. But if the creatures inside Rama are – er – malevolent – will it really make the slightest difference what we do?'

'They might ignore us if we go away.'

'What – after they've travelled billions of miles and thousands of years?'

The argument had reached the take-off point, and was now self-sustaining. Dr Bose sat back in his chair, said very little, and waited for the consensus to emerge.

It was just as he had predicted. Everyone agreed that, once he had opened the first door, it was inconceivable that Commander Norton should not open the second.

7

Two Wives

If his wives ever compared his videograms, Commander Norton thought with more amusement than concern, it would involve him in a lot of extra work. Now, he could make one long 'gram and dupe it, adding only brief personal messages and endearments before shooting the almost identical copies off to Mars and Earth.

Of course, it was highly unlikely that his wives ever would do such a thing; even at the concessionary rates allowed to spacemen's families, it would be expensive. And there would be no point in it; his families were on excellent terms with each other, and exchanged the usual greetings on birthdays and anniversaries. Yet, on the whole, perhaps it was just as well that the girls had never met, and probably never would. Myrna had been born on Mars and so could not tolerate the high gravity of Earth. And Caroline hated even the twenty-five minutes of the longest possible terrestrial journey.

'Sorry I'm a day late with this transmission,' said the Commander after he had finished the general-purpose preliminaries, 'but I've been away from the ship for the last thirty hours, believe it or not ...

'Don't be alarmed – everything is under control, going perfectly. It's taken us two days, but we're almost through the airlock complex. We could have done it in a couple of hours, if we'd known what we do now. But we took no chances, sent remote cameras ahead, and cycled all the locks a dozen times to make sure they wouldn't seize up behind us – *after* we'd gone through ...

'Each lock is a simple revolving cylinder with a slot on one side. You go in through this opening, crank the cylinder round a hundred and eighty degrees – and the slot then matches up with another door so that you can step out of it. Or float, in this case.

'The Ramans really made sure of things. There are three of these cylinder-locks, one after the other just inside the outer hull and below the entry pill-box. I can't imagine how even one would fail, unless someone blew it up with explosives, but if it did, there would be a second back-up, and then a third ...

'And *that's* only the beginning. The final lock opens into a straight corridor, almost half a kilometre long. It looks clean and tidy, like everything else we've seen; every few metres there are small ports that probably held lights, but now everything is completely black and, I don't mind telling you, scary. There are also two parallel slots, about a centimetre wide, cut in the walls and running the whole length of the tunnel. We suspect that some kind of shuttle runs inside these, to tow equipment – or people – back and forth. It would save us a lot of trouble if we could get it working ...

'I mentioned that the tunnel was half a kilometre long. Well, from our seismic soundings we knew that's about the thickness of the shell, so obviously we were almost through it. And at the end of the tunnel we weren't surprised to find another of those cylindrical airlocks.

'Yes, *and* another. *And* another. These people seem to have done everything in threes. We're in the final lock chamber now, awaiting the OK from Earth before we go through. The interior of Rama is only a few metres away. I'll be a lot happier when the suspense is over.

'You know Jerry Kirchoff, my Exec, who's got such a library of *real* books that he can't afford to emigrate from Earth? Well,

Jerry told me about a situation just like this, back at the beginning of the twenty-first – no, twentieth century. An archaeologist found the tomb of an Egyptian king, the first one that hadn't been looted by robbers. His workmen took months to dig their way in, chamber by chamber, until they came to the final wall. Then they broke through the masonry, and he held out a lantern and pushed his head inside. He found himself looking into a whole roomful of treasure – incredible stuff, gold and jewels ...

'Perhaps this place is also a tomb; it seems more and more likely. Even now, there's still not the slightest sound, or hint of any activity. Well, tomorrow we should know.'

Commander Norton switched the record to HOLD. What else, he wondered, should he say about the work before he began the separate personal messages to his families? Normally, he never went into so much detail, but these circumstances were scarcely normal. This might be the last 'gram he would ever send to those he loved; he owed it to them to explain what he was doing.

By the time they saw these images, and heard these words, he would be inside Rama – for better or for worse.

8
Through the Hub

Never before had Norton felt so strongly his kinship with that long dead Egyptologist. Not since Howard Carter had first peered into the tomb of Tutankhamen could any man have known a moment such as this – yet the comparison was almost laughably ludicrous.

Tutankhamen had been buried only yesterday – not even four thousand years ago; Rama might be older than mankind. That little tomb in the Valley of the Kings could have been lost in the corridors through which they had already passed, yet the space that lay beyond this final seal was at least a million times greater. And as for the treasure it might hold – that was beyond imagination.

No one had spoken over the radio circuits for at least five minutes; the well-trained team had not even reported verbally when all the checks were complete. Mercer had simply given him the OK sign and waved him towards the open tunnel. It was as if everyone realised that this was a moment for History, not to be spoiled by unnecessary small-talk. That suited Commander Norton, for at the moment he too had nothing to say. He flicked on the beam of his flashlight, triggered his jets, and drifted slowly down the short corridor, trailing his safety line behind him. Only seconds later, he was inside.

Inside *what*? All before him was total darkness; not a glimmer of light was reflected back from the beam. He had expected this, but he had not really believed it. All the calculations had shown that the far wall was tens of kilometres away; now his eyes told him that this was indeed the truth. As he drifted slowly into that darkness, he felt a sudden need for the reassurance of his safety line, stronger than any he had ever experienced before, even on his very first EVA. And that was ridiculous; he had looked out across the light-years and the megaparsecs without vertigo; why should he be disturbed by a few cubic kilometres of emptiness?

He was still queasily brooding over this problem when the momentum damper at the end of the line braked him gently to a halt, with a barely perceptible rebound. He swept the vainly-probing beam of the flashlight down from the nothingness ahead, to examine the surface from which he had emerged.

He might have been hovering over the centre of a small crater, which was itself a dimple in the base of a much larger one. On either side rose a complex of terraces and ramps – all geometrically precise and obviously artificial – which extended for as far as the beam could reach. About a hundred metres away he could see the exit of the other two airlock systems, identical with this one.

And that was all. There was nothing particularly exotic or alien about the scene: in fact, it bore a considerable resemblance to an abandoned mine. Norton felt a vague sense of disappoint-ment; after all this effort, there should have been some dramatic, even transcendental revelation. Then he reminded himself that he could see only a couple of hundred metres. The darkness beyond his field of view might yet contain more wonders than he cared to face.

He reported briefly to his anxiously-waiting companions, then added: 'I'm sending out the flare – two minutes delay. Here goes.'

With all his strength, he threw the little cylinder straight upwards – or outwards – and started to count seconds as it dwindled along the beam. Before he had reached the quarter minute it was out of sight; when he had got to a hundred he shielded his eyes and aimed the camera. He had always been good a estimating time; he was only two seconds off when the world exploded with light. And this time there was no cause for disappointment.

Even the millions of candlepower of the flare could not light up the whole of this enormous cavity, but now he could see enough to grasp its plan and appreciate its titanic scale. He was at one end of a hollow cylinder at least ten kilometres wide, and of indefinite length. From his viewpoint at the central axis he could see such a mass of detail on the curving walls surrounding him that his mind could not absorb more than a minute fraction of it; he was looking at the landscape of an entire world by a single flash of lightning, and he tried by a deliberate effort of will to freeze the image in his mind.

All round him, the terraced slopes of the 'crater' rose up until they merged into the solid wall that rimmed the sky. No – that impression was false; he must discard the instincts both of earth and of space, and reorientate himself to a new system of coordinates.

He was not at the lowest point of this strange, inside-out world, but the highest. From here, all directions were *down*, not up. If he moved away from this central axis, towards the curving wall which he must no longer think of as a wall, gravity would steadily increase. When he reached the inside surface of the cylinder, he could stand upright on it at any point, feet towards the stars and head towards the centre of the spinning drum. The concept was familiar enough; since the earliest dawn of space-flight, centrifugal force had been used to simulate gravity. It was only the scale of this application which was so overwhelming, so shocking. The largest of all spacestations, Syncsat Five, was less than two hundred metres in diameter. It would take some little while to grow accustomed to one a hundred times that size.

The tube of landscape which enclosed him was mottled with areas of light and shade that could have been forests, fields, frozen lakes or towns; the distance, and the fading illumination of the flare, made identification impossible. Narrow lines that could be highways, canals, or well-trained rivers formed a faintly visible geometrical network; and far along the cylinder, at the very limit of vision, was a band of deeper darkness. It formed a complete circle, ringing the interior of this world, and Norton suddenly recalled the myth of Oceanus, the sea which, the ancients believed, surrounded the Earth.

Here, perhaps, was an even stranger sea – not circular, but *cylindrical*. Before it became frozen in the inter-stellar night, did it have waves and tides and currents – and fish?

The flare guttered and died; the moment of revelation was over. But Norton knew that as long as he lived these images would be burned on his mind. Whatever discoveries the future might bring, they could never erase this first impression. And History could never take from him the privilege of being the first of all mankind to gaze upon the works of an alien civilization.

9
Reconnaissance

'We have now launched five long-delay flares down the axis of the cylinder, and so have a good photo-coverage of its full length. All the main features are mapped; though there are very few than we can identify, we've given them provisional names.

'The interior cavity is fifty kilometres long and sixteen wide. The two ends are bowl-shaped, with rather complicated geometries. We've called ours the Northern Hemisphere and are establishing our first base here at the axis.

'Radiating away from the central hub, a hundred and twenty degrees apart, are three ladders that are almost a kilometre long. They all end at a terrace or ring-shaped plateau, that runs right round the bowl. And leading on from *that*, continuing the direction of the ladders, are three enormous stairways, which go all the way down to the plain. If you imagine an umbrella with only three ribs, equally spaced, you'll have a good idea of this end of Rama.

'Each of those ribs is a stairway, very steep near the axis and then slowly flattening out as it approaches the plain below. The stairways – we've called them Alpha, Beta, Gamma – aren't continuous, but break at five more circular terraces. We estimate there must be between twenty and thirty thousand steps ... presumably they were only used for emergencies, since it's inconceivable that the Ramans – or whatever we're going to call them – had no better way of reaching the axis of their world.

'The Southern Hemisphere looks quite different; for one

thing, it has no stairways, and no flat central hub. Instead, there's a huge spike – kilometres long – jutting along the axis, with six smaller ones around it. The whole arrangement is very odd, and we can't imagine what it means.

'The fifty-kilometre-long, cylindrical section between the two bowls we've called the Central Plain. It may seem crazy to use the word "plain" to describe something so obviously curved, but we feel it's justified. It will appear flat to us when we get down there – just as the interior of a bottle must seem flat to an ant crawling round inside it.

'The most striking feature of the Central Plain is the ten-kilometre-wide dark band running completely round it at the half-way mark. It looks like ice, so we've christened it the Cylindrical Sea. Right out in the middle there's a large oval island, about ten kilometres long and three wide, and covered with tall structures. Because it reminds us of Old Manhattan, we've called it New York. Yet I don't think it's a city; it seems more like an enormous factory or chemical processing plant.

'But there are some cities – or at any rate, towns. At least six of them; if they were built for human beings, they could each hold about fifty thousand people. We've called them Rome, Peking, Paris, Moscow, London, Tokyo ... They are linked with highways and something that seems to be a rail system.

'There must be enough material for centuries of research in this frozen carcass of a world. We've four thousand square kilometres to explore, and only a few weeks to do it in. I wonder if we'll ever learn the answer to the two mysteries that have been haunting me ever since we got inside; who were they – *and what went wrong*?'

The recording ended. On Earth and Moon, the members of the Rama Committee relaxed, then started to examine the maps and photographs spread in front of them. Though they had already studied these for many hours, Commander Norton's voice added a dimension which no pictures could convey. He had actually been there – had looked with his own eyes across this extraordinary inside-out world, during the brief moments while its age-long night had been illuminated by the flares. And he was the man who would lead any expedition to explore it.

'Dr Perera, I believe you have some comments to make?'

Ambassador Bose wondered briefly if he should have first given the floor to Professor Davidson, as senior scientist and the only astronomer. But the old cosmologist still seemed to be in a mild state of shock, and was clearly out of his element. All his professional career he had looked upon the universe as an arena for the titanic impersonal forces of gravitation, magnetism, radiation; he had never believed that life played an important role in the scheme of things, and regarded its appearance on Earth, Mars and Jupiter as an accidental aberration.

But now there was proof that life not only existed outside the solar system, but had scaled heights far beyond anything that man had achieved, or could hope to reach for centuries to come. Moreover, the discovery of Rama challenged another dogma that Professor Olaf had preached for years. When pressed, he would reluctantly admit that life probably did exist in other star systems – but it was absurd, he had always maintained, to imagine that it could ever cross the interstellar gulfs ...

Perhaps the Ramans had indeed failed, if Commander Norton was correct in believing that their world was now a tomb. But at least they had attempted the feat, on a scale which indicated a high confidence in the outcome. If such a thing had happened once, it must surely have happened many times in this Galaxy of a hundred thousand million suns ... and someone, somewhere, would eventually succeed.

This was the thesis which, without proof but with considerable arm-waving, Dr Carlisle Perera had been preaching for years. He was now a very happy man, though also a most frustrated one. Rama had spectacularly confirmed his views – but he could never set foot inside it, or even see it with his own eyes.

If the devil had suddenly appeared and offered him the gift of instantaneous teleportation, he would have signed the contract without bothering to look at the small print.

'Yes, Mr Ambassador, I think I have some information of interest. What we have here is undoubtedly a "Space Ark". It's an old idea in the astronautical literature; I've been able to trace it back to the British physicist J. D. Bernal, who proposed this method of interstellar colonization in a book published in 1929 – yes, two hundred years ago. And the great Russian pioneer Tsiolkovski put forward somewhat similar proposals even earlier.

'If you want to go from one star system to another you have a number of choices. Assuming that the speed of light is an absolute limit – and that's *still* not completely settled, despite anything you may have heard to the contrary' – there was an indignant sniff, but no formal protest from Professor Davidson – 'you can make a fast trip in a small vessel, or a slow journey in a giant one.

'There seems no technical reason why spacecraft cannot reach ninety per cent, or more, of the speed of light. That would mean a travel time of five to ten years between neighbouring stars – tedious, perhaps, but not impracticable, especially for creatures whose life spans might be measured in centuries. One can imagine voyages of this duration, carried out in ships not much larger than ours.

'But perhaps such speeds are impossible, with reasonable payloads; remember, you have to carry the fuel to slow down at the end of the voyage, even if you're on a one-way trip. So it may make more sense to take your time – ten thousand, a hundred thousand years ...

'Bernal and others thought this could be done with mobile worldlets a few kilometres across, carrying thousands of passengers on journeys that would last for generations. Naturally, the system would have to be rigidly closed, recycling all food, air and other expendables. But, of course, that's just how the Earth operates – on a slightly larger scale.

'Some writers suggested that these Space Arks should be built in the form of concentric spheres; others proposed hollow, spinning cylinders so that centrifugal force could provide artificial gravity – exactly what we've found in Rama—'

Professor Davidson could not tolerate this sloppy talk.

'No such thing as centrifugal *force*. It's an engineer's phantom. There's only inertia.'

'You're quite right, of course,' admitted Perera, 'though it might be hard to convince a man who'd just been slung off a carousel. But mathematical rigour seems unnecessary—'

'Hear, hear,' interjected Dr Bose, with some exasperation. 'We all know what you mean, or think we do. Please don't destroy our illusions.'

'Well, I was merely pointing out that there's nothing conceptually novel about Rama, though its size is startling. Men have imagined such things for two hundred years.

'Now I'd like to address myself to another question. Exactly how long has Rama been travelling through space?

'We now have a very precise determination of its orbit and its velocity. Assuming that it's made no navigational changes, we can trace its position back for millions of years. We expected that it would be coming from the direction of a nearby star – but that isn't the case at all.

'It's more than *two hundred thousand years* since Rama passed near any star, and that particular one turns out to be an irregular variable – about the most unsuitable sun you could imagine for an inhabited solar system. It has a brightness range of over fifty to one; any planets would be alternately baked and frozen every few years.'

'A suggestion,' put in Dr Price. 'Perhaps that explains everything. Maybe this was once a normal sun and became unstable. That's why the Ramans had to find a new one.'

Dr Perera admired the old archaeologist, so he let her down lightly. But what would *she* say, he wondered, if he started pointing out the instantly obvious in her own speciality ...

'We did consider that,' he said gently. 'But if our present theories of stellar evolution are correct, this star could *never* have been stable – could never have had life-bearing planets. So Rama has been cruising through space for at least two hundred thousand years, and perhaps for more than a million.

'Now it's cold and dark and apparently dead, and I think I know why. The Ramans may have had no choice – perhaps they were indeed fleeing from some disaster – but they miscalculated.

'No closed ecology can be one hundred per cent efficient; there is always waste, loss – some degradation of the environment, and build-up of pollutants. It may take billions of years to poison and wear out a planet – but it will happen in the end. The oceans will dry up, the atmosphere will leak away ...

'By our standards, Rama is enormous – yet it is still a very tiny planet. My calculations, based on the leakage through its hull, and some reasonable guesses about the rate of biological turnover, indicate that its ecology could only survive for about a thousand years. At the most, I'll grant ten thousand ...

'That would be long enough, at the speed Rama is travelling, for a transit between the closely-packed suns in the heart of the Galaxy. But not out here, in the scattered population of the spiral arms. Rama is a ship which exhausted its provisions before it reached its goal. It's a derelict, drifting among the stars.

'There's just one serious objection to this theory, and I'll raise it before anybody else does. Rama's orbit is aimed so accurately at the solar system that coincidence seems ruled out. In fact, I'd say it's now heading much too close to the sun for comfort: *Endeavour* will have to break away long before perihelion, to avoid overheating.

'I don't pretend to understand this. Perhaps, there may be

some form of automatic terminal guidance still operating, steering Rama to the nearest suitable star ages after its builders are dead.

'And they *are* dead; I'll stake my reputation on that. All the samples we've taken from the interior are absolutely sterile – we've not found a single micro-organism. As for the talk you may have heard about suspended animation, you can ignore it. There are fundamental reasons why hibernation techniques will only work for a very few centuries – and we're dealing with time spans a thousand-fold longer.

'So the Pandorans and their sympathizers have nothing to worry about. For my part, I'm sorry. It would have been wonderful to have met another intelligent species.

'But at least we have answered one ancient question. We are not alone. The stars will never again be the same to us.'

10
Descent into Darkness

Commander Norton was sorely tempted – but as captain his first duty was to his ship. If anything went badly wrong on this initial probe, he might have to run for it.

So that left his second officer, Lieut-Commander Mercer, as the obvious choice. Norton willingly admitted that Karl was better suited for the mission.

The authority on life-support systems, Mercer had written some of the standard textbooks on the subject. He had personally checked out unnumerable types of equipment, often under hazardous conditions, and his biofeedback control was famous. At a moment's notice he could cut his pulse-rate by fifty per cent, and reduce respiration to almost zero for up to ten minutes. These useful little tricks had saved his life on more than one occasion.

Yet despite his great ability and intelligence, he was almost wholly lacking in imagination. To him the most dangerous experiments or missions were simply jobs that had to be done. He never took unnecessary risks, and had no use at all for what was commonly regarded as courage.

The two mottoes on his desk summed up his philosophy of life. One asked WHAT HAVE YOU FORGOTTEN? The other said HELP STAMP OUT BRAVERY. The fact that he was widely regarded as the bravest man in the Fleet was the only thing that ever made him angry.

Given Mercer, that automatically selected the next man – his inseparable companion Lt Joe Calvert. It was hard to see what the two had in common; the lightly-built, rather highly strung navigating officer was ten years younger than his stolid and imperturbable friend, who certainly did not share his passionate interest in the art of the primitive cinema.

But no one can predict where lightning will strike, and years ago Mercer and Calvert had established an apparently stable liaison. That was common enough; much more unusual was the fact that they also shared a wife back on Earth, who had borne each of them a child. Commander Norton hoped that he could meet her one day; she must be a very remarkable woman. The triangle had lasted for at least five years, and still seemed to be an equilateral one.

Two men were not enough for an exploring team; long ago it had been found that three was the optimum – for if one man was lost, two might still escape where a single survivor would be doomed. After a good deal of thought, Norton had chosen Technical Sergeant Willard Myron. A mechanical genius who could make anything work – or design something better if it wouldn't – Myron was the ideal man to identify alien pieces of equipment. On a long sabbatical from his regular job as Associate Professor at Astrotech, the Sergeant had refused to accept a commission on the grounds that he did not wish to block the promotion of more deserving career officers. No one took this explanation very seriously and it was generally agreed that Will rated zero for ambition. He might make it to Space Sergeant, but would never be a full professor. Myron, like count-less NCOs before him, had discovered the ideal compromise between power and responsibility.

As they drifted through the last airlock and floated out along the weightless axis of Rama, Lt Calvert found himself, as he so often did, in the middle of a movie flashback. He sometimes wondered if he should attempt to cure himself of this habit, but he could not see that it had any disadvantages. It could make even the dullest situations interesting and – who could tell? – one day it might save his life. He would remember what Fairbanks or Connery or Hiroshi had done in similar circumstances ...

This time, he was about to go over the top, in one of the early-twentieth-century wars; Mercer was the sergeant leading a three-man patrol on a night raid into no-man's land. It was not too difficult to imagine that they were at the bottom of an immense shell-crater, though one that had somehow become neatly tailored into a series of ascending terraces. The crater was flooded with light from three widely-spaced plasma-arcs, which gave an almost shadowless illumination over the whole interior. But beyond that – over the rim of the most distant terrace – was darkness and mystery.

In his mind's eye, Calvert knew perfectly well what lay there. First there was the flat circular plain over a kilometre across. Trisecting it into three equal parts, and looking very much like broad railroad tracks, were three wide ladders, their rungs recessed into the surface so that they would provide no obstruction to anything sliding over it. Since the arrangement was completely symmetrical, there was no reason to choose one ladder rather than another; that nearest to Airlock Alpha had been selected purely as a matter of convenience.

Though the rungs of the ladders were uncomfortably far apart, that presented no problem. Even at the rim of the Hub, half a kilometre from the axis, gravity was still barely one thirtieth of Earth's. Although they were carrying almost a hundred kilos of equipment and life-support gear, they would still be able to move easily hand-over-hand.

Commander Norton and the back-up team accompanied them along the guide ropes that had been stretched from Airlock Alpha to the rim of the crater; then, beyond the range of the floodlights, the darkness of Rama lay before them. All that could be seen in the dancing beams of the helmet lights was the first few hundred metres of the ladder, dwindling away across a flat and otherwise featureless plain.

And now, Karl Mercer told himself, I have to make my first decision. Am I going *up* that ladder, or *down* it?

The question was not a trivial one. They were still essentially in zero gravity, and the brain could select any reference system it pleased. By a simple effort of will, Mercer could convince himself that he was looking out across a horizontal plain, or up the face of a vertical wall, or over the edge of a sheer cliff. Not a few astronauts had experienced grave psychological problems by choosing the wrong coordinates when they started on a complicated job.

Mercer was determined to go head-first, for any other mode of locomotion would be awkward; moreover, this way he could more easily see what was in front of him. For the first few hundred metres, therefore, he would imagine he was climbing upwards; only when the increasing pull of gravity made it impossible to maintain the illusion would be switch his mental directions one hundred and eighty degrees.

He grasped the first rung and gently propelled himself along the ladder. Movement was as effortless as swimming along the seabed – more so, in fact, for there was no backward drag of water. It was so easy that there was a temptation to go too fast, but Mercer was much too experienced to hurry in a situation as novel as this.

In his earphones, he could hear the regular breathing of his two companions. He needed no other proof that they were in good shape, and wasted no time in conversation. Though he was tempted to look back, he decided not to risk it until they had reached the platform at the end of the ladder.

The rungs were spaced a uniform half metre apart, and for the first portion of the climb Mercer missed the alternate ones. But he counted them carefully, and at around two hundred noticed the first distinct sensations of weight. The spin of Rama was starting to make itself felt.

At rung four hundred, he estimated that his apparent weight was about five kilos. This was no problem, but it was now getting hard to pretend that he was climbing, when he was being firmly dragged *upwards*.

The five hundredth rung seemed a good place to pause. He could feel the muscles in his arms responding to the unaccustomed exercise, even though Rama was now doing all the work and he had merely to guide himself.

'Everything OK, Skipper,' he reported. 'We're just passing the halfway mark. Joe, Will – any problems?'

'I'm fine – what are you stopping for?' Joe Calvert answered.

'Same here,' added Sergeant Myron. 'But watch out for the Coriolis force. It's starting to build up.'

So Mercer had already noticed. When he let go of the rungs he had a distinct tendency to drift off to the right. He knew perfectly well that this was merely the effect of Rama's spin, but it seemed as if some mysterious force was gently pushing him away from the ladder.

Perhaps it was time to start going feet-first, now that 'down' was beginning to have a physical meaning. He would run the risk of a momentary disorientation.

'Watch out – I'm going to swing round.'

Holding firmly on to the rung, he used his arms to twist himself round a hundred and eighty degrees, and found himself momentarily blinded by the lights of his companions. Far above them – and now it really *was* above – he could see a fainter glow along the rim of the sheer cliff. Silhouetted against it were the figures of Commander Norton and the back-up team, watching him intently. They seemed very small and far away, and he gave them a reassuring wave.

He released his grip, and let Rama's still feeble pseudo-gravity take over. The drop from one rung to the next required more than two seconds; on Earth, in the same time, a man would have fallen thirty metres.

The rate of fall was so painfully slow that he hurried things up a trifle by pushing with his hands, gliding over spans of a dozen rungs at a time, and checking himself with his feet whenever he felt he was travelling too fast.

At rung seven hundred, he came to another halt and swung the beam of his helmet-lamp downwards; as he had calculated, the beginning of the stairway was only fifty metres below.

A few minutes later, they were on the first step. It was a strange experience, after months in space, to stand upright on a solid surface, and to feel it pressing against one's feet. Their weight was still less than ten kilogrammes, but that was enough to give a feeling of stability. When he closed his eyes, Mercer could believe that he once more had a real world beneath him.

The ledge or platform from which the stairway descended was about ten metres wide, and curved upwards on each side until it disappeared into the darkness. Mercer knew that it formed a complete circle and that if he walked along it for five kilometres he would come right back to his starting-point, having circumnavigated Rama.

At the fractional gravity that existed here, however, real walking was impossible; one could only bound along in giant strides. And therein lay danger.

The stairway that swooped down into the darkness, far below the range of their lights, would be deceptively easy to descend. But it would be essential to hold on to the tall handrail that flanked it on either side; too bold a step might send an incautious traveller arching far out into space. He would hit the surface again perhaps a hundred metres lower down; the impact would be harmless, but its consequences might not be – for the spin of Rama would have moved the stairway off to the left. And so a falling body would hit against the smooth curve that swept in an unbroken arc to the plain almost seven kilometres below.

That, Mercer told himself, would be a hell of a toboggan ride; the terminal speed, even in this gravity, could be several hundred kilometres an hour. Perhaps it would be possible to apply enough friction to check such a headlong descent; if so, this might even be the most convenient way to reach the inner surface of Rama. But some very cautious experimenting would be necessary first.

'Skipper,' reported Mercer, 'there were no problems getting down the ladder. If you agree, I'd like to continue towards the next platform. I want to time our rate of descent on the stairway.'

Norton replied without hesitation.

'Go ahead.' He did not need to add, 'Proceed with caution.'

It did not take Mercer long to make a fundamental discovery. It was impossible, at least at this one-twentieth-of-a-gravity level, to walk down the stairway in the normal manner. Any attempt to do so resulted in a slow-motion dream-like movement that was intolerably tedious; the only practical way was to ignore the steps, and to use the handrail to pull oneself downwards.

Calvert had come to the same conclusion.

'This stairway was built to walk *up*, not down!' he exclaimed. 'You can use the steps when you're moving against gravity, but they're just a nuisance in this direction. It may not be dignified, but I think the best way down is to slide along the handrail.'

'That's ridiculous,' protested Sergeant Myron. 'I can't believe the Ramans did it this way.'

'I doubt if they ever used this stairway – it's obviously only for emergencies. They must have had some mechanical transport system to get up here. A funicular, perhaps. That would explain those long slots running down from the Hub.'

'I always assumed they were drains – but I suppose they could be both. I wonder if it ever rained here?'

'Probably,' said Mercer. 'But I think Joe is right, and to hell with dignity. Here we go.'

The handrail – presumably it *was* designed for something like hands – was a smooth, flat, metal bar supported on widely-spaced pillars a metre high. Commander Mercer straddled it, carefully gauged the braking power he could exert with his hands, and let himself slide.

Very sedately, slowly picking up speed, he descended into the darkness, moving in the pool of light from his helmet-lamp. He had gone about fifty metres when he called the others to join him.

None would admit it, but they all felt like boys again, sliding down the banisters. In less than two minutes, they had made a kilometre descent in safety and comfort. Whenever they felt they were going too fast, a tightened grip on the handrail provided all the braking that was necessary.

'I hope you enjoyed yourselves,' Commander Norton called when they stepped off at the second platform. 'Climbing back won't be quite so easy.'

'That's what I want to check,' replied Mercer, who was walking experimentally back and forth, getting the feel of the increased gravity. 'It's already a tenth of a gee here – you really notice the difference.'

He walked – or, more accurately, glided – to the edge of the platform, and shone his helmet-light down the next section of the stairway. As far as his beam could reach, it appeared identical with the one above – though careful examination of photos had shown that the height of the steps steadily decreased with the rising gravity. The stair had apparently been designed so that the effort required to climb it was more or less constant at every point in its long curving sweep.

Mercer glanced up towards the Hub of Rama, now almost two kilometres above him. The little glow of light, and the tiny figures silhouetted against it, seemed horribly far away. For the first time, he was suddenly glad that he could not see the whole length of this enormous stairway. Despite his steady nerves and lack of imagination, he was not sure how he would react if he could see himself like an insect crawling up the face of a vertical saucer more than sixteen kilometres high – and with the upper half overhanging above him. Until this moment, he had regarded the darkness as a nuisance; now he almost welcomed it.

'There's no change of temperature,' he reported to Commander Norton. 'Still just below freezing. But the air-pressure is up, as we expected – around three hundred millibars. Even with this low oxygen content, it's almost breathable; further down there will be no problems at all. That will simplify exploration enormously. What a find – the first world on which we can walk without breathing gear! In fact, I'm going to take a sniff.'

Up on the Hub, Commander Norton stirred a little uneasily. But Mercer, of all men, knew exactly what he was doing. He would already have made enough tests to satisfy himself.

Mercer equalized pressure, unlatched the securing clip of his helmet, and opened it a crack. He took a cautious breath; then a deeper one.

The air of Rama was dead and musty, as if from a tomb so ancient that the last trace of physical corruption had disappeared ages ago. Even Mercer's ultra-sensitive nose, trained through years of testing life-support systems to and beyond the point of disaster, could detect no recognisable odours. There was a faint metallic tang, and he suddenly recalled that the first men on the Moon had reported a hint of burnt gunpowder when they repressurised the lunar module. Mercer imagined that the moon-dust-contaminated cabin on *Eagle* must have smelled rather like Rama.

He sealed the helmet again, and emptied his lungs of the alien air. He had extracted no sustenance from it; even a mountaineer acclimatised to the summit of Everest would die quickly here. But a few kilometres further down, it would be a different matter.

What else was there to do here? He could think of nothing, except the enjoyment of the gentle, unaccustomed gravity. But there was no point in growing used to that, since they would be returning immediately to the weightlessness of the Hub.

'We're coming back, Skipper,' he reported. 'There's no reason to go further – until we're ready to go *all* the way.'

'I agree. We'll be timing you, but take it easy.'

As he bounded up the steps, three or four at a stride, Mercer agreed that Calvert had been perfectly correct; these stairs were built to be walked *up*, not down. As long as one did not look back, and ignored the vertiginous steepness of the ascending curve, the climb was a delightful experience. After about two hundred steps, however, he began to feel some twinges in his calf muscles, and decided to slow down. The others had done the same; when he ventured a quick glance over his shoulder, they were considerably further down the slope.

The climb was wholly uneventful – merely an apparently endless succession of steps. When they stood once more on the highest platform, immediately beneath the ladder, they were barely winded, and it had taken them only ten minutes. They paused for another ten, then started on the last vertical kilometre.

Jump – catch hold of a rung – jump – catch – jump – catch ... it was easy, but so boringly repetitious that there was danger of becoming careless. Halfway up the ladder they rested for five minutes: by this time their arms as well as their legs had begun to ache. Once again, Mercer was glad that they could see so little of the vertical face to which they were clinging; it was not too difficult to pretend that the ladder only extended just a few metres beyond their circle of light, and would soon come to an end.

Jump – catch a rung – jump – then, quite suddenly, the ladder *really* ended. They were back at the weightless world of the axis, among their anxious friends. The whole trip had taken under an hour, and they felt a sense of modest achievement.

But it was much too soon to feel pleased with themselves. For all their efforts, they had traversed less than an eighth of that cyclopean stairway.

11
Men, Women and Monkeys

Some women, Commander Norton had decided long ago, should not be allowed aboard ship; weightlessness did things to their breasts that were too damn distracting. It was bad enough when they were motionless; but when they started to move, and sympathetic vibrations set in, it was more than any warm-blooded male should be asked to take. He was quite sure that at least one serious space accident had been caused by acute crew distraction, after the transit of a well-upholstered lady officer through the control cabin.

He had once mentioned this theory to Surgeon-Commander Laura Ernst, without revealing who had inspired his particular train of thought. There was no need; they knew each other much too well. On Earth, years ago, in a moment of mutual loneliness and depression, they had once made love. Probably they would never repeat the experience (but could one ever be *quite* sure of that?) because so much had changed for both of them. Yet whenever the well-built Surgeon oscillated into the Commander's cabin, he felt a fleeting echo of an old passion, she knew that he felt it, and everyone was happy.

'Bill,' she began, 'I've checked our mountaineers, and here's my verdict. Karl and Joe are in good shape – all indications normal for the work they've done. But Will shows signs of exhaustion and body-loss – I won't bother about the details. I don't believe he's been getting all the exercise he should, and he's not the only one. There's been some cheating in the centrifuge;

if there's any more, heads will roll. Please pass the word.'

'Yes, Ma'am. But there's some excuse. The men have been working very hard.'

'With their brains and fingers, certainly. But not with their bodies – not *real* work in kilogramme-metres. And that's what we'll be dealing with, if we're going to explore Rama.'

'Well, can we?'

'Yes, if we proceed with caution. Karl and I have worked out a very conservative profile – based on the assumption that we can dispense with breathing gear below Level Two. Of course, that's an incredible stroke of luck, and changes the whole logistics picture. I still can't get used to the idea of a world with oxygen … So we only need to supply food and water and thermosuits, and we're in business. Going down will be easy; it looks as if we can slide most of the way, on that very convenient banister.'

'I've got Chips working on a sled with parachute braking. Even if we can't risk it for crew, we can use it for stores and equipment.'

'Fine; *that* should do the trip in ten minutes; otherwise it will take about an hour.

'Climbing up is harder to estimate; I'd like to allow six hours, including two one-hour periods. Later, as we get experience – *and* develop some muscles – we may be able to cut this back considerably.'

'What about psychological factors?'

'Hard to assess, in such a novel environment. Darkness may be the biggest problem.'

'I'll establish searchlights on the Hub. Besides its own lamps, any party down there will always have a beam playing on it.'

'Good – that should be a great help.'

'One other point: should we play safe and send a party only halfway down the stair – and back – or should we go the whole way on the first attempt?'

'If we had plenty of time, I'd be cautious. But time is short, and I can see no danger in going all the way – and looking around when we get there.'

'Thanks, Laura – that's all I want to know. I'll get the Exec working on the details. And I'll order all hands to the centrifuge – twenty minutes a day at half a gee. Will that satisfy you?'

'No. It's point six gee down there in Rama, and I want a safety margin. Make it three quarters—'

'Ouch!'

'– for ten minutes—'

'I'll settle for that—'

'– *twice* a day.'

'Laura, you're a cruel, hard woman. But so be it. I'll break the news just before dinner. That should spoil a few appetites.'

It was the first time that Commander Norton had ever seen Karl Mercer slightly ill at ease. He had spent the fifteen minutes discussing the logistics problem in his usual competent manner, but something was obviously worrying him. His captain, who had a shrewd idea of what it was, waited patiently until he brought it out.

'Skipper,' Karl said at length, 'are you *sure* you should lead this party? If anything goes wrong, I'm considerably more expendable. And I've been further inside Rama than anyone else – even if only by fifty metres.'

'Granted. But it's time the commander led his troops, and we've decided that there's no greater risk on this trip than on the last. At the first sign of trouble, I'll be back up that stairway fast enough to qualify for the Lunar Olympics.'

He waited for any further objections, but none came, though Karl still looked unhappy. So he took pity on him and added gently: 'And I bet Joe will beat me to the top.'

The big man relaxed, and a slow grin spread across his face. 'All the same, Bill, I wish you'd taken someone else.'

'I wanted *one* man who'd been down before, and we can't

both go. As for Herr Doktor Professor Sergeant Myron, Laura says he's still two kilos overweight. Even shaving off that moustache didn't help.'

'Who's your number three?'

'I still haven't decided. That depends on Laura.'

'She wants to go herself.'

'Who doesn't? But if she turns up at the top of her own fitness list, I'll be very suspicious.'

As Lieut-Commander Mercer gathered up his papers and launched himself out of the cabin, Norton felt a brief stab of envy. Almost all the crew – about eighty-five per cent, by his minimum estimate – had worked out some sort of emotional accommodation. He had known ships where the captain had done the same, but that was not his way. Though discipline aboard the *Endeavour* was based very largely on the mutual respect between highly trained and intelligent men and women, the commander needed something more to underline his position. His responsibility was unique, and demanded a certain degree of isolation, even from his closest friends. Any liaison could be damaging to morale, for it was almost impossible to avoid charges of favouritism. For this reason, affairs spanning more than two degrees of rank were firmly discouraged; but apart from this, the only rule regulating shipboard sex was 'So long as they don't do it in the corridors and frighten the simps'.

There were four superchimps aboard *Endeavour*, though strictly speaking the name was inaccurate, because the ship's non-human crew was not based on chimpanzee stock. In zero gravity, a prehensile tail is an enormous advantage, and all attempts to supply these to humans had turned into embarrassing failures. After equally unsatisfactory results with the great apes, the Superchimpanzee Corporation had turned to the monkey kingdom.

Blackie, Blondie, Goldie and Brownie had family trees whose branches included the most intelligent of the Old and New

World monkeys, plus synthetic genes that had never existed in nature. Their rearing and education had probably cost as much as that of the average spaceman, and they were worth it. Each weighed less than thirty kilos and consumed only half the food and oxygen of a human being, but each could replace 2.75 men for house-keeping, elementary cooking, tool-carrying and dozens of other routine jobs.

That 2.75 was the Corporation's claim, based on innumerable time-and-motion studies. The figure, though surprising and frequently challenged, appeared to be accurate, for simps were quite happy to work fifteen hours a day and did not get bored by the most menial and repetitious tasks. So they freed human beings for human work; and on a spaceship, that was a matter of vital importance.

Unlike the monkeys who were their nearest relatives *Endeavour*'s simps were docile, obedient and uninquisitive. Being cloned, they were also sexless, which eliminated awkward behavioural problems. Carefully house-trained vegetarians, they were very clean and didn't smell; they would have made perfect pets, except that nobody could possibly have afforded them.

Despite these advantages, having simps on board involved certain problems. They had to have their own quarters – inevitably labelled 'The Monkey House'. Their little mess-room was always spotless, and was well-equipped with TV, games equipment and programmed teaching machines. To avoid accidents, they were absolutely forbidden to enter the ship's technical areas; the entrances to all these were colour-coded in red, and the simps were conditioned so that it was psychologically impossible for them to pass the visual barriers.

There was also a communications problem. Though they had an equivalent IQ of sixty, and could understand several hundred words of English, they were unable to talk. It had proved impossible to give useful vocal chords either to apes or monkeys, and they therefore had to express themselves in sign language.

The basic signs were obvious and easily learned, so that everyone on board ship could understand routine messages. But the only man who could speak fluent Simpish was their handler – Chief Steward McAndrews.

It was a standing joke that Sergeant Ravi McAndrews *looked* rather like a simp – which was hardly an insult, for with their short, tinted pelts and graceful movements they were very handsome animals. They were also affectionate, and everyone on board had his favourite; Commander Norton's was the aptly-named Goldie.

But the warm relationship which one could so easily establish with simps created another problem, often used as a powerful argument against their employment in space. Since they could only be trained for routine, low-grade tasks, they were worse than useless in an emergency; they could then be a danger to themselves and to their human companions. In particular, teaching them to use spacesuits had proved impossible, the concepts involved being quite beyond their understanding.

No one liked to talk about it, but everybody knew what had to be done if a hull was breached or the order came to abandon ship. It had happened only once; then the simp handler had carried out his instructions more than adequately. He was found with his charges, killed by the same poison. Thereafter the job of euthing was transferred to the chief medical officer, who it was felt would have less emotional involvement.

Norton was very thankful that this responsibility, at least, did not fall upon the captain's shoulders. He had known men he would have killed with far fewer qualms than he would Goldie.

12
The Stairway of the Gods

In the clear, cold atmosphere of Rama, the beam of the search-light was completely invisible. Three kilometres down from the central Hub, the hundred-metre wide oval of light lay across a section of that colossal stairway. A brilliant oasis in the surrounding darkness, it was sweeping slowly towards the curved plain still five kilometres below; and in its centre moved a trio of ant-like figures, casting long shadows before them.

It had been, just as they had hoped and expected, a completely uneventful descent. They had paused briefly at the first platform, and Norton had walked a few hundred metres along the narrow, curving ledge before starting the slide down to the second level. Here they had discarded their oxygen gear, and revelled in the strange luxury of being able to breathe without mechanical aids. Now they could explore in comfort, freed from the greatest danger that confronts a man in space, and forgetting all worries about suit integrity and oxygen reserve.

By the time they had reached the fifth level, and there was only one more section to go, gravity had reached almost half its terrestrial value. Rama's centrifugal spin was at last exerting its real strength; they were surrendering themselves to the implacable force which rules every planet, and which can exert a merciless price for the smallest slip. It was still very easy to go downwards; but the thought of the return, up those thousands upon thousands of steps, was already beginning to prey upon their minds.

The stairway had long ago ceased its vertiginous downward plunge and was now flattening out towards the horizontal. The gradient was now only about one in five; at the beginning, it had been five in one. Normal walking was now both physically, and psychologically, acceptable; only the lowered gravity reminded them that they were not descending some great stairway on Earth. Norton had once visited the ruins of an Aztec temple, and the feelings he had then experienced came echoing back to him – amplified a hundred times. Here was the same sense of awe and mystery, and the sadness of the irrevocably vanished past. Yet the scale here was so much greater, both in time and space, that the mind was unable to do it justice; after a while, it ceased to respond. Norton wondered if, sooner or later, he would take even Rama for granted.

And there was another respect in which the parallel with terrestrial ruins failed completely. Rama was hundreds of times older than any structure that had survived on Earth – even the Great Pyramid. *But everything looked absolutely new; there was no sign of wear and tear.*

Norton had puzzled over this a good deal, and had arrived at a tentative explanation. Everything that they had so far examined was part of an emergency back-up system, very seldom put to actual use. He could not imagine that the Ramans – unless they were physical fitness fanatics of the kind not uncommon on Earth – ever walked up and down this incredible stairway, or its two identical companions completing the invisible Y far above his head. Perhaps they had only been required during the actual construction of Rama, and had served no purpose since that distant day. That theory would do for the moment, yet it did not feel right. There was something wrong, somewhere …

They did not slide for the last kilometre but went down the steps two at a time in long, gentle strides; this way, Norton decided, they would give more exercise to muscles that would soon have to be used. And so the end of the stairway came upon them almost unawares; suddenly, there were no more steps – only a flat plain, dull grey in the now weakening beam of the Hub searchlight, fading away into the darkness a few hundred metres ahead.

Norton looked back along the beam, towards its source up on the axis more than eight kilometres away. He knew that Mercer would be watching through the telescope, so he waved to him cheerfully.

'Captain here,' he reported over the radio. 'Everyone in fine shape – no problems. Proceeding as planned.'

'Good,' replied Mercer. 'We'll be watching.'

There was a brief silence; then a new voice cut in. 'This is the Exec, on board ship. Really, Skipper, this isn't good enough. You know the news services have been screaming at us for the last week. I don't expect deathless prose, but can't you do better than that?'

'I'll try,' Norton chuckled. 'But remember there's nothing to see yet. It's like – well, being on a huge, darkened stage, with a single spotlight. The first few hundred steps of the stairway rise out of it until they disappear into the darkness overhead. What we can see of the plain looks perfectly flat – the curvature's too small to be visible over this limited area. And that's about it.'

'Like to give any impressions?'

'Well, it's still very cold – below freezing – and we're glad of our thermosuits. And *quiet* of course, quieter than anything I've ever known on Earth, or in space, where there's always some background noise. Here, every sound is swallowed up; the space around us is so enormous that there aren't any echoes. It's weird, but I hope we'll get used to it.'

'Thanks, Skipper. Anyone else – Joe, Boris?'

Lt Joe Calvert, never at a loss for words, was happy to oblige.

'I can't help thinking that this is the first time – *ever* – that we've been able to walk on another world, breathing its natural atmosphere – though I suppose "natural" is hardly the word you can apply to a place like this. Still, Rama must resemble the world of its builders; our own spaceships are all miniature earths. Two examples are damned poor statistics, but does this mean that all intelligent life-forms are oxygen eaters? What we've seen of their work suggests that the Ramans were humanoid, though perhaps about fifty per cent taller than we are. Wouldn't you agree, Boris?'

Is Joe teasing Boris? Norton asked himself. I wonder how he's going to react? ...

To all his shipmates, Boris Rodrigo was something of an enigma. The quiet, dignified communications officer was popular with the rest of the crew, but he never entered fully into their activities and always seemed a little apart – marching to the music of a different drummer.

As indeed he was, being a devout member of the Fifth Church of Christ, Cosmonaut. Norton had never been able to discover what had happened to the earlier four, and he was equally in the dark about the Church's rituals and ceremonies. But the main tenet of its faith was well known: it believed that Jesus Christ was a visitor from space, and had constructed an entire theology on that assumption.

It was perhaps not surprising that an unusually high proportion of the Church's devotees worked in space in some capacity or other. Invariably, they were efficient, conscientious and absolutely reliable. They were universally respected and even liked, especially as they made no attempt to convert others. Yet there was also something slightly spooky about them; Norton could never understand how men with advanced scientific and technical training could possibly believe some of the things he had heard Christers state as incontrovertible facts.

As he waited for Lt Rodrigo to answer Joe's possibly loaded question, the commander had a sudden insight into his own hidden motives. He had chosen Brois because he was physically fit, technically qualified, and completely dependable. At the same time, he wondered if some part of his mind had not selected the lieutenant out of an almost mischievous curiosity. How could a man with such religious beliefs react to the awesome reality of Rama? Suppose he encountered something that confounded his theology ... or, for that matter, confirmed it?

But Boris Rodrigo, with his usual caution, refused to be drawn.

'They were certainly oxygen breathers, and they *could* be humanoid. But let's wait and see. With any luck, we should discover what they were like. There may be pictures, statues – perhaps even bodies, over in those towns. If they are towns.'

'And the nearest is only eight kilometres away,' said Joe Calvert hopefully.

Yes, thought the commander, but it's also eight kilometres back – and then there's that overwhelming stairway to climb again. Can we take the risk?

A quick sortie to the 'town' which they had named Paris had been among the first of his contingency plans, and now he had to make his decision. They had ample food and water for a stay of twenty-four hours; they would always be in full view of the back-up team on the Hub, and any kind of accident seemed virtually impossible on this smooth, gently curving, metal plain. The only foreseeable danger was exhaustion; when they got to Paris, which they could do easily enough, could they do more than take a few photographs and perhaps collect some small artefacts, before they had to return?

But even such a brief foray would be worth it; there was so little time, as Rama hurtled sunwards towards a perihelion too dangerous for *Endeavour* to match.

In any case, part of the decision was not his to make. Up in the ship, Dr Ernst would be watching the outputs of the bio-telemetering sensors attached to his body. If she turned thumbs-down, that would be that.

'Laura, what do you think?'

'Take thirty minutes' rest, and a five hundred calorie energy module. Then you can start.'

'Thanks, Doc,' interjected Joe Calvert. 'Now I can die happy. I always wanted to see Paris. Montmartre, here we come.'

13
The Plain of Rama

After those interminable stairs, it was a strange luxury to walk once more on a horizontal surface. Directly ahead, the ground was indeed completely flat; to right and left, at the limits of the floodlit area, the rising curve could just be detected. They might have been walking along a very wide, shallow valley; it was quite impossible to believe that they were really crawling along the inside of a huge cylinder, and that beyond this little oasis of light the land rose up to meet – no, to *become* – the sky.

Though they all felt a sense of confidence and subdued excitement, after a while the almost palpable silence of Rama began to weigh heavily upon them. Every footstep, every word, vanished instantly into the unreverberant void; after they had gone little more than half a kilometre, Lt Calvert could stand it no longer.

Among his minor accomplishments was a talent now rare, though many thought not rare enough – the art of whistling. With or without encouragement he could reproduce the themes from most of the movies of the last two hundred years. He started appropriately with Heigh-ho, heigh-ho, 'tis off to work we go, found that he couldn't stay down comfortably in the bass with Disney's marching dwarfs, and switched quickly to River Kwai. Then he progressed, more or less chronologically, through half a dozen epics, culminating with the theme from Sid Krassman's famous late-twentieth-century *Napoleon*.

It was a good try, but it didn't work, even as a morale-builder. Rama needed the grandeur of Bach or Beethoven or Sibelius or Tuan Sun, not the trivia of popular entertainment. Norton was on the point of suggesting that Joe save his breath for later exertions, when the young officer realised the inappropriateness of his efforts. Thereafter, apart from an occasional consultation with the ship, they marched on in silence. Rama had won this round.

On his initial traverse, Norton had allowed for one detour. Paris lay straight ahead, halfway between the foot of the stairway and the shore of the Cylindrical Sea, but only a kilometre to the right of their track was a very prominent, and rather mysterious, feature which had been christened the Straight Valley. It was a long groove or trench, forty metres deep and a hundred wide, with gently sloping sides; it had been provisionally identified as an irrigation ditch or canal. Like the stairway itself, it had two similar counterparts, equally spaced around the curve of Rama.

The three valleys were almost ten kilometres long, and stopped abruptly just before they reached the Sea – which was strange, if they were intended to carry water. And on the other side of the Sea the pattern was repeated: three more ten-kilometre-trenches continued on to the South Polar region.

They reached the end of the Straight Valley after only fifteen minutes' comfortable walking, and stood for a while staring thoughtfully into its depths. The perfectly smooth walls sloped down at an angle of sixty degrees; there were no steps or foot-holds. Filling the bottom was a sheet of flat, white material that looked very much like ice. A specimen could settle a good many arguments; Norton decided to get one.

With Calvert and Rodrigo acting as anchors and paying out a safety rope, he rapelled slowly down the steep incline. When he reached the bottom, he fully expected to find the familiar slippery feel of ice underfoot, but he was mistaken. The friction was too great; his footing was secure. This material was some kind of glass or transparent crystal; when he touched it with his fingertips, it was cold, hard and unyielding.

Turning his back to the searchlight and shielding his eyes from its glare, Norton tried to peer into the crystalline depths, as one may attempt to gaze through the ice of a frozen lake. But he could see nothing; even when he tried the concentrated beam of his own helmet-lamp, he was no more successful. This stuff was translucent, but not transparent. If it was a frozen liquid, it had a melting-point very much higher than water.

He tapped it gently with the hammer from his geology kit; the tool rebounded with a dull, unmusical 'clunk'. He tapped harder, with no more result, and was about to exert his full strength when some impulse made him desist.

It seemed most unlikely that he could crack this material; but what if he did? He would be like a vandal, smashing some enormous plate-glass window. There would be a better opportunity later, and at least he had discovered valuable information. It now seemed more unlikely than ever that this was a canal; it was simply a peculiar trench that stopped and started abruptly, but led nowhere. And if at any time it had carried liquid, where were the stains, the encrustations of dried-up sediment, that one would expect? Everything was bright and clean, as if the builders had left only yesterday ...

Once again he was face to face with the fundamental mystery of Rama, and this time it was impossible to evade it. Commander Norton was a reasonably imaginative man, but he would never have reached his present position if he had been liable to the wilder flights of fancy. Yet now, for the first time, he had a sense – not exactly of foreboding, but of anticipation. Things were not what they seemed; there was something very, very odd about a place that was simultaneously brand new – and a million years old.

Very thoughtfully, he began to walk slowly along the length of the little valley, while his companions, still holding the rope that was attached to his waist, followed him along the rim. He did not expect to make any further discoveries, but he wanted to let his curious emotional state run its course. For something else was worrying him; and it had nothing to do with the inexplicable newness of Rama.

He had walked no more than a dozen metres when it hit him like a thunderbolt.

He knew this place. *He had been here before.* Even on Earth, or some familiar planet, that experience is disquieting, though it is not particularly rare. Most men have known it at some time or other, and usually they dismiss it as the memory of a forgotten photograph, a pure coincidence – or, if they are mystically inclined, some form of telepathy from another mind, or even a flashback from their own future.

But to recognise a spot which *no* other human being can possibly have seen – that is quite shocking. For several seconds, Commander Norton stood rooted to the smooth crystalline surface on which he had been walking, trying to straighten out his emotions. His well-ordered universe had been turned upside down, and he had a dizzying glimpse of those mysteries at the edge of existence which he had successfully ignored for most of his life.

Then, to his immense relief, common sense came to the rescue. The disturbing sensation of *déjà-vu* faded out, to be replaced by a real and identifiable memory from his youth.

It was true – he had once stood between such steeply sloping walls, watching them drive into the distance until they seemed to converge at a point indefinitely far ahead. But they had been covered with neatly trimmed grass; and underfoot had been broken stone, not smooth crystal.

It had happened thirty years ago, during a summer vacation in England. Largely because of another student (he could remember her face – but he had forgotten her name) he had taken a course of industrial archaeology, then very popular among science and engineering graduates. They had explored abandoned coal-mines and cotton mills, climbed over ruined blast-furnaces and steam-engines, goggled unbelievingly at primitive (and still dangerous) nuclear reactors, and driven priceless turbine-powered antiques along restored motor roads.

Not everything that they saw was genuine; much had been lost during the centuries, for men seldom bother to preserve the commonplace articles of everyday life. But where it was necessary to make copies, they had been reconstructed with loving care.

And so young Bill Norton had found himself bowling along, at an exhilarating hundred kilometres an hour, while he furiously shoveled precious coal into the firebox of a locomotive that looked two hundred years old, but was actually younger than he was. The thirty-kilometre stretch of the Great Western Railway, however, was quite genuine, though it had required a good deal of excavating to get it back into commission.

Whistle screaming, they had plunged into a hillside and raced through a smoky, flame-lit darkness. An astonishingly long time later, they had burst out of the tunnel into a deep, perfectly straight cutting between steep grassy banks. The long-forgotten vista was almost identical with the one before him now.

'What is it, Skipper?' called Lt Rodrigo. 'Have you found something?'

As Norton dragged himself back to present reality, some of the oppression lifted from his mind. There was mystery here – yes; but it might not be beyond human understanding. He had learned a lesson, though it was not one that he could readily impart to others. At all costs, he must not let Rama overwhelm him. That way lay failure – perhaps even madness.

'No,' he answered, 'there's nothing down here. Haul me up – we'll head straight to Paris.'

14
Storm Warning

'I've called this meeting of the Committee,' said His Excellency the Ambassador of Mars to the United Planets, 'because Dr Perera has something important to tell us. He insists that we get in touch with Commander Norton right away, using the priority channel we've been able to establish after, I might say, a good deal of difficulty. Dr Perera's statement is rather technical, and before we come to it I think a summary of the present position might be in order; Dr Price has prepared one. Oh yes – some apologies for absence. Sir Lewis Sands is unable to be with us because he's chairing a conference, and Dr Taylor asks to be excused.'

He was rather pleased about that last abstention. The anthropologist had rapidly lost interest in Rama, when it became obvious that it would present little scope for him. Like many others, he had been bitterly disappointed to find that the mobile wordlet was dead; now there would be no opportunity for sensational books and viddies about Raman rituals and behavioural patterns. Others might dig up skeletons and classify artifacts; *that* sort of thing did not appeal to Conrad Taylor. Perhaps the only discovery that would bring him back in a hurry would be some highly explicit works of art, like the notorious frescoes of Thera and Pompeii.

Thelma Price, the archaelogist, took exactly the opposite point of view. She preferred excavations and ruins uncluttered by inhabitants who might interfere with dispassionate, scientific studies. The bed of the Mediterranean had been ideal – at least until the city planners and landscape artists had started getting in the way. And Rama would have been perfect, except for the maddening detail that it was a hundred million kilometres away and she would never be able to visit it in person.

'As you all know,' she began, 'Commander Norton has completed one traverse of almost thirty kilometres, without encountering any problems. He explored the curious trench shown on your maps as the Straight Valley; its purpose is still quite unknown, but it's clearly important as it runs the full length of Rama – except for the break at the Cylindrical Sea – and there are two other identical structures a hundred and twenty degrees apart round the circumference of the world.

'Then the party turned left – or East, if we adopt the North Pole convention – until they reached Paris. As you'll see from this photograph, taken by a telescope camera at the Hub, it's a group of several hundred buildings, with wide streets between them.

'Now *these* photographs were taken by Commander Norton's group when they reached the site. If Paris is a city, it's a very peculiar one. Note that none of the buildings have windows, or even doors! They are all plain rectangular structures, an identical thirty-five metres high. And they appear to have been extruded out of the ground – there are no seams or joints – look at this close-up of the base of a wall – there's a smooth transition into the ground.

'My own feeling is that this place is not a residential area, but a storage or supply depot. In support of that theory, look at this photo …

'These narrow slots or grooves, about five centimetres wide, run along all the streets, and there's one leading to every building – going straight into the wall. There's a striking resemblance to the street-car tracks of the early twentieth century; they are obviously part of some transport system.

'We've never considered it necessary to have public transport direct to every house. It would be economically absurd – people can always walk a few hundred metres. But if these buildings are used for the storage of heavy materials, it would make sense.'

'May I ask a question?' said the Ambassador for Earth.

'Of course, Sir Robert.'

'Commander Norton couldn't get into a single building?'

'No; when you listen to his report, you can tell he was quite frustrated. At one time he decided that the buildings could only be entered from underground; then he discovered the grooves of the transport system, and changed his mind.'

'Did he try to break in?'

'There was no way he could, without explosives or heavy tools. And he doesn't want to do that until all other approaches have failed.'

'I have it!' Dennis Solomons suddenly interjected. 'Cocooning!'

'I beg your pardon?'

'It's a technique developed a couple of hundred years ago,' continued the science historian. 'Another name for it is moth-balling. When you have something you want to preserve, you seal it inside a plastic envelope, and then pump in an inert gas. The original use was to protect military equipment between wars; it was once applied to whole ships. It's still widely used in museums that are short of storage space; no one knows what's inside some of the hundred-year-old cocoons in the Smithsonian basement.'

Patience was not one of Carlisle Perera's virtues; he was aching to drop his bombshell, and could restrain himself no longer.

'*Please*, Mr Ambassador! This is all very interesting, but I feel my information is rather more urgent.'

'If there are no other points – very well, Dr Perera.'

The exobiologist, unlike Conrad Taylor, had not found Rama

a disappointment. It was true that he no longer expected to find life – but sooner or later, he had been quite sure, some remains would be discovered of the creatures who had built this fantastic world. The exploration had barely begun, although the time available was horribly brief before *Endeavour* would be forced to escape from her present sun-grazing orbit.

But now, if his calculations were correct, Man's contact with Rama would be even shorter than he had feared. For one detail had been overlooked – because it was so large that no one had noticed it before.

'According to our latest information,' Perera began, 'one party is now on its way to the Cylindrical Sea, while Commander Norton has another group setting up a supply base at the foot of Stairway Alpha. When that's established, he intends to have at least two exploratory missions operating at all times. In this way he hopes to use his limited manpower at maximum efficiency.

'It's a good plan, but there may be no time to carry it out. In fact, I would advise an immediate alert, and a preparation for total withdrawal at twelve hours' notice. Let me explain …

'It's surprising how few people have commented on a rather obvious anomaly about Rama. It's now well inside the orbit of Venus – yet the interior is still frozen. But the temperature of an object in direct sunlight at this point is about five hundred degrees!

'The reason of course, is that Rama hasn't had time to warm up. It must have cooled down to near absolute zero – two hundred and seventy below – while it was in interstellar space. Now, as it approaches the sun, the outer hull is already almost as hot as molten lead. But the inside will stay cold, until the heat works its way through that kilometre of rock.

'There's some kind of fancy dessert with a hot exterior and ice-cream in the middle – I don't remember what it's called—'

'Baked Alaska. It's a favourite at UP banquets, unfortunately.'

'Thank you, Sir Robert. That's the situation in Rama at the moment, but it won't last. All these weeks, the solar heat has been working its way through, and we expect a sharp temperature rise to begin in a few hours. *That's* not the problem; by the time we'll have to leave anyway, it will be no more than comfortably tropical.'

"Then what's the difficulty?"

'I can answer in one word, Mr Ambassador. *Hurricanes.*'

15
The Edge of the Sea

There were now more than twenty men and women inside Rama – six of them down on the plain, the rest ferrying equipment and expendables through the airlock system and down the stairway. The ship itself was almost deserted, with the minimum possible staff on duty; the joke went around that *Endeavour* was really being run by the four simps and that Goldie had been given the rank of Acting-Commander.

For these first explorations, Norton had established a number of ground-rules; the most important dated back to the earliest days of man's space-faring. Every group, he had decided, must contain one person with prior experience. But not *more* than one. In that way, everybody would have an opportunity of learning as quickly as possible.

And so the first party to head for the Cylindrical Sea, though it was led by Surgeon-Commander Laura Ernst, had as its one-time veteran Lt Boris Rodrigo, just back from Paris. The third member, Sergeant Pieter Rousseau, had been with the back-up teams at the Hub; he was an expert on space reconnaissance instrumentation, but on this trip he would have to depend on his own eyes and a small portable telescope.

From the foot of Stairway Alpha to the edge of the Sea was just under fifteen kilometres – or an Earth-equivalent of eight under the low gravity of Rama. Laura Ernst, who had to prove that she lived up to her own standards, set a brisk pace. They stopped for thirty minutes at the mid-way mark, and made the whole trip in a completely uneventful three hours.

It was also quite monotonous, walking forward in the beam of the searchlight through the anechoic darkness of Rama. As the pool of light advanced with them, it slowly elongated into a long, narrow ellipse; this foreshortening of the beam was the only visible sign of progress. If the observers up on the Hub had not given them continual distance checks, they could not have guessed whether they had travelled one kilometre, or five, or ten. They just plodded onwards through the million-year-old night, over an apparently seamless metal surface.

But at last, far ahead at the limits of the now weakening beam, there was something new. On a normal world, it would have been a horizon; as they approached, they could see that the plain on which they were walking came to an abrupt stop. They were nearing the edge of the Sea.

'Only a hundred metres,' said Hub Control. 'Better slow down.'

That was hardly necessary, yet they had already done so. It was a sheer straight drop of fifty metres from the level of the plain to that of the Sea – if it was a sea, and not another sheet of that mysterious crystalline material. Although Norton had impressed upon everyone the danger of taking anything for granted in Rama, few doubted that the Sea was really made of ice. But for what conceivable reason was the cliff on the southern shore five hundred metres high, instead of the fifty here?

It was as if they were approaching the edge of the world; their oval of light, cut off abruptly ahead of them, became shorter and shorter. But far out on the curved screen of the Sea their monstrous foreshortened shadows had appeared, magnifying and exaggerating every movement. Those shadows had been their companions every step of the way, as they marched down the beam, but now that they were broken at the edge of the cliff they no longer seemed part of them. They might have been creatures of the Cylindrical Sea, waiting to deal with any intruders into their domain.

Because they were now standing on the edge of a fifty-metre cliff, it was possible for the first time to appreciate the curvature of Rama. But no one had ever seen a frozen lake bent upwards into a cylindrical surface; that was distinctly unsettling, and the eye did its best to find some other interpretation. It seemed to Dr Ernst, who had once made a study of visual illusions, that half the time she was really looking at a *horizontally* curving bay, not a surface that soared up into the sky. It required a deliberate effort of will to accept the fantastic truth.

Only in the line directly ahead, parallel to the axis of Rama, was normalcy preserved. In this direction alone was there agreement between vision and logic. Here – for the next few kilometres at least – Rama looked flat, and *was* flat ... And out there, beyond their distorted shadows and the outer limit of the beam, lay the island that dominated the Cylindrical Sea.

'Hub Control,' Dr Ernst radioed, 'please aim your beam at New York.'

The night of Rama fell suddenly upon them, as the oval of light went sliding out to sea. Conscious of the now invisible cliff at their feet, they all stepped back a few metres. Then, as if by some magical stage transformation, the towers of New York sprang into view.

The resemblance to old-time Manhattan was only superficial; this star-born echo of Earth's past possessed its own unique identity. The more Dr Ernst stared at it, the more certain she became that it was not a city at all.

The real New York, like all of Man's habitations, had never been finished; still less had it been designed. *This* place, however, had an overall symmetry and pattern, though one so complex that it eluded the mind. It had been conceived and planned by some controlling intelligence – and then it had been completed, like a machine devised for some specific purpose. After that, there was no possibility of growth or change.

The beam of the searchlight slowly tracked along those distant towers and domes and interlocked spheres and criss-crossed tubes. Sometimes there would be a brilliant reflection as some flat surface shot the light back towards them; the first time this happened, they were all taken by surprise. It was exactly as if, over there on that strange island, someone was signaling to them ...

But there was nothing that they could see here that was not already shown in greater detail on photographs taken from the Hub. After a few minutes, they called for the light to return to them, and began to walk eastwards along the edge of the cliff. It had been plausibly theorized that, somewhere, there must surely be a flight of steps, or a ramp, leading down to the Sea. And one crewman, who was a keen sailor, had raised an interesting conjecture.

'Where there's a sea,' Sergeant Ruby Barnes had predicted, 'there must be docks and harbours – and ships. You can learn everything about a culture by studying the way it builds boats.' Her colleagues thought this a rather restricted point of view, but at least it was a stimulating one.

Dr Ernst had almost given up the search, and was preparing to make a descent by rope, when Lt Rodrigo spotted the narrow stairway. It could easily have been over-looked in the shadowed darkness below the edge of the cliff, for there was no guard-rail or other indication of its presence. And it seemed to lead no-where; it ran down the fifty-metre vertical wall at a steep angle, and disappeared below the surface of the Sea.

They scanned the flight of steps with their helmet-lights, could see no conceivable hazard, and Dr Ernst got Commander Norton's permission to descend. A minute later, she was cautiously testing the surface of the Sea.

Her foot slithered almost frictionlessly back and forth. The material felt exactly like ice. It *was* ice.

When she struck it with her hammer, a familiar pattern of cracks radiated from the impact point, and she had no difficulty in collecting as many pieces as she wished. Some had already melted when she held up the sample holder to the light; the liquid appeared to be slightly turbid water, and she took a cautious sniff.

'Is that safe?' Rodrigo called down, with a trace of anxiety.

'Believe me, Boris,' she answered, 'if there are any pathogens around here that have slipped through my detectors, our insurance policies lapsed a week ago.'

But Boris had a point. Despite all the tests that had been carried out, there was a very slight risk that this substance might be poisonous, or might carry some unknown disease. In normal circumstances, Dr Ernst would not have taken even this minuscule chance. Now, however, time was short and the stakes were enormous. If it became necessary to quarantine *Endeavour*, that would be a very small price to pay for her cargo of knowledge.

'It's water, but I wouldn't care to drink it – it smells like an algae culture that's gone bad. I can hardly wait to get it to the lab.'

'Is the ice safe to walk on?'

'Yes, solid as a rock.'

'Then we can get to New York.'

'Can we, Pieter? Have you ever tried to walk across four kilometers of ice?'

'Oh – I see what you mean. Just imagine what Stores would say, if we asked for a set of skates! Not that many of us would know how to use them, even if we had any aboard.'

'And there's another problem,' put in Boris Rodrigo. 'Do you realize that the temperature is already above freezing? Before long, that ice is going to melt. How many spacemen can swim four kilometres? Certainly not this one ...'

Dr Ernst rejoined them at the edge of the cliff, and held up the small sample bottle in triumph.

'It's a long walk for a few cc's of dirty water, but it may teach us more about Rama than anything we've found so far. Let's head for home.'

They turned towards the distant lights of the Hub, moving with the gentle, loping strides which had proved the most comfortable means of walking under this reduced gravity. Often they looked back, drawn by the hidden enigma of the island out there in the centre of the frozen sea.

And just once, Dr Ernst thought she felt the faint suspicion of a breeze against her cheek.

It did not come again, and she quickly forgot all about it.

16
Kealakekua

'As you know perfectly well, Dr Perera,' said Ambassador Bose in a tone of patient resignation, 'few of us share your knowledge of mathematical meteorology. So please take pity on our ignorance.'

'With pleasure,' answered the exobiologist, quite unabashed. 'I can explain it best by telling you what is going to happen inside Rama – very soon.

'The temperature is now about to rise, as the solar heat pulse reaches the interior. According to the latest information I've received, it's already above freezing point. The Cylindrical Sea will soon start to thaw; and unlike bodies of water on Earth, it will melt from the bottom upwards. That may produce some odd effects; but I'm much more concerned with the atmosphere.

'As it's heated, the air inside Rama will expand – and will attempt to rise towards the central axis. And this is the problem. At ground level, although it's apparently stationary, it's actually sharing the spin of Rama – over eight hundred kilometres an hour. As it rises towards the axis it will try to retain that speed – and it won't be able to do so, of course. The result will be violent winds and turbulence; I estimate velocities of between two and three hundred kilometres an hour.

'Incidentally, very much the same thing occurs on Earth. The heated air at the Equator – which shares the Earth's sixteen-hundred-kilometres-an-hour spin – runs into the same problem when it rises and flows north and south.'

'Ah, the Trade Winds! I remember that from my geography lessons.'

'Exactly, Sir Robert. Rama will have Trade Winds, with a vengeance. I believe they'll last only a few hours, and then some kind of equilibrium will be restored. Meanwhile, I should advise Commander Norton to evacuate – as soon as possible. Here is the message I propose sending.'

With a little imagination, Commander Norton told himself, he could pretend that this was an improvised night camp at the foot of some mountain in a remote region of Asia or America. The clutter of sleeping pads, collapsible chairs and tables, portable power plant, lighting equipment, electrosan toilets, and miscellaneous scientific apparatus would not have looked out of place on Earth – especially as there were men and women working here without life support systems.

Establishing Camp Alpha had been very hard work, for everything had had to be man-handled through the chain of airlocks, sledded down the slope from the Hub, and then retrieved and unpacked. Sometimes, when the braking parachutes had failed, a consignment had ended up a good kilometre away out on the plain. Despite this, several crew members had asked permission to make the ride; Norton had firmly forbidden it. In an emergency, however, he might be prepared to reconsider the ban.

Almost all this equipment would stay here, for the labour of carrying it back was unthinkable – in fact, impossible. There were times when Commander Norton felt an irrational shame at leaving so much human litter in this strangely immaculate place. When they finally departed, he was prepared to sacrifice some of their precious time to leave everything in good order. Improbable though it was, perhaps millions of years hence, when Rama shot through some other star system, it might have visitors again. He would like to give them a good impression of Earth.

Meanwhile, he had a rather more immediate problem. During the last twenty-four hours he had received almost identical messages from both Mars and Earth. It seemed an odd coincidence; perhaps they had been commiserating with each other, as wives who lived safely on different planets were liable to do under sufficient provocation. Rather pointedly, they had reminded him that even though he was now a great hero, he still had family responsibilities.

The Commander picked up a collapsible chair, and walked out of the pool of light into the darkness surrounding the camp. It was the only way he could get any privacy, and he could also think better away from the turmoil. Deliberately turning his back on the organised confusion behind him, he began to speak into the recorder slung around his neck.

'Original for personal file, dupes to Mars and Earth. Hello, darling – yes, I know I've been a lousy correspondent, but I haven't been aboard ship for a week. Apart from a skeleton crew, we're all camping inside Rama, at the foot of the stairway we've christened Alpha.

'I have three parties out now, scouting the plain, but we've made disappointingly slow progress, because everything has to be done on foot. If only we had some means of transport! I'd be very happy to settle for a few electric bicycles ... they'd be perfect for the job.

'You've met my medical officer, Surgeon-Commander Ernst—' He paused uncertainly; Laura had met *one* of his wives, but which? Better cut that out—

Erasing the sentence, he began again.

'My MO, Surgeon-Commander Ernst, led the first group to reach the Cylindrical Sea, fifteen kilometres from here. She found that it was frozen water, as we'd expected – but you wouldn't want to drink it. Dr Ernst says it's a dilute organic soup, containing traces of almost any carbon compound you care to name, as well as phosphates and nitrates and dozens of metallic salts. There's not the slightest sign of life – not even any dead micro-organisms. So we still know nothing about the biochemistry of the Ramans ... though it was probably not wildly different from ours.'

Something brushed lightly against his hair; he had been too busy to get it cut, and would have to do something about that before he next put on a space-helmet ...

'You've seen the viddies of Paris and the other towns we've explored on this side of the Sea ... London, Rome, Moscow. It's impossible to believe that they were ever built for anything to *live* in. Paris looks like a giant storage depot. London is a collection of cylinders linked together by pipes connected to what are obviously pumping stations. Everything is sealed up, and there's no way of finding what's inside without explosives or lasers. We won't try these until there are no alternatives.

'As for Rome and Moscow—'

'Excuse me, Skipper. Priority from Earth.'

What now? Norton asked himself. Can't a man get a few minutes to talk to his families?

He took the message from the Sergeant, and scanned it quickly, just to satisfy himself that it was not immediate. Then he read it again, more slowly.

What the devil was the Rama Committee? And why had he never heard of it? He knew that all sorts of associations, societies, and professional groups – some serious, some completely crackpot – had been trying to get in touch with him; Mission Control had done a good job of protection, and would not have forwarded this message unless it was considered important.

'Two-hundred-kilometre winds – probably sudden onset.' – well, that was something to think about. But it was hard to take it too seriously, on this utterly calm night; and it would be ridiculous to run away like frightened mice, when they were just starting effective exploration.

Commander Norton lifted a hand to brush aside his hair,

which had somehow fallen into his eyes again. Then he froze, the gesture uncompleted.

He *had* felt a trace of wind, several times in the last hour. It was so slight that he had completely ignored it; after all, he was the commander of a *space*ship, not a sailing ship. Until now the movement of air had not been of the slightest professional concern. What would the long-dead captain of that earlier *Endeavour* have done in a situation such as this?

Norton had asked himself that question at every moment of crisis in the last few years. It was his secret, which he had never revealed to anyone. And like most of the important things in life, it had come about quite by accident.

He had been captain of *Endeavour* for several months before he realised that it was named after one of the most famous ships in history. True, during the last four hundred years there had been a dozen *Endeavours* of sea and two of space, but the ancestor of them all was the 370-ton Whitby collier that Captain James Cook, RN, had sailed round the world between 1768 and 1771.

With a mild interest that had quickly turned to an absorbing curiosity – almost an obsession – Norton had begun to read everything he could find about Cook. He was now probably the world's leading authority on the greatest explorer of all time, and knew whole sections of the *Journals* by heart.

It still seemed incredible that one man could have done so much, with such primitive equipment. But Cook had been not only a supreme navigator, but a scientist and – in an age of brutal discipline – a humanitarian. He treated his own men with kindness, which was unusual; what was quite unheard of was that he behaved in exactly the same way to the often hostile savages in the new lands he discovered.

It was Norton's private dream, which he knew he would never achieve, to retrace at least one of Cook's voyages around the world. He had made a limited but spectacular start, which would certainly have astonished the Captain, when he once flew a polar orbit directly above the Great Barrier Reef. It had been early morning on a clear day, and from four hundred kilometres up he had had a superb view of that deadly wall of coral, marked by its line of white foam along the Queensland coast.

He had taken just under five minutes to travel the whole two thousand kilometres of the Reef. In a single glance he could span weeks of perilous voyaging for that first *Endeavour*. And through the telescope, he had caught a glimpse of Cooktown and the estuary where the ship had been dragged ashore for repairs, after her near-fatal encounter with the Reef.

A year later, a visit to the Hawaii Deep-Space Tracking Station had given him an even more unforgettable experience. He had taken the hydrofoil to Kealakekua Bay, and as he moved swiftly past the bleak volcanic cliffs, he felt a depth of emotion that had surprised and even disconcerted him. The guide had led his group of scientists, engineers and astronauts past the glittering metal pylon that had replaced the earlier monument, destroyed by the Great Tsunami of '68. They had walked on for a few more yards across black, slippery lava to the small plaque at the water's edge. Little waves were breaking over it, but Norton scarcely noticed them as he bent down to read the words:

NEAR THIS SPOT
CAPTAIN JAMES COOK
WAS KILLED
14 FEBRUARY, 1779
ORIGINAL TABLET DEDICATED 28 AUGUST, 1928
BY COOK SESQUICENTENNIAL COMMISSION
REPLACED BY TRICENTENNIAL COMMISSION
14 FEBRUARY, 2079

That was years ago, and a hundred million kilometres away. But at moments like this, Cook's reassuring presence seemed very close. In the secret depths of his mind, he would ask: 'Well, Captain – what is *your* advice?' It was a little game he played, on occasions when there were not enough facts for sound judgement, and one had to rely on intuition. That had been part of Cook's genius; he always made the right choice – until the very end, at Kealakekua Bay.

The Sergeant waited patiently, while his Commander stared silently out into the night of Rama. It was no longer unbroken, for at two spots about four kilometres away, the faint patches of light of exploring parties could be clearly seen.

In an emergency, I can recall them within the hour, Norton told himself. And that, surely, should be good enough.

He turned to the Sergeant, 'Take this message. Rama Committee, care of Spacecom. Appreciate your advice and will take precautions. Please specify meaning of phrase "sudden onset". Respectfully, Norton, Commander, *Endeavour*.'

He waited until the Sergeant had disappeared towards the blazing lights of the camp, then switched on his recorder again. But the train of thought was broken, and he could not get back into the mood. The letter would have to wait for some other time.

It was not often that Captain Cook came to his aid when he was neglecting his duty. But he suddenly remembered how rarely and briefly poor Elizabeth Cook had seen her husband in sixteen years of married life. Yet she had borne him six children – and outlived them all.

His wives, never more than ten minutes away at the speed of light, had nothing to complain about …

17
Spring

During the first 'nights' on Rama, it had not been easy to sleep. The darkness and the mysteries it concealed were oppressive, but even more unsettling was the silence. Absence of noise is not a natural condition; all human senses require some input. If they are deprived of it, the mind manufactures its own substitutes.

And so many sleepers had complained of strange noises – even of voices – which were obviously illusions, because those awake had heard nothing. Surgeon-Commander Ernst had prescribed a very simple and effective cure; during the sleeping period, the camp was now lulled by gentle, unobtrusive background music.

This night, Commander Norton found the cure inadequate. He kept straining his ears into the darkness, and he knew what he was listening for. But though a very faint breeze did caress his face from time to time, there was no sound that could possibly be taken for that of a distant, rising wind. Nor did either of the exploring parties report anything unusual.

At last, around Ship's midnight, he went to sleep. There was always a man on watch at the communications console, in case of any urgent messages. No other precautions seemed necessary.

Not even a hurricane could have created the sound that did wake him, and the whole camp, in a single instant. It seemed that the sky was falling, or that Rama had split open and was tearing itself apart. First there was a rending crack, then a long-drawn-out series of crystalline crashes like a million glass-houses being demolished. It lasted for minutes, though it seemed like hours; it was still continuing, apparently moving away into the distance, when Norton got to the message centre.

'Hub Control! What's happened?'

'Just a moment, Skipper. It's over by the Sea. We're getting the light on it.'

Eight kilometres overhead, on the axis of Rama, the searchlight began to swing its beam out across the plain. It reached the edge of the Sea, then started to track along it, scanning around the interior of the world. A quarter of the way round the cylindrical surface, it stopped.

Up there in the sky – or what the mind still persisted in calling the sky – something extraordinary was happening. At first, it seemed to Norton that the Sea was boiling. It was no longer static and frozen in the grip of an eternal winter; a huge area, kilometers across, was in turbulent movement. And it was changing colour; a broad band of white was marching across the ice.

Suddenly a slab perhaps a quarter of a kilometre on a side began to tilt upwards like an opening door. Slowly and majestically, it reared into the sky, glittering and sparkling in the beam of the searchlight. Then it slid back and vanished underneath the surface, while a tidal wave of foaming water raced outwards in all directions from its point of submergence.

Not until then did Commander Norton fully realize what was happening. *The ice was breaking up.* All these days and weeks, the Sea had been thawing, far down in the depths. It was hard to concentrate because of the crashing roar that still filled the world and echoed round the sky, but he tried to think of a reason for so dramatic a convulsion. When a frozen lake or river thawed on Earth, it was nothing like this ...

But of course! It was obvious enough, now that it had happened. The Sea was thawing from *beneath* as the solar heat seeped through the hull of Rama. And when ice turns into water, it occupies less volume ...

So the Sea had been sinking below the upper layer of ice, leaving it unsupported. Day by day the strain had been building up; now the band of ice that encircled the equator of Rama was collapsing, like a bridge that had lost its central pier. It was splintering into hundreds of floating islands, that would crash and jostle into each other until they too melted. Norton's blood ran suddenly cold, when he remembered the plans that were being made to reach New York by sledge ...

The tumult was swiftly subsiding; a temporary stalemate had been reached in the war between ice and water. In a few hours, as the temperature continued to rise, the water would win and the last vestiges of ice would disappear. But in the long run, ice would be the victor, as Rama rounded the sun and set forth once more into the interstellar night.

Norton remembered to start breathing again; then he called the party nearest the Sea. To his relief, Lieutenant Rodrigo answered at once. No, the water hadn't reached them. No tidal wave had come sloshing over the edge of the cliff. 'So now we know,' he added very calmly, 'why there *is* a cliff.' Norton agreed silently; but that hardly explains, he thought to himself, why the cliff on the southern shore is ten times higher ...

The Hub searchlight continued to scan round the world. The awakened Sea was steadily calming, and the boiling white foam no longer raced outwards from capsizing ice-floes. In fifteen minutes, the main disturbance was over.

But Rama was no longer silent; it had awakened from its sleep, and ever and again there came the sound of grinding ice as one berg collided with another.

Spring had been a little late, Norton told himself, but winter had ended.

And there was that breeze again, stronger than ever. Rama had given him enough warnings; it was time to go.

As he neared the halfway mark, Commander Norton once again

felt gratitude to the darkness that concealed the view above – and below. Though he knew that more than ten thousand steps still lay ahead of him, and could picture the steeply ascending curve in his mind's eye, the fact that he could see only a small portion of it made the prospect more bearable.

This was his second ascent, and he had learned from his mistakes on the first. The great temptation was to climb too quickly in this low gravity; every step was so easy that it was very hard to adopt a slow, plodding rhythm. But unless one did this, after the first few thousand steps strange aches developed in the thighs and calves. Muscles that one never knew existed started to protest, and it was necessary to take longer and longer periods of rest. Towards the end he had spent more time resting than climbing, and even then it was not enough. He had suffered painful leg-cramps for the next two days, and would have been almost incapacitated had he not been back in the zero-gravity environment of the ship.

So this time he had started with almost painful slowness, moving like an old man. He had been the last to leave the plain, and the others were strung out along the half-kilometre of stairway above him; he could see their lights moving up the invisble slope ahead.

He felt sick at heart at the failure of his mission, and even now hoped that this was only a temporary retreat. When they reached the Hub, they could wait until any atmospheric disturbances had ceased. Presumably, it would be a dead calm there, as at the centre of a cyclone, and they could wait out the expected storm in safety.

Once again, he was jumping to conclusions, drawing dangerous analogies from Earth. The meteorology of a whole world, even under steady-state conditions, was a matter of enormous complexity. After several centuries of study, terrestrial weather-forecasting was still not absolutely reliable. And Rama was not merely a completely novel system; it was also undergoing rapid changes, for the temperature had risen several degrees in the last few hours. Yet still there was no sign of the promised hurricane, though there had been a few feeble gusts from apparently random directions.

They had now climbed five kilometres, which in this low and steadily diminishing gravity was equivalent to less than two on Earth. At the third level, three kilometres from the axis, they rested for an hour, taking light refreshments and massaging leg muscles. This was the last point at which they could breathe in comfort; like old-time Himalayan mountaineers, they had left their oxygen supplies here, and now put them on for the final ascent.

An hour later, they had reached the top of the stairway – and the beginning of the ladder. Ahead lay the last, vertical kilometre, fortunately in a gravity field only a few per cent of Earth's. Another thirty-minute rest, a careful check of oxygen, and they were ready for the final lap.

Once again, Norton made sure that all his men were safely ahead of him, spaced out at twenty-metre intervals along the ladder. From now on, it would be a slow, steady haul, extremely boring. The best technique was to empty the mind of all thoughts and to count the rungs as they drifted by – one hundred, two hundred, three hundred, four hundred ...

He had just reached twelve hundred and fifty when he suddenly realised that something was wrong. The light shining on the vertical surface immediately in front of his eyes was the wrong colour – and it was much too bright.

Commander Norton did not even have time to check his ascent, or to call a warning to his men. Everything happened in less than a second.

In a soundless concussion of light, dawn burst upon Rama.

18
Dawn

The light was so brilliant that for a full minute Norton had to keep his eyes clenched tightly shut. Then he risked opening them, and stared through barely-parted lids at the wall a few centimetres in front of his face. He blinked several times, waited for the involuntary tears to drain away, and then turned slowly to behold the dawn.

He could endure the sight for only a few seconds; then he was forced to close his eyes again. It was not the glare that was intolerable – he could grow accustomed to that – but the awesome spectacle of Rama, now seen for the first time in its entirety.

Norton had known exactly what to expect; nevertheless the sight had stunned him. He was seized by a spasm of uncontrollable trembling; his hands tightened round the rungs of the ladder with the violence of a drowning man clutching at a lifebelt. The muscles of his forearms began to knot, yet at the same time his legs – already fatigued by hours of steady climbing – seemed about to give way. If it had not been for the low gravity, he might have fallen.

Then his training took over, and he began to apply the first remedy for panic. Still keeping his eyes closed and trying to forget the monstrous spectacle around him, he started to take deep, long breaths, filling his lungs with oxygen and washing the poisons of fatigue out of his system.

Presently he felt much better, but he did not open his eyes until he had performed one more action. It took a major effort of will to force his right hand to open – he had to talk to it like a disobedient child – but presently he manoeuvred it down to his waist, unclipped the safety belt from his harness, and hooked the buckle to the nearest rung. Now, whatever happened, he could not fall.

Norton took several more deep breaths; then – still keeping his eyes closed – he switched on his radio. He hoped his voice sounded calm and authoritative as he called: 'Captain here. Is everyone OK?'

As he checked off the names one by one, and received answers – even if somewhat tremulous ones – from everybody, his own confidence and self-control came swiftly back to him. All his men were safe, and were looking to him for leadership. He was the commander once more.

'Keep your eyes closed until you're quite sure you can take it,' he called. 'The view is – overwhelming. If anyone finds that it's too much, keep on climbing without looking back. Remember, you'll soon be at zero gravity, so you can't possibly fall.'

It was hardly necessary to point out such an elementary fact to trained spacemen, but Norton had to remind himself of it every few seconds. The thought of zero-gravity was a kind of talisman, protecting him from harm. Whatever his eyes told him, Rama could not drag him down to destruction on the plain eight kilometres below.

It became an urgent matter of pride and self-esteem that he should open his eyes once more and look at the world around him. But first, he had to get his body under control.

He let go of the ladder with *both* hands, and hooked his left arm under a rung. Clenching and unclenching his fists, he waited until the muscle cramps had faded away; then, when he felt quite comfortable, he opened his eyes and slowly turned to face Rama.

His first impression was one of blueness. The glare that filled the sky could not have been mistaken for sunlight; it might have been that of an electric arc. So Rama's sun, Norton told himself, must be hotter than ours. That should interest the astronomers . . .

And now he understood the purpose of those mysterious trenches, the Straight Valley and its five companions; they were nothing less than gigantic strip-lights. Rama had six linear suns, symmetrically ranged around its interior. From each, a broad fan of light was aimed across the central axis, to shine upon the far side of the world. Norton wondered if they could be switched alternately to produce a cycle of light and darkness, or whether this was a planet of perpetual day.

Too much staring at those blinding bars of light had made his eyes hurt again; he was not sorry to have a good excuse to close them for a while. It was not until then, when he had almost recovered from this initial visual shock, that he was able to devote himself to a much more serious problem.

Who, or what, had switched on the lights of Rama?

This world was sterile, by the most sensitive tests that man could apply to it. But now something was happening that could not be explained by the action of natural forces. There might not be life here, but there could be consciousness, awareness; robots might be waking after a sleep of aeons. Perhaps this outburst of light was an unprogrammed, random spasm – a last dying gasp of machines that were responding wildly to the warmth of a new sun, and would soon lapse again into quiescence, this time for ever.

Yet Norton could not believe such a simple explanation. Bits of the jigsaw puzzle were beginning to fall into place, though many were still missing. The absence of all signs of wear, for example – the feeling of *newness*, as if Rama had just been created . . .

These thoughts might have inspired fear, even terror. Somehow, they did nothing of the sort. On the contrary, Norton felt a sense of exhilaration – almost of delight. There was far more here to discover than they had ever dared to hope. 'Wait,' he said to himself, 'until the Rama Committee hears about *this*!'

Then, with a calm determination, he opened his eyes again and began a careful inventory of everything he saw.

First, he had to establish some kind of reference system. He was looking at the largest enclosed space ever seen by man, and needed a mental map to find his way around it.

The feeble gravity was very little help, for with an effort of will he could switch Up and Down in any direction he pleased. But some directions were psychologically dangerous; whenever his mind skirted these, he had to vector it hastily away.

Safest of all was to imagine that he was at the bowl-shaped bottom of a gigantic well, sixteen kilometres wide and fifty deep. The advantage of this image was that there could be no danger of falling further; nevertheless, it had some serious defects.

He could pretend that the scattered towns and cities, and the differently coloured and textured areas, were all securely fixed to the towering walls. The various complex structures that could be seen hanging from the dome overhead were perhaps no more disconcerting than the pendent candelabra in some great concert-hall on Earth. What was quite unacceptable was the Cylindrical Sea ...

There it was, halfway up the well-shaft – a band of water, wrapped completely round it, with no visible means of support. There could be no doubt that it *was* water; it was a vivid blue, flecked with brilliant sparkles from the few remaining ice-floes. But a vertical sea forming a complete circle twenty kilometres up in the sky was such an unsettling phenomenon that after a while he began to seek an alternative.

That was when his mind switched the scene through ninety degrees. Instantly, the deep well became a long tunnel, capped at either end. 'Down' was obviously in the direction of the ladder and the stairway he had just ascended; and now with this perspective, Norton was at last able to appreciate the true vision of the architects who had built this place.

He was clinging to the face of a curving sixteen-kilometre-high cliff, the upper half of which overhung completely until it merged into the arched roof of what was now the sky. Beneath him, the ladder descended more than five hundred metres, until it ended at the first ledge or terrace. There the stairway began, continuing almost vertically at first in this low-gravity regime, then slowly becoming less and less steep until, after breaking at five more platforms, it reached the distant plain. For the first two or three kilometres he could see the individual steps, but thereafter they had merged into a continuous band.

The downward swoop of that immense stairway was so overwhelming that it was impossible to appreciate its true scale. Norton had once flown round Mount Everest, and had been awed by its size. He reminded himself that this stairway was as high as the Himalayas, but the comparison was meaningless.

And no comparison at all was possible with the other two stairways, Beta and Gamma, which slanted up into the sky and then curved far out over his head. Norton had now acquired enough confidence to lean back and glance up at them – briefly. Then he tried to forget that they were there ...

For too much thinking along those lines evoked yet a third image of Rama, which he was anxious to avoid at all costs. This was the viewpoint that regarded it once again at a vertical cylinder or well – but now he was at the *top*, not the bottom, like a fly crawling upside down on a domed ceiling, with a fifty-kilometre drop immediately below. Every time Norton found this image creeping up on him, it needed all his willpower not to cling to the ladder again in mindless panic.

In time, he was sure, all these fears would ebb. The wonder and strangeness of Rama would banish its terrors, at least for men who were trained to face the realities of space. Perhaps no one who had never left Earth, and had never seen the stars all around him, could endure these vistas. But if any men could accept them, Norton told himself with grim determination, it would be the captain and crew of *Endeavour*.

He looked at his chronometer. This pause had lasted only two minutes, but it had seemed a lifetime. Exerting barely enough effort to overcome his inertia and the fading gravitational field, he started to pull himself slowly up the last hundred metres of the ladder. Just before he entered the airlock and turned his back upon Rama, he made one final swift survey of the interior.

It had changed, even in the last few minutes; a mist was rising from the Sea. For the first few hundred metres the ghostly white columns were tilted sharply forward in the direction of Rama's spin; then they started to dissolve in a swirl of turbulence, as the uprushing air tried to jettison its excess velocity. The Trade Winds of this cylindrical world were beginning to etch their patterns in its sky; the first tropical storm in unknown ages was about to break.

19
A Warning from Mercury

It was the first time in weeks that every member of the Rama Committee had made himself available. Professor Solomons had emerged from the depths of the Pacific, where he had been studying mining operations along the mid-ocean trenches. And to nobody's surprise, Dr Taylor had reappeared, now that there was at least a possibility that Rama held something more newsworthy than lifeless artifacts.

The Chairman had fully expected Dr Carlisle Perera to be even more dogmatically assertive than usual, now that his prediction of a Raman hurricane had been confirmed. To His Excellency's great surprise, Perera was remarkably subdued, and accepted the congratulations of his colleagues in a manner as near to embarrassment as he was ever likely to achieve.

The exobiologist, in fact, was deeply mortified. The spectacular break-up of the Cylindrical Sea was a much more obvious phenomenon than the hurricane winds – yet he had completely overlooked it. To have remembered that hot air rises, but to have forgotten that hot ice contracts, was not an achievement of which he could be very proud. However, he would soon get over it, and revert to his normal Olympian self-confidence.

When the Chairman offered him the floor, and asked what further climatic changes he expected, he was very careful to hedge his bets.

'You must realise,' he explained, 'that the meteorology of a world as strange as Rama may have many other surprises. But if my calculations are correct, there will be no further storms, and conditions will soon be stable. There will be a slow temperature rise until perihelion – and beyond – but that won't concern us, as *Endeavour* will have had to leave long before then.'

'So it should soon be safe to go back inside?'

'Er – probably. We should certainly know in forty-eight hours.'

'A return is imperative,' said the Ambassador for Mercury. 'We have to learn everything we possibly can about Rama. The situation has now changed completely.'

'I think we know what you mean, but would you care to elaborate?'

'Of course. Until now, we have assumed that Rama is lifeless – or at any rate uncontrolled. But we can no longer pretend that it is a derelict. Even if there are no life-forms aboard, it may be directed by robot mechanisms, programmed to carry out some mission – perhaps one highly disadvantageous to us. Unpalatable though it may be, we must consider the question of self-defence.'

There was a babble of protesting voices, and the Chairman had to hold up his hand to restore order.

'Let His Excellency finish!' he pleaded. 'Whether we like the idea or not, it should be considered seriously.'

'With all due respect to the Ambassador,' said Dr Conrad Taylor in his most disrespectful voice, 'I think we can rule out as naïve the fear of malevolent intervention. Creatures as advanced as the Ramans must have correspondingly developed morals. Otherwise, they would have destroyed themselves – as we nearly did in the twentieth century. I've made that quite clear in my new book *Ethos and Cosmos*. I hope you received your copy.'

'Yes, thank you, though I'm afraid the pressure of other matters has not allowed me to read beyond the introduction. However, I'm familiar with the general thesis. We may have no malevolent intentions towards an ant-heap. But if we want to build a house on the same site ...'

'This is as bad as the Pandora Party! It's nothing less than interstellar xenophobia!'

'Please, *gentlemen*! This is getting us nowhere. Mr Ambassador, you still have the floor.'

The Chairman glared across three hundred and eighty thousand kilometres of space at Conrad Taylor, who reluctantly subsided, like a volcano biding its time.

'Thank you,' said the Ambassador for Mercury. 'The danger may be unlikely, but where the future of the human race is involved, we can take no chances. And, if I may say so, we Hermians may be particularly concerned. We may have more cause for alarm than anyone else.'

Dr Taylor snorted audibly, but was quelled by another glare from the Moon.

'Why Mercury, more than any other planet?' asked the Chairman.

'Look at the dynamics of the situation. Rama is already inside our orbit. It is only an assumption that it will go round the sun and head on out again into space. Suppose it carries out a braking manoeuvre? If it does so, this will be at perihelion, about thirty days from now. My scientists tell me that if the entire velocity change is carried out there, Rama will end up in a circular orbit only twenty-five million kilometres from the sun. From there, it could dominate the solar system.'

For a long time nobody – not even Conrad Taylor – spoke a word. All the members of the Committee were marshalling their thoughts about those difficult people the Hermians, so ably represented here by their Ambassador.

To most people, Mercury was a fairly good approximation of Hell; at least, it would do until something worse came along. But the Hermians were proud of their bizarre planet, with its days longer than its years, its double sunrises and sunsets, its rivers of molten metal ... By comparison, the Moon and Mars had been almost trivial challenges. Not until men landed on Venus (if they ever did) would they encounter an environment more hostile than that of Mercury.

And yet this world had turned out to be, in many ways, the key to the solar system. This seemed obvious in retrospect, but the Space Age had been almost a century old before the fact was realised. Now the Hermians never let anyone forget it.

Long before men reached the planet, Mercury's abnormal density hinted at the heavy elements it contained; even so, its wealth was still a source of astonishment, and had postponed for a thousand years any fears that the key metals of human civilisation would be exhausted. And these treasures were in the best possible place, where the power of the Sun was ten times greater than on frigid Earth.

Unlimited energy – unlimited metal; *that* was Mercury. Its great magnetic launchers could catapult manufactured products to any point in the solar system. It could also export energy, in synthetic transuranium isotopes or pure radiation. It had even been proposed that Hermian lasers would one day thaw out gigantic Jupiter, but this idea had not been well received on the other worlds. A technology that could cook Jupiter had too many tempting possibilities for interplanetary blackmail.

That such a concern had ever been expressed said a good deal about the general attitude towards the Hermians. They were respected for their toughness and engineering skills, and admired for the way in which they had conquered so fearsome a world. But they were not liked, and still less were they completely trusted.

At the same time, it was possible to appreciate their point of view. The Hermians, it was often joked, some times behaved as if the Sun was their personal property. They were bound to it in an intimate love-hate relationship – as the Vikings had once been linked to the sea, the Nepalese to the Himalayas, the Eskimos to the Tundra. They would be most unhappy if something came between them and the natural force that dominated and controlled their lives.

At last, the Chairman broke the long silence. He still remembered the sun of India, and shuddered to contemplate the sun of Mercury. So he took the Hermians very seriously indeed, even though he considered them uncouth technological barbarians.

'I think there is some merit in your argument, Mr Ambassador,' he said slowly. 'Have you any proposals?'

'Yes, sir. Before we know what action to take, we must have the facts. We know the geography of Rama – if one can use that term – but we have no idea of its capabilities. And the key to the whole problem is this: does Rama have a propulsion system? *Can it change orbit?* I'd be very interested in Dr Perera's views.'

'I've given the subject a good deal of thought,' answered the exobiologist. 'Of course, Rama must have been given its original impetus by some launching device, but that could have been an external booster. If it does have onboard propulsion, we've found no trace of it. Certainly there are no rocket exhausts, or anything similar, anywhere on the outer shell.'

'They could be hidden.'

'True, but there would seem little point in it. And where are the propellant tanks, the energy sources? The main hull is solid – we've checked that with seismic surveys. The cavities in the northern cap are all accounted for by the airlock systems.

'That leaves the southern end of Rama, which Commander Norton has been unable to reach, owing to that ten-kilometre-wide band of water. There are all sorts of curious mechanisms and structures up on the South Pole – you've seen the photographs. What they are is anybody's guess.

'But I'm reasonably sure of this. If Rama does have a propulsion system, it's something completely outside our present knowledge. In fact, it would have to be the fabulous "Space Drive" people have been talking about for two hundred years.'

'You wouldn't rule that out?'

'Certainly not. If we can prove that Rama has a Space Drive – even if we learn nothing about its mode of operation – that would be a major discovery. At least we'd know that such a thing is possible.'

'What *is* a Space Drive?' asked the Ambassador for Earth, rather plaintively.

'Any kind of propulsion system, Sir Robert, that doesn't work on the rocket principle. Anti-gravity – if it is possible – would do very nicely. At present, we don't know where to look for such a drive, and most scientists doubt if it exists.'

'It doesn't,' Professor Davidson interjected. 'Newton settled *that*. You can't have action without reaction. Space Drives are nonsense. Take it from me.'

'You may be right,' Perera replied with unusual blandness. 'But if Rama doesn't have a Space Drive, it has no drive at all. There's simply no room for a conventional propulsion system, with its enormous fuel tanks.'

'It's hard to imagine a whole world being pushed around,' said Dennis Solomons. 'What would happen to the objects inside it? Everything would have to be bolted down. Most inconvenient.'

'Well, the acceleration would probably be very low. The biggest problem would be the water in the Cylindrical Sea. How would you stop that from ...'

Perera's voice suddenly faded away, and his eyes glazed over. He seemed to be in the throes of an incipient epileptic fit, or even a heart attack. His colleagues looked at him in alarm; then he made a sudden recovery, banged his fist on the table and shouted: 'Of course! That explains everything! The southern cliff – *now* it makes sense!'

'Not to me,' grumbled the Lunar Ambassador, speaking for all the diplomats present.

'Look at this longitudinal cross-section of Rama,' Perera continued excitedly, unfolding his map. 'Have you got your copies? The Cylindrical Sea is enclosed between two cliffs, which completely circle the interior of Rama. The one on the north is only fifty metres high. The southern one, on the other hand, is almost half a kilometre high. Why the big difference? No one's been able to think of a sensible reason.

'But suppose Rama *is* able to propel itself – accelerating so that the northern end is forward. The water in the Sea would tend to move back; the level at the south would rise – perhaps hundreds of metres. Hence the cliff. Let's see—'

Perera started scribbling furiously. After an astonishingly short time – it could not have been more than twenty seconds – he looked up in triumph.

'Knowing the height of those cliffs, we can calculate the maximum acceleration Rama can take. If it was more than two per cent of a gravity, the Sea would slosh over into the southern continent.'

'A fiftieth of a gee? That's not very much.'

'It is – for a mass of ten million megatons. And it's all you need for astronomical manoeuvring.'

'Thank you very much, Dr Perera,' said the Hermian Ambassador. 'You've given us a lot to think about. Mr Chairman – can we impress on Commander Norton the importance of looking at the South Polar region?'

'He's doing his best. The Sea is the obstacle, of course. They're trying to build some kind of raft – so that they can at least reach New York.'

'The South Pole may be even more important. Meanwhile, I am going to bring these matters to the attention of the General Assembly. Do I have your approval?'

There were no objections, not even from Dr Taylor. But just as the Committee members were about to switch out of circuit, Sir Lewis raised his hand.

The old historian very seldom spoke; when he did, everyone listened.

'Suppose we do find that Rama is – *active* – and has these capabilities. There is an old saying in military affairs that capability does not imply intention.'

'How long should we wait to find what its intentions are?' asked the Hermian. 'When we discover them, it may be far too late.'

'It is already too late. There is nothing we can do to affect Rama. Indeed, I doubt if there ever was.'

'I do not admit that, Sir Lewis. There are many things we can do – if it proves necessary. But the time is desperately short. Rama is a cosmic egg, being warmed by the fires of the sun. It may hatch at any moment.'

The Chairman of the Committee looked at the Ambassador for Mercury in frank astonishment. He had seldom been so surprised in his diplomatic career.

He would never have dreamed that a Hermian was capable of such a poetic flight of imagination.

20
Book of Revelation

When one of his crew called him 'Commander', or, worse still 'Mister Norton', there was always something serious afoot. He could not recall that Boris Rodrigo had ever before addressed him in such a fashion, so this must be doubly serious. Even in normal times, Lieut-Commander Rodrigo was a very grave and sober person.

'What's the problem, Boris?' he asked when the cabin door closed behind them.

'I'd like permission, commander, to use Ship Priority for a direct message to Earth.'

This *was* unusual, though not unprecedented. Routine signals went to the nearest planetary relay – at the moment, they were working through Mercury – and even though the transit time was only a matter of minutes, it was often five or six hours before a message arrived at the desk of the person for whom it was intended. Ninety-nine per cent of the time, that was quite good enough; but in an emergency more direct, and much more expensive, channels could be employed, at the captain's discretion.

'You know, of course, that you have to give me a good reason. All our available bandwidth is already clogged with data transmissions. Is this a personal emergency?'

'No, Commander. It is much more important than *that*. I want to send a message to the Mother Church.'

Uh-uh, said Norton to himself. How do I handle this?

'I'd be glad if you'll explain.'

It was not mere curiosity that prompted Norton's request – though that was certainly present. If he gave Boris the priority he asked, he would have to justify his action.

The calm, blue eyes stared into his. He had never known Boris to lose control, to be other than completely self-assured. All the Cosmo-Christers were like this; it was one of the benefits of their faith, and it helped to make them good spacemen. Sometimes, however, their unquestioning certainty was just a little annoying to those unfortunates who had not been vouch-safed the Revelation.

'It concerns the purpose of Rama, Commander. I believe I have discovered it.'

'Go on.'

'Look at the situation. Here is a completely empty, lifeless world – yet it is suitable for human beings. It has water, and an atmosphere we can breathe. It comes from the remote depths of space, aimed precisely at the solar system – something quite incredible, if it was a matter of pure chance. And it appears not only new; *it looks as if it has never been used.*'

We've all been through this dozens of times, Norton told himself. What could Boris add to it?

'Our faith has told us to expect such a visitation though we do not know exactly what form it will take. The Bible gives hints. If this is not the Second Coming, it may be the Second Judgement; the story of Noah describes the first. I believe that Rama is a cosmic Ark, sent here to save – those who are worthy of salvation.'

There was silence for quite a while in the Captain's cabin. It was not that Norton was at a loss for words; rather, he could think of too many questions, but he was not sure which ones it would be tactful to ask.

Finally he remarked, in as mild and non-committal a voice as he could manage: 'That's a very interesting concept, and though

I don't go along with your faith, it's a tantalisingly plausible one.' He was not being hypocritical or flattering; stripped of its religious overtones, Rodrigo's theory was at least as convincing as half a dozen others he had heard. Suppose some catastrophe was about to befall the human race, and a benevolent higher intelligence knew all about it? That would explain everything, very neatly. However, there were still a few problems ...

'A couple of questions, Boris. Rama will be at perihelion in three weeks; then it will round the sun and leave the solar system just as fast as it came in. There's not much time for a Day of Judgement, or for shipping across those who are, er, selected – however *that's* going to be done.'

'Very true. So when it reaches perihelion, Rama will have to decelerate and go into a parking orbit – probably one with aphelion at Earth's orbit. There it might make another velocity change, and rendezvous with Earth.'

This was disturbingly persuasive. If Rama wished to remain in the solar system, it was going the right way about it. The most efficient way to slow down was to get as close to the sun as possible, and carry out the braking manoeuvre there. If there was any truth in Rodrigo's theory – or some variant of it – it would soon be put to the test.

'One other point, Boris. What's controlling Rama now?'

'There is no doctrine to advise on that. It could be a pure robot. Or it could be – a spirit. That would explain why there are no signs of biological life-forms.'

The Haunted Asteroid; why had that phrase popped up from the depths of memory? Then he recalled a silly story he had read years ago; he thought it best not to ask Boris if he had ever run into it. He doubted if the other's tastes ran to that sort of reading.

'I'll tell you what we'll do, Boris,' said Norton, abruptly making up his mind. He wanted to terminate this interview before it got too difficult, and thought he had found a good compromise.

'Can you sum up your ideas in less than – oh, a thousand bits?'

'Yes, I think so.'

'Well, if you can make it sound like a straightforward scientific theory, I'll send it, top priority, to the Rama Committee. Then a copy can go to your Church at the same time, and everyone will be happy.'

'Thank you, Commander, I really appreciate it.'

'Oh, I'm not doing this to save my conscience. I'd just like to see what the Committee makes of it. Even if I don't agree with you all along the line, you may have hit on something important.'

'Well, we'll know at perihelion, won't we?'

'Yes. We'll know at perihelion.'

When Boris Rodrigo had left, Norton called the bridge and gave necessary authorisation. He thought he had solved the problem rather neatly; besides, just suppose that Boris *was* right.

He might have increased his chances of being among the saved.

21
After the Storm

As they drifted along the now familiar corridor of the Alpha Airlock complex, Norton wondered if they had let impatience overcome caution. They had waited aboard *Endeavour* for forty-eight hours – two precious days – ready for instant departure if events should justify it. But nothing had happened; the instruments left in Rama had detected no unusual activity. Frustratingly, the television camera on the Hub had been blinded by a fog which had reduced visibility to a few metres and had only now started to retreat.

When they operated the final airlock door, and floated out into the cat's-cradle of guide-ropes around the Hub, Norton was struck first by the change in the light. It was no longer harshly blue, but was much more mellow and gentle, reminding him of a bright, hazy day on Earth.

He looked outwards along the axis of the world – and could see nothing except a glowing, featureless tunnel of white, reaching all the way to those strange mountains at the South Pole. The interior of Rama was completely blanketed with clouds, and nowhere was a break visible in the overcast. The top of the layer was quite sharply defined; it formed a smaller cylinder inside the larger one of this spinning world, leaving a central core, five or six kilometers wide, quite clear except for a few stray wisps of cirrus.

The immense tube of cloud was lit from underneath by the six artificial suns of Rama. The locations of the three on this

Northern continent were clearly defined by diffuse strips of light, but those on the far side of the Cylindrical Sea merged together into a continuous, glowing band.

What is happening down beneath those clouds? Norton asked himself. But at least the storm, which had centrifuged them into such perfect symmetry about the axis of Rama, had now died away. Unless there were some other surprises, it would be safe to descend.

It seemed appropriate, on this return visit, to use the team that had made the first deep penetration into Rama. Sergeant Myron – like every other member of *Endeavour*'s crew – now fully met Surgeon-Commander Ernst's physical requirements; he even maintained, with convincing sincerity, that he was never going to wear his old uniforms again.

As Norton watched Mercer, Calvert and Myron 'swimming' quickly and confidently down the ladder, he reminded himself how much had changed. That first time they had descended in cold and darkness; now they were going towards light and warmth. And on all earlier visits, they had been confident that Rama was dead. That might yet be true, in a biological sense. But something was stirring; and Boris Rodrigo's phrase would do as well as any other. The spirit of Rama was awake.

When they had reached the platform at the foot of the ladder and were preparing to start down the stairway, Mercer carried out his usual routine test of the atmosphere. There were some things that he never took for granted; even when the people around him were breathing perfectly comfortably, without aids, he had been known to stop for an air check before opening his helmet. When asked to justify such excessive caution, he had answered: 'Because human senses aren't good enough, that's why. You may think you're fine, but you could fall flat on your face with the next deep breath.'

He looked at his meter, and said 'Damn!'

'What's the trouble?' asked Calvert.

'It's broken – reading too high. Odd; I've never known that to happen before. I'll check it on my breathing circuit.'

He plugged the compact little analyser into the test point of his oxygen supply, then stood in thoughtful silence for a while. His companions looked at him with anxious concern; anything that upset Karl was to be taken very seriously indeed.

He unplugged the meter, used it to sample the Rama atmosphere again, then called Hub Control.

'Skipper! Will you take an O_2 reading?'

There was a much longer pause than the request justified. Then Norton radioed back: 'I think there's something wrong with my meter.'

A slow smile spread across Mercer's face.

'It's up fifty per cent, isn't it?'

'Yes, what does that mean?'

'It means that we can all take off our masks. Isn't that convenient?'

'I'm not sure,' replied Norton, echoing the sarcasm in Mercer's voice. 'It seems too good to be true.' There was no need to say any more. Like all spacemen, Commander Norton had a profound suspicion of things that were too good to be true.

Mercer cracked his mask open a trifle, and took a cautious sniff. For the first time at this altitude, the air was perfectly breathable. The musty, dead smell had gone; so had the excessive dryness, which in the past had caused several respiratory complaints. Humidity was now an astonishing eighty per cent; doubtless the thawing of the Sea was responsible for this. There was a muggy feeling in the air, though not an unpleasant one. It was like a summer evening. Mercer told himself, on some tropical coast. The climate inside Rama had improved dramatically during the last few days ...

And why? The increased humidity was no problem; the startling rise in oxygen was much more difficult to explain.

As he recommended the descent, Mercer began a whole series of mental calculations. He had not arrived at any satisfactory result by the time they entered the cloud layer.

It was a dramatic experience, for the transition was very abrupt. At one moment they were sliding downwards in clear air, gripping the smooth metal of the handrail so that they would not gain speed too swiftly in this quarter-of-a-gravity region. Then, suddenly, they shot into a blinding white fog, and visibility dropped to a few metres. Mercer put on the brakes so quickly that Calvert almost bumped into him – and Myron *did* bump into Calvert, nearly knocking him off the rail.

'Take it easy,' said Mercer. 'Spread out so we can just see each other. And don't let yourself build up speed, in case I have to stop suddenly.'

In eerie silence, they continued to glide downwards through the fog. Calvert could just see Mercer as a vague shadow ten metres ahead, and when he looked back, Myron was at the same distance behind him. In some ways, this was even spookier than descending in the complete darkness of the Raman night; then, at least, the searchlight beams had shown them what lay ahead. But *this* was like diving in poor visibility in the open sea.

It was impossible to tell how far they had travelled, and Calvert guessed they had almost reached the fourth level when Mercer suddenly braked again. When they had bunched together, he whispered: 'Listen! Don't you hear something?'

'Yes,' said Myron, after a minute. 'It sounds like the wind.'

Calvert was not so sure. He turned his head back and forth, trying to locate the direction of the very faint murmur that had come to them through the fog, then abandoned the attempt as hopeless.

They continued the slide, reached the fourth level, and started on towards the fifth. All the while the sound grew louder – and more hauntingly familiar. They were half-way down the fourth stairway before Myron called out: 'Now do you recognise it?'

They would have identified it long ago, but it was not a sound they would ever have associated with any world except Earth. Coming out of the fog, from a source whose distance could not be guessed, was the steady thunder of falling water.

A few minutes later, the cloud ceiling ended as abruptly as it had begun. They shot out into the blinding glare of the Raman day, made more brilliant by the light reflected from the low-hanging clouds. There was the familiar curving plain – now made more acceptable to mind and senses, because its full circle could no longer be seen. It was not too difficult to pretend that they were looking along a broad valley, and that the upward sweep of the Sea was really an *outward* one.

They halted at the fifth and penultimate platform, to report that they were through the cloud cover and to make a careful survey. As far as they could tell, nothing had changed down there on the plain; but up here on the Northern dome, Rama had brought forth another wonder.

So there was the origin of the sound they had heard. Descending from some hidden source in the clouds three or four kilometres away was a waterfall, and for long minutes they stared at it silently, almost unable to believe their eyes. Logic told them that on this spinning world no falling object could move in a straight line, but there was something horribly unnatural about a curving waterfall that curved sideways, to end many kilometres away from the point directly below its source ...

'If Galileo had been born in this world,' said Mercer at length, 'he'd have gone crazy working out the laws of dynamics.'

'I thought I knew them,' Calvert replied, 'and I'm going crazy anyway. Doesn't it upset you, Prof?'

'Why should it?' said Sergeant Myron. 'It's a perfectly straightforward demonstration of the Coriolis Effect. I wish I could show it to some of my students.'

Mercer was staring thoughtfully at the globe-circling band of the Cylindrical Sea.

'Have you noticed what's happened to the water?' he said at last.

'Why – it's no longer so blue. I'd call it pea-green. What does that signify?'

'Perhaps the same thing that it does on Earth. Laura called the Sea an organic soup waiting to be shaken into life. Maybe that's exactly what's happened.'

'In a couple of days! It took millions of years on Earth.'

'Three hundred and seventy-five million, according to the latest estimate. So *that's* where the oxygen's come from. Rama's shot through the anerobic stage and has got to photosynthetic plants – in about forty-eight hours. I wonder what it will produce tomorrow?'

22
To Sail the Cylindrical Sea

When they reached the foot of the stairway, they had another shock. At first, it appeared that something had gone through the camp, overturning equipment, even collecting smaller objects and carrying them away. But after a brief examination, their alarm was replaced by a rather shame-faced annoyance.

The culprit was only the wind; though they had tied down all loose objects before they left, some ropes must have parted during exceptionally strong gusts. It was several days before they were able to retrieve all their scattered property.

Otherwise, there seemed no major changes. Even the silence of Rama had returned, now that the ephemeral storms of spring were over. And out there at the edge of the plain was a calm sea, waiting for the first ship in a million years.

'Shouldn't one christen a new boat with a bottle of champagne?'

'Even if we had any on board, I wouldn't allow such a criminal waste. Anyway, it's too late. We've already launched the thing.'

'At least it does float. You've won your bet, Jimmy. I'll settle when we get back to Earth.'

'It's got to have a name. Any ideas?'

The subject of these unflattering comments was now bobbing beside the steps leading down into the Cylindrical Sea. It was a small raft, constructed from six empty storage drums held together by a light metal framework. Building it, assembling it at

Camp Alpha and hauling it on demountable wheels across more than ten kilometres of plain had absorbed the crew's entire energies for several days. It was a gamble that had better pay off.

The prize was worth the risk. The enigmatic towers of New York, gleaming there in the shadowless light five kilometres away, had taunted them ever since they had entered Rama. No one doubted that the city – or whatever it might be – was the real heart of this world. If they did nothing else, they must reach New York.

'We still don't have a name. Skipper – what about it?'

Norton laughed, then became suddenly serious.

'I've got one for you. Call it *Resolution*.'

'Why?'

'That was one of Cook's ships. It's a good name – may she live up to it.'

There was a thoughtful silence; then Sergeant Barnes, who had been principally responsible for the design, asked for three volunteers. Everyone present held up a hand.

'Sorry – we only have four life-jackets. Boris, Jimmy, Pieter – you've all done some sailing. Let's try her out.'

No one thought it in the least peculiar that an Executive Sergeant was now taking charge of the proceedings. Ruby Barnes had the only Master's Certificate aboard, so that settled the matter. She had navigated racing trimarans across the Pacific, and it did not seem likely that a few kilometres of dead-calm water could present much of a challenge to her skills.

Ever since she had set eyes upon the Sea, she had been determined to make this voyage. In all the thousands of years that man had had dealings with the waters of his own world, no sailor had ever faced anything remotely like this. In the last few days a silly little jingle had been running through her mind, and she could not get rid of it. 'To sail the Cylindrical Sea …' Well, that was precisely what she was going to do.

Her passengers took their places on the improvised bucket

seats, and Ruby opened the throttle. The twenty-kilowatt motor started to whirr, the chain-drives of the reduction gear blurred, and *Resolution* surged away to the cheers of the spectators.

Ruby had hoped to get fifteen kph with this load, but would settle for anything over ten. A half-kilometre course had been measured along the cliff, and she made the round trip in five and a half minutes. Allowing for turning time, this worked out at twelve kph; she was quite happy with that.

With no power, but with three energetic paddlers helping her own more skilful blade, Ruby was able to get a quarter of this speed. So even if the motor broke down, they could get back to shore in a couple of hours. The heavy-duty power cells could provide enough energy to circumnavigate the world; she was carrying two spares, to be on the safe side. And now that the fog had completely burned away, even such a cautious mariner as Ruby was prepared to put to sea without a compass.

She saluted smartly as she stepped ashore.

'Maiden voyage of *Resolution* successfully completed, Sir. Now awaiting your instructions.'

'Very good ... Admiral. When will you be ready to sail?'

'As soon as stores can be loaded aboard, and the Harbour Master gives us clearance.'

'Then we leave at dawn.'

'Aye, aye, Sir.'

Five kilometres of water does not seem very much on a map; it is very different when one is in the middle of it. They had been cruising for only ten minutes, and the fifty-metre cliff facing the Northern Continent already seemed a surprising distance away. Yet, mysteriously, New York hardly appeared much closer than before ...

But most of the time they paid little attention to the land; they were still too engrossed in the wonder of the Sea. They no longer made the nervous jokes that had punctuated the start of the voyage; this new experience was too overwhelming.

Every time, Norton told himself, he felt that he had grown accustomed to Rama, it produced some new wonder. As *Resolution* hummed steadily forward, it seemed that they were caught in the trough of a gigantic wave – a wave which curved up on either side until it became vertical – then overhung until the two flanks met in a liquid arch sixteen kilometres above their heads. Despite everything that reason and logic told them, none of the voyagers could for long throw off the impression that at any minute those millions of tons of water would come crashing down from the sky.

Yet despite this, their main feeling was one of exhilaration; there was a sense of danger, without any *real* danger. Unless, of course, the Sea itself produced any more surprises.

That was a different possibility, for as Mercer had guessed, the water was now alive. Every spoonful contained thousands of spherical, single-celled micro-organisms, similar to the earliest forms of plankton that had existed in the oceans of Earth.

Yet they showed puzzling differences; they lacked a nucleus, as well as many of the other minimum requirements of even the most primitive terrestrial life-forms. And although Laura Ernst – now doubling as research scientist as well as ship's doctor – had proved that they definitely generated oxygen, there were far too few of them to account for the augmentation of Rama's atmosphere. They should have existed in billions, not mere thousands.

Then she discovered that their numbers were dwindling rapidly, and must have been far higher during the first hours of the Raman dawn. It was as if there had been a brief explosion of life, recapitulating on a trillion-fold swifter time-scale the early history of Earth. Now, perhaps, it had exhausted itself; the drifting micro-organisms were disintegrating, releasing their stores of chemicals back into the Sea.

'If you have to swim for it,' Dr Ernst had warned the mariners, 'keep your mouths closed. A few drops won't matter – if you spit them out right away. But all those weird organo-metallic salts add up to a fairly poisonous package, and I'd hate to have to work out an antidote.'

This danger, fortunately, seemed very unlikely. *Resolution* could stay afloat if any two of her buoyancy tanks were punctured. (When told of this, Joe Calvert had muttered darkly: 'Remember the *Titanic!*') And even if she sank, the crude but efficient life-jackets would keep their heads above water. Although Laura had been reluctant to give a firm ruling on this, she did not think that a few hours' immersion in the Sea would be fatal; but she did not recommend it.

After twenty minutes of steady progress, New York was no longer a distant island. It was becoming a real place, and details which they had seen only through telescopes and photo-enlargements were now revealing themselves as massive, solid structures. It was now strikingly apparent that the 'city', like so much of Rama, was triplicated; it consisted of three identical, circular complexes or super-structures, rising from a long, oval foundation. Photographs taken from the Hub also indicated that each complex was *itself* divided into three equal components, like a pie sliced into 120-degree portions. This would greatly simplify the task of exploration; presumably they had to examine only one ninth of New York to have seen the whole of it. Even this would be a formidable undertaking; it would mean investigating at least a square kilometre of buildings and machinery, some of which towered hundreds of metres into the air.

The Ramans, it seemed, had brought the art of triple-redundancy to a high degree of perfection. This was demonstrated in the airlock system, the stairways at the Hub, the artificial suns. And where it really mattered, they had even taken the next step. New York appeared to be an example of triple-triple redundancy.

Ruby was steering *Resolution* towards the central complex,

where a flight of steps led up from the water to the very top of the wall or levee which surrounded the island. There was even a conveniently-placed mooring post to which boats could be tied; when she saw this, Ruby became quite excited. Now she would never be content until she found one of the craft in which the Ramans sailed their extraordinary sea.

Norton was the first to step ashore; he looked back at his three companions and said: 'Wait here on the boat until I get to the top of the wall. When I wave, Pieter and Boris will join me. You stay at the helm, Ruby, so that we can cast off at a moment's notice. If anything happens to me, report to Karl and follow his instructions. Use your best judgement – but no heroics. Understood?'

'Yes, Skipper. Good luck!'

Commander Norton did not really believe in luck; he never got into a situation until he had analysed all the factors involved and had secured his line of retreat. But once again Rama was forcing him to break some of his cherished rules. Almost every factor here was unknown – as unknown as the Pacific and the Great Barrier Reef had been to his hero, three and a half centuries ago ... Yes, he could do with all the luck that happened to be lying around.

The stairway was a virtual duplicate of the one down which they had descended on the other side of the Sea; doubtless his friends over there were looking straight across at him through their telescopes. And 'straight' was now the correct word; in this one direction, parallel to the axis of Rama, the Sea was indeed completely flat. It might well be the only body of water in the universe of which this was true, for on all other worlds, every sea or lake must follow the surface of a sphere, with equal curvature in all directions.

'Nearly at the top,' he reported, speaking for the record and for his intently listening second-in-command, five kilometres away, 'still completely quiet – radiation normal. I'm holding the meter above my head, just in case this wall is acting as a shield for anything. And if there are any hostiles on the other side, they'll shoot that first.'

He was joking, of course. And yet – why take any chances, when it was just as easy to avoid them?

When he took the last step, he found that the flat-topped embankment was about ten metres thick; on the inner side, an alternating series of ramps and stairways led down to the main level of the city, twenty metres below. In effect, he was standing on a high wall which completely surrounded New York, and so was able to get a grandstand view of it.

It was a view almost stunning in its complexity, and his first act was to make a slow panoramic scan with his camera. Then he waved to his companions and radioed back across the Sea: 'No sign of any activity – everything quiet. Come on up – we'll start exploring.'

23
NY, Rama

It was not a city; it was a machine. Norton had come to that conclusion in ten minutes, and saw no reason to change it after they had made a complete traverse of the island. A city – whatever the nature of its occupants – surely had to provide some form of accommodation: there was nothing here of that nature, unless it was underground. And if that was the case, where were the entrances, the stairways, the elevators? He had not found anything that even qualified as a simple door ...

The closest analogy he had ever seen to this place on Earth was a giant chemical processing plant. However, there were no stockpiles of raw materials, or any indications of a transport system to move them around. Nor could he imagine where the finished product would emerge – still less what that product could possibly be. It was all very baffling, and more than a little frustrating.

'Anybody care to make a guess?' he said at last, to all who might be listening. 'If this is a factory, what does it make? And where does it get its raw materials?'

'I've a suggestion, Skipper,' said Karl Mercer, over on the far shore. 'Suppose it uses the Sea. According to Doc, that contains just about anything you can think of.'

It was a plausible answer, and Norton had already considered it. There could well be buried pipes leading to the Sea – in fact, there *must* be, for any conceivable chemical plant would require large quantities of water. But he had a suspicion of plausible answers; they were so often wrong.

'That's a good idea, Karl; but what does New York *do* with its seawater?'

For a long time, nobody answered from ship, Hub or Northern plain. Then an unexpected voice spoke.

'That's easy, Skipper. But you're all going to laugh at me.'

'No, we're not, Ravi. Go ahead.'

Sergeant Ravi McAndrews, Chief Steward and Simp Master, was the last person on this ship who would normally get involved in a technical discussion. His IQ was modest and his scientific knowledge was minimal, but he was no fool and had a natural shrewdness which everyone respected.

'Well, it's a factory all right, Skipper, and maybe the Sea provides the raw material ... after all, that's how it all happened on Earth, though in a different way ... I believe New York is a factory for making – Ramans.'

Somebody, somewhere, snickered, but became quickly silent and did not identify himself.

'You know, Ravi,' said his commander at last, 'that theory is crazy enough to be true. And I'm not sure if I want to see it tested ... at least, until I get back to the mainland.'

This celestial New York was just about as wide as the island of Manhattan, but its geometry was totally different. There were few straight thoroughfares; it was a maze of short, concentric arcs, with radial spokes linking them. Luckily, it was impossible to lose one's bearings inside Rama; a single glance at the sky was enough to establish the north-south axis of the world.

They paused at almost every intersection to make a panoramic scan. When all these hundreds of pictures were sorted out, it would be a tedious but fairly straightforward job to construct an accurate scale model of the city. Norton suspected that the resulting jigsaw puzzle would keep scientists busy for generations.

It was even harder to get used to the silence here than it had been out on the plain of Rama. A city-machine should make some sound; yet there was not even the faintest of electric hums, or the slightest whisper of mechanical motion. Several times Norton put his ear to the ground, or to the side of a building, and listened intently. He could hear nothing except the pounding of his own blood.

The machines were sleeping: they were not even ticking over. Would they ever wake again, and for what purpose? Everything was in perfect condition, as usual. It was easy to believe that the closing of a single circuit, in some patient, hidden computer, would bring all this maze back to life.

When at last they had reached the far side of the city, they climbed to the top of the surrounding levee and looked across the southern branch of the Sea. For a long time Norton stared at the five-hundred-metre cliff that barred them from almost half of Rama – and, judging from their telescopic surveys, the most complex and varied half. From this angle, it appeared an ominous, forbidding black, and it was easy to think of it as a prison wall surrounding a whole continent. Nowhere along its entire circle was there a flight of stairways or any other means of access.

He wondered how the Ramans reached their southern land from New York. Probably there was an underground transport system running beneath the Sea, but they must also have aircraft as well; there were many open areas here in the city that could be used for landing. To discover a Raman vehicle would be a major accomplishment – especially if they could learn to operate it. (Though could any conceivable power-source still be functioning, after several hundred thousand years?) There were numerous structures that had the functional look of hangars or garages, but they were all smooth and windowless, as if they had been sprayed with sealant. Sooner or later, Norton had told himself grimly, we'll be forced to use explosives, and laser beams. He was determined to put off this decision to the last possible moment.

His reluctance to use brute force was based partly on pride, partly on fear. He did not wish to behave like a technological barbarian, smashing what he could not understand. After all, he was an uninvited visitor in this world, and should act accordingly.

As for his fear – perhaps that was too strong a word; apprehension might be better. The Ramans seemed to have planned for everything; he was not anxious to discover the precautions they had taken to guard their property. When he sailed back to the mainland, it would be with empty hands.

24
Dragonfly

Lieutenant James Pak was the most junior officer on board *Endeavour*, and this was only his fourth mission into deep space. He was ambitious, and due for promotion; he had also committed a serious breach of regulations. No wonder, therefore, that he took a long time to make up his mind.

It would be a gamble; if he lost, he could be in deep trouble. He could not only be risking his career; he might even be risking his neck. But if he succeeded, he would be a hero. What finally convinced him was neither of these arguments; it was the certainty that, if he did nothing at all, he would spend the rest of his life brooding over his lost opportunity. Nevertheless, he was still hesitant when he asked the Captain for a private meeting.

What is it *this* time? Norton asked himself, as he analysed the uncertain expression of the young officer's face. He remembered his delicate interview with Boris Rodrigo; no, it wouldn't be anything like that. Jimmy was certainly not the religious type; the only interests he had ever shown outside his work were sport and sex, preferably combined.

It could hardly be the former, and Norton hoped it was not the latter. He had encountered most of the problems that a commanding officer could encounter in this department – except the classical one of an unscheduled birth during a mission. Though this situation was the subject of innumerable jokes, it had never happened yet; but such gross incompetence was probably only a matter of time.

'Well, Jimmy, what is it?'

'I have an idea, Commander. I know how to reach the southern continent – even to the South Pole.'

'I'm listening. How do you propose to do it?'

'Er – by flying there.'

'Jimmy, I've had at least five proposals to do that – more if you count crazy suggestions from Earth. We've looked into the possibility of adapting our spacesuit propulsors, but air drag would make them hopelessly inefficient. They'd run out of fuel before they could go ten kilometres.'

'I know that. But I have the answer.'

Lt Pak's attitude was a curious mixture of complete confidence and barely suppressed nervousness. Norton was quite baffled; what was the kid worried about? Surely he knew his commanding officer well enough to be certain that no reasonable proposal would be laughed out of court.

'Well, go on. If it works, I'll see your promotion is retroactive.'

That little half-promise, half-joke didn't go down as well as he had hoped. Jimmy gave a rather sickly smile, made several false starts, then decided on an oblique approach to the subject.

'You know, Commander, that I was in the Lunar Olympics last year.'

'Of course. Sorry you didn't win.'

'It was bad equipment; I know what went wrong. I have friends on Mars who've been working on it, in secret. We want to give everyone a surprise.'

'Mars? But I didn't know …'

'Not many people do – the sport's still new there; it's only been tried in the Xante Sportsdome. But the best aerodynamicists in the solar system are on Mars; if you can fly in *that* atmosphere, you can fly anywhere.

'Now, my idea was that if the Martians could build a good

machine, with all their know-how, it would *really* perform on the Moon – where gravity is only half as strong.'

'That seems plausible, but how does it help us?'

Norton was beginning to guess, but he wanted to give Jimmy plenty of rope.

'Well, I formed a syndicate with some friends in Lowell City. They've built a fully aerobatic flyer with some refinements that no one has ever seen before. In lunar gravity, under the Olympic dome, it should create a sensation.'

'And win you the gold medal.'

'I hope so.'

'Let me see if I follow your train of thought correctly. A sky-bike that could enter the Lunar Olympics, at a sixth of a gravity, would be even more sensational inside Rama, with no gravity at all. You could fly it right along the axis, from the North Pole to the South – and back again.'

'Yes – easily. The one-way trip would take three hours, non-stop. But of course you could rest whenever you wanted to, as long as you kept near the axis.'

'It's a brilliant idea, and I congratulate you. What a pity sky-bikes aren't part of regular Space Survey equipment.'

Jimmy seemed to have some difficulty in finding words. He opened his mouths everal times, but nothing happened.

'All right, Jimmy. As a matter of morbid interest, and purely off the record, how did you smuggle the thing aboard?'

'Er – "Recreational Stores".'

'Well, you weren't lying. And what about the weight?'

'It's only twenty kilogrammes.'

'*Only!* Still, that's not as bad as I thought. In fact, I'm astonished you can build a bike for that weight.'

'Some have been only fifteen, but they were too fragile and usually folded up when they made a turn. There's no danger of *Dragonfly* doing that. As I said, she's fully aerobatic.'

'*Dragonfly* – nice name. So tell me just how you plan to use her; then I can decide whether a promotion or a court martial is in order. Or both.'

25
Maiden Flight

Dragonfly was certainly a good name. The long, tapering wings were almost invisible, except when the light struck them from certain angles and was refracted into rainbow hues. It was as if a soap-bubble had been wrapped round a delicate tracery of aerofoil sections; the envelope enclosing the little flyer was an organic film only a few molecules thick, yet strong enough to control and direct the movements of a fifty-kph air flow.

The pilot – who was also the powerplant and the guidance system – sat on a tiny seat at the centre of gravity, in a semi-reclining position to reduce air resistance. Control was by a single stick which could be moved backwards and forwards, right and left; the only 'instrument' was a piece of weighted ribbon attached to the leading edge, to show the direction of the relative wind.

Once the flyer had been assembled at the Hub, Jimmy Pak would allow no one to touch it. Clumsy handling could snap one of the single-fibre structural members, and those glittering wings were an almost irresistible attraction to prying fingers. It was hard to believe that there was *really* something there …

As he watched Jimmy climb into the contraption, Commander Norton began to have second thoughts. If one of those wire-sized struts snapped when *Dragonfly* was on the other side of the Cylindrical Sea, Jimmy would have no way of getting back – even if he was able to make a safe landing. They were also breaking one of the most sacrosanct rules of space exploration;

a man was going *alone* into unknown territory, beyond all possibility of help. The only consolation was that he would be in full view and communication all the time; they would know exactly what had happened to him, if he did meet with disaster.

Yet this opportunity was far too good to miss; if one believed in fate or destiny, it would be challenging the gods themselves to neglect the only chance they might ever have of reaching the far side of Rama, and seeing at close quarters the mysteries of the South Pole. Jimmy knew what he was attempting, far better than anyone in the crew could tell him. This was precisely the sort of risk that had to be taken; if it failed, that was the luck of the game. You couldn't win them all ...

'Now listen to me carefully, Jimmy,' said Surgeon-Commander Ernst. 'It's very important not to over-exert yourself. Remember, the oxygen level here at the axis is still very low. If you feel breathless at any time, stop and hyperventilate for thirty seconds – but no longer.'

Jimmy nodded absentmindedly as he tested the controls. The whole rudder-elevator assembly, which formed a single unit on an outrigger five metres behind the rudimentary cockpit, began to twist around; then the flap-shaped ailerons, halfway along the wing, moved alternately up and down.

'Do you want me to swing the prop?' asked Joe Calvert, unable to suppress memories of two-hundred-year-old war movies. 'Ignition! Contact!' Probably no one except Jimmy knew what he was talking about, but it helped to relieve the tension.

Very slowly, Jimmy started to move the foot-pedals. The flimsy, broad fan of the airscrew – like the wing, a delicate skeleton covered with shimmering film – began to turn. By the time it had made a few revolutions, it had disappeared completely; and *Dragonfly* was on her way.

She moved straight outwards from the Hub, moving slowly along the axis of Rama. When she had travelled a hundred metres, Jimmy stopped pedalling; it was strange to see an obviously aerodynamic vehicle hanging motionless in mid-air. This must be the first time such a thing had ever happened, except possibly on a very limited scale inside one of the larger space-stations.

'How does she handle?' Norton called.

'Response good, stability poor. But I know what the trouble is – no gravity. We'll be better off a kilometre lower down.'

'Now wait a minute – is that safe?'

By losing altitude, Jimmy would be sacrificing his main advantage. As long as he stayed precisely on the axis, he – and *Dragonfly* – would be completely weightless. He could hover effortlessly, or even go to sleep if he wished. But as soon as he moved away from the central line around which Rama spun, the pseudo-weight of centrifugal force would reappear.

And so, unless he could maintain himself at this altitude, he would continue to lose height – and at the same time, *to gain weight*. It would be an accelerating process, which could end in catastrophe. The gravity down on the plain of Rama was twice that in which *Dragonfly* had been designed to operate. Jimmy might be able to make a safe landing; he could certainly never take off again.

But he had already considered all this, and he answered confidently enough: 'I can manage a tenth of a gee without any trouble. And she'll handle more easily in denser air.'

In a slow, leisurely spiral, *Dragonfly* drifted across the sky, roughly following the line of Stairway Alpha down towards the plain. From some angles, the little sky-bike was almost invisible; Jimmy seemed to be sitting in mid-air pedalling furiously. Sometimes he moved into spurts of up to thirty kilometres an hour; then he would coast to a halt, getting the feel of the controls, before accelerating again. And he was always very careful to keep a safe distance from the curving end of Rama.

It was soon obvious that *Dragonfly* handled much better at lower altitudes; she no longer rolled around at any angle, but stabilized so that her wings were parallel to the plain seven kilometres below. Jimmy completed several wide orbits, then started to climb upwards again. He finally halted a few metres above his waiting colleagues and realised, a little belatedly, that he was not quite sure how to land this gossamer craft.

'Shall we throw you a rope?' Norton asked half-seriously.

'No, Skipper – I've got to work this out myself. I won't have anyone to help me at the other end.'

He sat thinking for a while, then started to ease *Dragonfly* towards the Hub with short bursts of power. She quickly lost momentum between each, as air drag brought her to rest again. When he was only five metres away, and the sky-bike was still barely moving, Jimmy abandoned ship. He let himself float towards the nearest safety line in the Hub webwork, grasped it, then swung around in time to catch the approaching bike with his hands. The manoeuvre was so neatly executed that it drew a round of applause.

'For my *next* act—' Joe Calvert began.

Jimmy was quick to disclaim any credit.

'That was messy,' he said. 'But now I know how to do it. I'll take a sticky-bomb on a twenty-metre line; then I'll be able to pull myself in wherever I want to.'

'Give me your wrist, Jimmy,' ordered the Doctor, 'and blow into this bag. I'll want a blood sample, too. Did you have any difficulty in breathing?'

'Only at this altitude. Hey, what do you want the blood for?'

'Sugar level; then I can tell how much energy you've used. We've got to make sure you carry enough fuel for the mission. By the way, what's the endurance record for sky-biking?'

'Two hours twenty-five minutes three point six seconds. On the Moon, of course – a two kilometre circuit in the Olympic Dome.'

'And you think you can keep it up for six hours?'

'Easily, since I can stop for a rest at any time. Sky-biking on the Moon is at least twice as hard as it is here.'

'OK Jimmy – back to the lab. I'll give you a Go-No-Go as soon as I've analysed these samples. I don't want to raise false hopes – but I think you can make it.'

A large smile of satisfaction spread across Jimmy Pak's ivory-hued countenance. As he followed Surgeon-Commander Ernst to the airlock, he called back to his companions: 'Hands off, *please*! I don't want anyone putting his fist through the wings.'

'I'll see to that, Jimmy,' promised the Commander. '*Dragonfly* is off limits to *everybody* – including myself.'

26
The Voice of Rama

The real magnitude of his adventure did not hit Jimmy Pak until he reached the coast of the Cylindrical Sea. Until now, he had been over known territory; barring a catastrophic structural failure, he could always land and walk back to base in a few hours.

That option no longer existed. If he came down in the Sea, he would probably drown, quite unpleasantly, in its poisonous waters. And even if he made a safe landing in the southern continent, it might be impossible to rescue him before *Endeavour* had to break away from Rama's sunward orbit.

He was also acutely aware that the foreseeable disasters were the ones most unlikely to happen. The totally unknown region over which he was flying might produce any number of surprises; suppose there were flying creatures here, who objected to his intrusion? He would hate to engage in a dog-fight with anything larger than a pigeon. A few well-placed pecks could destroy *Dragonfly*'s aerodynamics.

Yet, if there were no hazards, there would be no achievement – no sense of adventure. Millions of men would gladly have traded places with him now. He was going not only where no one had ever been before – but where no one would ever go again. In all of history, he would be the only human being to visit the southern regions of Rama. Whenever he felt fear brushing against his mind, he could remember that.

He had now grown accustomed to sitting in mid-air, with the world wrapped around him. Because he had dropped two kilometres below the central axis, he had acquired a definite sense of 'up' and 'down'. The ground was only six kilometres below, but the arch of the sky was ten kilometres overhead. The 'city' of London was hanging up there near the zenith; New York, on the other hand, was the right way up, directly ahead.

'*Dragonfly*,' said Hub Control, 'you're getting a little low. Twenty-two hundred metres from the axis.'

"Thanks,' he replied. 'I'll gain altitude. Let me know when I'm back at twenty.'

This was something he'd have to watch. There was a natural tendency to lose height – and he had no instruments to tell him exactly where he was. If he got too far away from the zero-gravity of the axis, he might never be able to climb back to it. Fortunately, there was a wide margin for error, and there was always some-one watching his progress through a telescope at the Hub.

He was now well out over the Sea, pedalling along at a steady twenty kilometres an hour. In five minutes, he would be over New York; already the island looked rather like a ship, sailing for ever round and round the Cylindrical Sea.

When he reached New York, he flew a circle over it, stopping several times so that his little TV camera could send back steady, vibration-free images. The panorama of buildings, towers, in-dustrial plants, power stations – or whatever they were – was fascinating but essentially meaningless. No matter how long he stared at its complexity, he was unlikely to learn anything. The camera would record far more details than he could possibly assimilate; and one day – perhaps years hence – some student might find in them the key to Rama's secrets.

After leaving New York, he crossed the other half of the Sea in only fifteen minutes. Though he was not aware of it, he had been flying fast over water, but as soon as he reached the south coast he unconsciously relaxed and his speed dropped by several kilometres an hour. He might be in wholly alien territory – but at least he was over land.

As soon as he had crossed the great cliff that formed the Sea's southern limit, he panned the TV camera completely round the circle of the world.

'Beautiful!' said Hub Control. 'This will keep the map-makers happy. How are you feeling?'

'I'm fine – just a little fatigue, but no more than I expected. How far do you make me from the Pole?'

'Fifteen point six kilometres.'

'Tell me when I'm at ten; I'll take a rest then. And make sure I don't get low again. I'll start climbing when I've five to go.'

Twenty minutes later the world was closing in upon him; he had come to the end of the cylindrical section, and was entering the southern dome.

He had studied it for hours through the telescopes at the other end of Rama, and had learned its geography by heart. Even so, that had not fully prepared him for the spectacle all around him.

In almost every way the southern and northern ends of Rama differed completely. Here was no triad of stairways, no series of narrow, concentric plateaux, no sweeping curve from hub to plain. Instead, there was an immense central spike, more than five kilometres long, extending along the axis. Six smaller ones, half this size, were equally spaced around it; the whole assembly looked like a group of remarkable symmetrical stalactites, hanging from the roof of a cave. Or, inverting the point of view, the spires of some Cambodian temple, set at the bottom of a crater ...

Linking these slender, tapering towers, and curving down from them to merge eventually in the cylindrical plain, were flying buttresses that looked massive enough to bear the weight of a world. And this, perhaps, was their function, if they were indeed the elements of some exotic drive units, as some had suggested.

Lieutenant Pak approached the central spike cautiously,

stopped pedalling while he was still a hundred metres away, and let *Dragonfly* drift to rest. He checked the radiation level, and found only Rama's very low background. There might be forces at work here which no human instruments could detect, but that was another unavoidable risk.

'What can you see?' Hub Control asked anxiously.

'Just Big Horn – it's absolutely smooth – no markings – and the point's so sharp you could use it as a needle. I'm almost scared to go near it.'

He was only half joking. It seemed incredible that so massive an object should taper to such a geometrically perfect point. Jimmy had seen collections of insects impaled upon pins, and he had no desire for his own *Dragonfly* to meet a similar fate.

He pedalled slowly forward until the spike had flared out to several metres in diameter, then stopped again. Opening a small container, he rather gingerly extracted a sphere about as big as a baseball, and tossed it towards the spike. As it drifted away, it played out a barely visible thread.

The sticky-bomb hit the smoothly curving surface – and did not rebound. Jimmy gave the thread an experimental twitch, then a harder tug. Like a fisherman hauling in his catch, he slowly wound *Dragonfly* across to the tip of the appropriately christened 'Big Horn', until he was able to put out his hand and make contact with it.

'I suppose you could call this some kind of touchdown,' he reported to Hub Control. 'It feels like glass – almost friction-less, and slightly warm. The sticky-bomb worked fine. Now I'm trying the mike ... let's see if the suction pad holds as well ... plugging in the leads ... anything coming through?

There was a long pause from the Hub; then Control said disgustedly: 'Not a damn thing, except the usual thermal noises. Will you tap it with a piece of metal? Then at least we'll find if it's hollow.'

'OK. Now what?'

'We'd like you to fly along the spike, making a complete scan every half-kilometre, and looking out for anything unusual. Then, if you're sure it's safe, you might go across to one of the Little Horns. But only if you're certain you can get back to zero gee without any problems.'

'Three kilometres from the axis – that's slightly above lunar gravity. *Dragonfly* was designed for that. I'll just have to work harder.'

'Jimmy, this is the Captain. I've got second thoughts on that. Judging by your pictures, the smaller spikes are just the same as the big one. Get the best coverage of them you can with the zoom lens. I don't want you leaving the low-gravity region ... unless you see something that looks very important. Then we'll talk it over.'

'OK, Skipper,' said Jimmy, and perhaps there was just a trace of relief in his voice. 'I'll stay close to Big Horn. Here we go again.'

He felt he was dropping straight downwards into a narrow valley between a group of incredibly tall and slender mountains. Big Horn now towered a kilometre above him, and the six spikes of the Little Horns were looming up all around. The complex of buttresses and flying arches which surrounded the lower slopes was approaching rapidly; he wondered if he could make a safe landing somewhere down there in that Cyclopean architecture. He could no longer land on Big Horn itself, for the gravity on its widening slopes was now too powerful to be counteracted by the feeble force of the sticky-bomb.

As he came even closer to the South Pole, he began to feel more and more like a sparrow flying beneath the vaulted roof of some great cathedral – though no cathedral ever built had been even one hundredth the size of this place. He wondered if it was indeed a religious shrine, or something remotely analogous, but quickly dismissed the idea. Nowhere in Rama had there been any trace of artistic expression; everything was purely functional. Perhaps the Ramans felt that they already knew the ultimate secrets of the universe, and were no longer haunted by the yearnings and aspirations that drove mankind.

That was a chilling thought, quite alien to Jimmy's usual not-very-profound philosophy; he felt an urgent need to resume contact, and reported his situation back to his distant friends.

'Say again, *Dragonfly*,' replied Hub Control. 'We can't understand you – your transmission is garbled.'

'I repeat – I'm near the base of Little Horn number Six, and am using the sticky-bomb to haul myself in.'

'Understand only partially. Can you hear me?'

'Yes, perfectly. Repeat, perfectly.'

'Please start counting numbers.'

'One, two, three, four ...'

'Got part of that. Give us beacon for fifteen seconds, then go back to voice.'

'Here it is.'

Jimmy switched on the low-powered beacon which would locate him anywhere inside Rama, and counted off the seconds. When he went over to voice again he asked plaintively: 'What's happening? Can you hear me now?'

Presumably Hub didn't, because the controller then asked for fifteen seconds of TV. Not until Jimmy had repeated the question twice did the message get through.

'Glad you can hear us OK, Jimmy. But there's something very peculiar happening at your end. Listen.'

Over the radio, he heard the familiar whistle of his own beacon, played back to him. For a moment it was perfectly normal; then a weird distortion crept into it. The thousand-cycle whistle became modulated by a deep, throbbing pulse so low that it was almost beneath the threshold of hearing; it was a kind of *basso-profundo* flutter in which each individual vibration could be heard. And the modulation was itself modulated; it rose and fell, rose and fell with a period of about five seconds.

Never for a moment did it occur to Jimmy that there was something wrong with his radio transmitter. This was from outside; though what it was, and what it meant, was beyond his imagination.

Hub Control was not much wiser, but at least it had a theory.

'We think you must be in some kind of very intense field – probably magnetic – with a frequency of about ten cycles. It may be strong enough to be dangerous. Suggest you get out right away – it may only be local. Switch on your beacon again, and we'll play it back to you. Then you can tell when you're getting clear of the interference.'

Jimmy hastily jerked the sticky-bomb loose and abandoned his attempt to land. He swung *Dragonfly* round in a wide circle, listening as he did so to the sound that wavered in his earphones. After flying only a few metres, he could tell that its intensity was falling rapidly; as Hub Control had guessed, it was extremely localized.

He paused for a moment at the last spot where he could hear it, like a faint throbbing deep in his brain. So might a primitive savage have listened in awestruck ignorance to the low humming of a giant power transformer. And even the savage might have guessed that the sound he heard was merely the stray leakage from colossal energies, fully controlled, but biding their time . . .

Whatever this sound meant, Jimmy was glad to be clear of it. This was no place, among the overwhelming architecture of the South Pole, for a lone man to listen to the voice of Rama.

27
Electric Wind

As Jimmy turned homewards, the northern end of Rama seemed incredibly far away. Even the three giant stairways were barely visible, as a faint Y etched on the dome that closed the world. The band of the Cylindrical Sea was a wide and menacing barrier, waiting to swallow him up if, like Icarus, his fragile wings should fail.

But he had come all this way with no problems, and though he was feeling slightly tired he now felt that he had nothing to worry about. He had not even touched his food or water, and had been too excited to rest. On the return journey, he would relax and take it easy. He was also cheered by the thought that the homeward trip could be twenty kilometres shorter than the outward one, for as long as he cleared the Sea, he could make an emergency landing anywhere in the northern continent. That would be a nuisance, because he would have a long walk – and much worse, would have to abandon *Dragonfly* – but it gave him a very comforting safety margin.

He was now gaining altitude, climbing back towards the central spike; Big Horn's tapering needle still stretched for a kilometre ahead of him, and sometimes he felt it was the axis on which this whole world turned.

He had almost reached the tip of Big Horn when he became aware of a curious sensation; a feeling of foreboding, and indeed of physical as well as psychological discomfort, had come over him. He suddenly recalled – and this did nothing at all to help

– a phrase he had once come across: '*Someone is walking over your grave.*'

At first he shrugged it off, and continued his steady pedalling. He certainly had no intention of reporting anything as tenuous as a vague malaise to Hub Control, but as it grew steadily worse he was tempted to do so. It could not possibly be psychological; if it was, his mind was much more powerful than he realised. For he could, quite literally, feel his skin beginning to crawl ...

Now seriously alarmed, he stopped in mid-air and began to consider the situation. What made it all the more peculiar was the fact that this depressed heavy feeling was not completely novel; he had known it before, but could not remember where.

He looked around him. Nothing had changed. The great spike of Big Horn was a few hundred metres above, with the other side of Rama spanning the sky beyond that. Eight kilometres below lay the complicated patchwork of the Southern continent, full of wonders that no other man would ever see. In all the utterly alien yet now familiar landscape, he could find no cause for his discomfort.

Something was tickling the back of his hand; for a moment, he thought an insect had landed there, and brushed it away without looking. He had only half-completed the swift motion when he realised what he was doing and checked himself, feeling slightly foolish. Of course, no one had ever seen an insect in Rama ...

He lifted his hand, and stared at it, mildly puzzled because the tickling sensation was still there. It was then that he noticed that every individual hair was standing straight upright. All the way up his forearm it was the same – and so it was with his head, when he checked with an exploring hand.

So *that* was the trouble. He was in a tremendously powerful electric field; the oppressed, heavy sensation he had felt was that which sometimes precedes a thunderstorm on Earth.

The sudden realisation of his predicament brought Jimmy

very near to panic. Never before in his life had he been in real physical danger. Like all spacemen, he had known moments of frustration with bulky equipment, and times when, owing to mistakes or inexperience, he had wrongly believed he was in a perilous situation. But none of these episodes had lasted more than a few minutes, and usually he was able to laugh at them almost at once.

This time there was no quick way out. He felt naked and alone in a suddenly hostile sky, surrounded by titanic forces which might discharge their furies at any moment. *Dragonfly* – already fragile enough – now seemed more insubstantial than the finest gossamer. The first detonation of the gathering storm would blast her to fragments.

'Hub Control,' he said urgently. 'There's a static charge building up around me. I think there's going to be a thunderstorm at any moment.'

He had barely finished speaking when there was a flicker of light behind him; by the time he had counted ten, the first crackling rumble arrived. Three kilometres – that put it back around the Little Horns. He looked towards them and saw that every one of the six needles seemed to be on fire. Brush discharges, hundreds of metres long, were dancing from their points, as if they were giant lightning conductors.

What was happening back there could take place on an even larger scale near the tapering spike of Big Horn. His best move would be to get as far as possible from this dangerous structure, and to seek clear air. He started to pedal again, accelerating as swiftly as he could without putting too great a strain on *Dragonfly*. At the same time he began to lose altitude; even though this would mean entering the region of higher gravity, he was now prepared to take such a risk. Eight kilometres was much too far from the ground for his peace of mind.

The ominous black spike of Big Horn was still free of visible discharges, but he did not doubt that tremendous potentials were building up there. From time to time the thunder still reverberated behind him, rolling round and round the circumference of the world. It suddenly occurred to Jimmy how strange it was to have such a storm in a perfectly clear sky; then he realised that this was not a meteorological phenomenon at all. In fact, it might be only a trivial leakage of energy from some hidden source, deep in the southern cap of Rama. But why *now*? And, even more important – *what next*?

He was now well past the tip of Big Horn, and hoped that he would soon be beyond the range of any lightning discharges. But now he had another problem; the air was becoming turbulent, and he had difficulty in controlling *Dragonfly*. A wind seemed to have sprung up from nowhere, and if conditions became much worse the bike's fragile skeleton would be endangered. He pedalled grimly on, trying to smooth out the buffeting by variations in power and movements of his body. Because *Dragonfly* was almost an extension of himself, he was partly successful; but he did not like the faint creaks of protest that came from the main spar, nor the way in which the wings twisted with every gust.

And there was something else that worried him – a faint rushing sound, steadily growing in strength, that seemed to come from the direction of Big Horn. It sounded like gas escaping from a valve under pressure, and he wondered if it had anything to do with the turbulence which he was battling. Whatever its cause, it gave him yet further grounds for disquiet.

From time to time he reported these phenomena, rather briefly and breathlessly, to Hub Control. No one there could give him any advice, or even suggest what might be happening; but it was reassuring to hear the voices of his friends, even though he was now beginning to fear that he would never see them again.

The turbulence was still increasing. It almost felt as if he was entering a jet stream – which he had once done, in search of a record, while flying a high-altitude glider on Earth. But what could possible create a jet stream inside Rama?

He had asked himself the right question; as soon as he had formulated it, he knew the answer.

The sound he had heard was the electric wind carrying away the tremendous ionisation that must be building up around Big Horn. Charged air was spraying out along the axis of Rama, and more air was flowing into the low-pressure region behind. He looked back at that gigantic and now doubly threatening needle, trying to visualise the boundaries of the gale that was blowing from it. Perhaps the best tactic would be to fly by ear, getting as far as possible away from the ominous hissing.

Rama spared him the necessity of choice. A sheet of flame burst out behind him, filling the sky. He had time to see it split into six ribbons of fire, stretching from the tip of Big Horn to each of the Little Horns. Then the concussion reached him.

28
Icarus

Jimmy Pak had barely time to radio: 'The wing's buckling – I'm going to crash – I'm going to crash!' when *Dragonfly* started to fold up gracefully around him. The left wing snapped cleanly in the middle, and the outer section drifted away like a gently falling leaf. The right wing put up a more complicated perform-ance. It twisted round at the root, and angled back so sharply that its tip became entangled in the tail. Jimmy felt that he was sitting in a broken kite, slowly falling down the sky.

Yet he was not quite helpless; the airscrew still worked, and while he had power there was still some measure of control. He had perhaps five minutes in which to use it.

Was there any hope of reaching the Sea? No – it was much too far away. Then he remembered that he was still thinking in terrestrial terms; though he was a good swimmer, it would be hours before he could possibly be rescued, and in that time the poisonous waters would undoubtedly have killed him. His only hope was to come down on land; the problem of the sheer southern cliff he would think about later – if there was any 'later'.

He was falling very slowly, here in this tenth-of-a-gravity zone, but would soon start to accelerate as he got further away from the axis. However, air-drag would complicate the situa-tion, and would prevent him from building up too swift a rate of descent. *Dragonfly*, even without power, would act as a crude parachute. The few kilogrammes of thrust he could still provide might make all the difference between life and death; that was his only hope.

Hub had stopped talking; his friends could see exactly what was happening to him and knew that there was no way their words could help. Jimmy was now doing the most skilful flying of his life; it was too bad, he thought with grim humour, that his audience was so small, and could not appreciate the finer details of his performance.

He was going down in a wide spiral, and as long as its pitch remained fairly flat his chances of survival were good. His pedalling was helping to keep *Dragonfly* airborne, though he was afraid to exert maximum power in case the broken wings came completely adrift. And every time he swung southwards, he could appreciate the fantastic display that Rama had kindly arranged for his benefit.

The streamers of lightning still played from the tip of Big Horn down to the lesser peaks beneath, but now the whole pattern was rotating. The six-pronged crown of fire was turning against the spin of Rama, making one revolution every few seconds. Jimmy felt that he was watching a giant electric motor in operation, and perhaps that was not hopelessly far from the truth.

He was halfway down to the plain, still orbiting in a flat spiral, when the firework display suddenly ceased. He could feel the tension drain from the sky and knew, without looking, that the hairs on his arms were no longer straining upright. There was nothing to distract or hinder him now, during the last few minutes of his fight for life.

Now that he could be certain of the general area in which he must land, he started to study it intently. Much of this region was a checkerboard of totally conflicting environments, as if a mad landscape gardener had been given a free hand and told to exercise his imagination to the utmost. The squares of the checkerboard were almost a kilometre on a side, and though most of them were flat he could not be sure if they were solid, their colours and textures varied so greatly. He decided to wait until the last possible minute before making a decision – if indeed he had any choice.

When there were a few hundred metres to go, he made a last call to the Hub.

'I've still got some control – will be down in half a minute – will call you then.'

That was optimistic, and everyone knew it. But he refused to say goodbye; he wanted his comrades to know that he had gone down fighting, and without fear.

Indeed, he felt very little fear, and this surprised him, for he had never thought of himself as a particularly brave man. It was almost as if he was watching the struggles of a complete stranger, and was not himself personally involved. Rather, he was studying an interesting problem in aerodynamics, and changing various parameters to see what would happen. Almost the only emotion he felt was a certain remote regret for lost opportunities – of which the most important was the forthcoming Lunar Olympics. One future at least was decided; *Dragonfly* would never show her paces on the Moon.

A hundred metres to go; his ground speed seemed acceptable, but how fast was he falling? And here was one piece of luck – the terrain was completely flat. He would put forth all his strength in a final burst of power, starting – NOW!

The right wing, having done its duty, finally tore off at the roots. *Dragonfly* started to roll over, and he tried to correct by throwing the weight of his body against the spin. He was looking directly at the curving arch of landscape sixteen kilometres away when he hit.

It seemed altogether unfair and unreasonable that the sky should be so hard.

29
First Contact

When Jimmy Pak returned to consciousness, the first thing he became aware of was a splitting headache. He almost welcomed it; at least it proved that he was still alive.

Then he tried to move, and at once a wide selection of aches and pains brought themselves to his attention. But as far as he could tell, nothing seemed to be broken.

After that, he risked opening his eyes, but closed them at once when he found himself staring straight into the band of light along the ceiling of the world. As a cure for headache, that view was not recommended.

He was still lying there, regaining his strength and wondering how soon it would be safe to open his eyes, when there was a sudden crunching noise from close at hand. Turning his head very slowly towards the source of the sound, he risked a look – and almost lost consciousness again.

Not more than five metres away, a large crab-like creature was apparently dining on the wreckage of poor *Dragonfly*. When Jimmy recovered his wits he rolled slowly and quietly away from the monster, expecting at every moment to be seized by its claws, when it discovered that more appetizing fare was available. However, it took not the slightest notice of him; when he had increased their mutual separation to ten metres, he cautiously propped himself up in a sitting position.

From this greater distance, the thing did not appear quite so formidable. It had a low, flat body about two metres long and one wide, supported on six triple-jointed legs. Jimmy saw that he was mistaken in assuming that it had been eating *Dragonfly*; in fact, he could not see any sign of a mouth. The creature was actually doing a neat job of demolition, using scissor-like claws to chop the sky-bike into small pieces. A whole row of manipulators, which looked uncannily like tiny human hands, then transferred the fragments to a steadily growing pile on the animal's back.

But *was* it an animal? Though that had been Jimmy's first reaction, now he had second thoughts. There was a purposeful-ness about its behaviour which suggested fairly high intelligence; he could see no reason why any creature of pure instincts should carefully collect the scattered pieces of his sky-bike – unless, perhaps, it was gathering material for a nest.

Keeping a wary eye on the crab, which still ignored him completely, Jimmy struggled to his feet. A few wavering steps demonstrated that he could still walk, though he was not sure if he would outdistance those six legs. Then he switched on his radio, never doubting that it would be operating. A crash that *he* could survive would not even have been noticed by its solid-state electronics.

'Hub Control,' he said softly. 'Can you receive me?'

'Thank God! Are you OK?'

'Just a bit shaken. Take a look at this.'

He turned his camera towards the crab, just in time to record the final demolition of *Dragonfly*'s wing.

'What the devil is it – and why is it chewing up your bike?'

'Wish I knew. It's finished with *Dragonfly*. I'm going to back away, in case it wants to start on me.'

Jimmy slowly retreated, never taking his eyes off the crab. It was now moving round and round in a steadily widening spiral, apparently searching for fragments it might have overlooked, and so Jimmy was able to get an overall view of it for the first time.

Now that the initial shock had worn off, he could appreciate that it was quite a handsome beast. The name 'crab' which he had automatically given it was perhaps a little misleading; if it had not been so impossibly large, he might have called it a beetle. Its carapace had a beautiful metallic sheen; in fact, he would almost have been prepared to swear that it *was* metal.

That was an interesting idea. Could it be a robot, and not an animal? He stared at the crab intently with this thought in mind, analysing all the details of its anatomy. Where it should have had a mouth was a collection of manipulators that reminded Jimmy strongly of the multi-purpose knives that are the delight of all red-blooded boys; there were pinchers, probes, rasps and even something that looked like a drill. But none of this was decisive. On Earth, the insect world had matched all these tools, and many more. The animal-or-robot question remained in perfect balance in his mind.

The eyes, which might have settled the matter, left it even more ambiguous. They were so deeply recessed in protective hoods that it was impossible to tell whether their lenses were made of crystal or jelly. They were quite expressionless, and of a startlingly vivid blue. Though they had been directed towards Jimmy several times, they had never shown the slightest flicker of interest. In his perhaps biased opinion, that decided the level of the creature's intelligence. An entity – robot or animal – which could ignore a human being could not be very bright.

It had now stopped its circling, and stood still for a few seconds, as if listening to some inaudible message. Then it set off, with a curious rolling gait, in the general direction of the Sea. It moved in a perfectly straight line at a steady four or five kilometres an hour, and had already travelled a couple of hundred metres before Jimmy's still slightly-shocked mind registered the fact that the last sad relics of his beloved *Dragonfly* were being carried away from him. He set off in a hot and indignant pursuit.

His action was not wholly illogical. The crab was heading towards the Sea – and if any rescue was possible, it could only be from this direction. Moreover, he wanted to discover what the creature would do with its trophy; that should reveal something about its motivation and intelligence.

Because he was still bruised and stiff, it took Jimmy several minutes to catch up with the purposefully-moving crab. When he had done so, he followed it at a respectful distance, until he felt sure that it did not resent his presence. It was then that he noticed his water-flask and emergency ration pack among the debris of *Dragonfly*, and instantly felt both hungry and thirsty.

There, scuttling away from him at a remorseless five kilometres an hour, was the only food and drink in all this half of the world. Whatever the risk, he had to get hold of it.

He cautiously closed in on the crab, approaching from right rear. While he kept station with it, he studied the complicated rhythm of its legs, until he could anticipate where they would be at any moment. When he was ready, he muttered a quick 'Excuse *me*,' and shot swiftly in to grab his property. Jimmy had never dreamed that he would one day have to exercise the skills of a pickpocket, and was delighted with his success. He was out again in less than a second, and the crab never slackened its steady pace.

He dropped back a dozen metres, moistened his lips from the flask, and started to chew a bar of meat concentrate. The little victory made him feel much happier; now he could even risk thinking about his sombre future.

While there was life, there was hope; yet he could imagine no way in which he could possibly be rescued. Even if his colleagues crossed the Sea, how could he reach them, half a kilometre below? 'We'll find a way down *somehow*,' Hub Control had promised. 'That cliff can't go right round the world, without a break anywhere.' He had been tempted to answer 'Why not?', but had thought better of it.

One of the strangest things about walking inside Rama was that you could always see your destination. Here, the curve of the world did not hide – it *revealed*. For some time Jimmy had been aware of the crab's objective; up there in the land which seemed to rise before him was a half-kilometre-wide pit. It was one of three in the southern continent; from the Hub, it had been impossible to see how deep they were. All had been named after prominent lunar craters, and he was approaching Copernicus. The name was hardly appropriate, for there were no surrounding hills and no central peaks. This Copernicus was merely a deep shaft or well, with perfectly vertical sides.

When he came close enough to look into it, Jimmy was able to see a pool of ominous, leaden-green water at least half a kilometre below. This would put it just about level with the Sea, and he wondered if they were connected.

Winding down the interior of the well was a spiral ramp, completely recessed into the sheer wall, so that the effect was rather like that of rifling in an immense gun-barrel. There seemed to be a remarkable number of turns; not until Jimmy had traced them for several revolutions, getting more and more confused in the process, did he realise that there was not one ramp but *three*, totally independent and 120 degrees apart. In any other background than Rama, the whole concept would have been an impressive architectural *tour de force*.

The three ramps led straight down into the pool and disappeared beneath its opaque surface. Near the waterline Jimmy could see a group of black tunnels or caves; they looked rather sinister, and he wondered if they were inhabited. Perhaps the Ramans were amphibious ...

As the crab approached the edge of the well, Jimmy assumed that it was going to descend one of the ramps – perhaps taking the wreckage of *Dragonfly* to some entity who would be able to evaluate it. Instead, the creature walked straight to the brink, extended almost half its body over the gulf without any sign of hesitation, though an error of a few centimetres would have been disastrous – and gave a brisk shrug. The fragments of *Dragonfly* went fluttering down into the depths; there were tears in Jimmy's eyes as he watched them go. So much, he thought bitterly, for *this* creature's intelligence.

Having disposed of the garbage, the crab swung around and started to walk towards Jimmy, standing only about ten metres away. Am I going to get the same treatment? He wondered. He hoped the camera was not too unsteady as he showed Hub Control the rapidly approaching monster. 'What do you advise?' he whispered anxiously, without much hope that he would get a useful answer. It was some small consolation to realise that he was making history, and his mind raced through the approved patterns for such a meeting. Until now, all of these had been purely theoretical. He would be the first man to check them in practice.

'Don't run until you're sure it's hostile', Hub Control whispered back at him. Run where? Jimmy asked himself. He thought he could out-distance the thing in a hundred metre sprint, but had a sick certainty that it could wear him down over the long haul.

Slowly, Jimmy held up his outstretched hands. Men had been arguing for two hundred years about this gesture; would every creature, everywhere in the universe, interpret this as 'See – no weapons?' But no one could think of anything better.

The crab showed no reaction whatsoever, nor did it slacken its pace. Ignoring Jimmy completely, it walked straight past him and headed purposefully into the south. Feeling extremely foolish, the acting representative of *Homo sapiens* watched his First Contact stride away across the Raman plain, totally indifferent to his presence.

He had seldom been so humiliated in his life. Then Jimmy's sense of humour came to his rescue. After all, it was no great matter to have been ignored by an animated garbage truck.

It would have been worse if it had greeted him as a long-lost brother ...

He walked back to the rim of Copernicus, and stared down into its opaque waters. For the first time, he noticed that vague shapes – some of them quite large – were moving slowly back and forth beneath the surface. Presently one of them headed towards the nearest spiral ramp, and something that looked like a multi-legged tank started on the long ascent. At the rate it was going, Jimmy decided, it would take almost an hour to get here; if it was a threat, it was a very slow-moving one.

Then he noticed a flicker of much more rapid movement, near those cave-like openings down by the waterline. Something was travelling very swiftly along the ramp, but he could not focus clearly upon it, or discern any definite shape. It was as if he was looking at a small whirlwind or 'dust-devil', about the size of a man ...

He blinked and shook his head, keeping his eyes closed for several seconds. When he opened them again, the apparition was gone.

Perhaps the impact had shaken him up more than he had realised; this was the first time he had ever suffered from visual hallucinations. He would not mention it to Hub Control.

Nor would he bother to explore those ramps, as he had half-thought of doing. It would obviously be a waste of energy.

The spinning phantom he had merely imagined seeing had nothing to do with his decision.

Nothing at all; for, of course, Jimmy did not believe in ghosts.

30
The Flower

Jimmy's exertions had made him thirsty, and he was acutely conscious of the fact that in all this land there was no water that a man could drink. With the contents of his flask, he could probably survive a week – but for what purpose? The best brains of Earth would soon be focused on his problem; doubtless Commander Norton would be bombarded with suggestions. But he could imagine no way in which he could lower himself down the face of that half-kilometre cliff. Even it he had a long rough rope, there was nothing to which he could attach it.

Nevertheless, it was foolish – and unmanly – to give up without a struggle. Any help would have to come from the Sea, and while he was marching towards it he could carry on with his job as if nothing had happened. No one else would ever observe and photograph the varied terrain through which he must pass, and that would guarantee a posthumous immortality. Though he would have preferred many other honours, that was better than nothing.

He was only three kilometres from the Sea as poor *Dragonfly* could have flown, but it seemed unlikely that he could reach it in a straight line; some of the terrain ahead of him might prove too great an obstacle. That was no problem, however, as there were plenty of alternative routes. Jimmy could see them all, spread out on the great curving map that swept up and away from him on either side.

He had plenty of time; he would start with the most interesting scenery, even if it took him off his direct route. About a kilometre away towards the right was a square that glittered like cut glass – or a gigantic display of jewellery. It was probably this thought that triggered Jimmy's footsteps. Even a doomed man might reasonably be expected to take some slight interest in a few thousand square metres of gems.

He was not particularly disappointed when they turned out to be quartz crystals, millions of them, set in a bed of sand. The adjacent square of the checkerboard was rather more interesting, being covered with an apparently random pattern of hollow metal columns, set very close together and ranging in height from less than one to more than five metres. It was completely impassable; only a tank could have crashed through that forest of tubes.

Jimmy walked between the crystals and the columns until he came to the first crossroads. The square on the right was a huge rug or tapestry made of woven wire; he tried to prise a strand loose, but was unable to break it.

On the left was a tessellation of hexagonal tiles, so smoothly inlaid that there were no visible joints between them. It would have appeared a continuous surface, had the tiles not been coloured all the hues of the rainbow. Jimmy spent many minutes trying to find two adjacent tiles of the same colour, to see if he could then distinguish their boundaries, but he could not find a single example of such coincidence.

As he did a slow pan right around the crossroads, he said plaintively to Hub Control: 'What do *you* think this is? I feel I'm trapped in a giant jigsaw puzzle. Or is this the Raman Art Gallery?'

'We're as baffled as you, Jimmy. But there's never been any sign that the Ramans go in for art. Let's wait until we have some more examples before we jump to any conclusions.'

The two examples he found at the next crossroads were not much help. One was completely blank – a smooth, neutral grey, hard but slippery to the touch. The other was a soft sponge, perforated with billions upon billions of tiny holes. He tested it with his foot, and the whole surface undulated sickeningly beneath him like a barely stabilised quicksand.

At the next cross-roads he encountered something strikingly like a ploughed field – except that the furrows were a uniform metre in depth, and the material of which they were made had the texture of a file or rasp. But he paid little attention to this, because the square adjacent to it was the most thought-provoking of all that he had so far met. At last there was something that he could understand; and it was more than a little disturbing.

The entire square was surrounded by a fence, so conventional that he would not have looked at it twice had he seen it on Earth. There were posts – apparently of metal – five metres apart, with six strands of wire strung taut between them.

Beyond this fence was a second, identical one – and beyond that, a third. It was another typical example of Raman redundancy; whatever was penned inside this enclosure would have no chance of breaking out. There was no entrance – no gates that could be swung open to drive in the beast, or beasts, that were presumably kept here. Instead, there was a single hole, like a smaller version of Copernicus, in the centre of the square.

Even in different circumstances, Jimmy would probably not have hesitated, but now he had nothing to lose. He quickly scaled all three fences, walked over to the hole, and peered into it.

Unlike Copernicus, this well was only fifty metres deep. There were three tunnel exits at the bottom, each of which looked large enough to accommodate an elephant. And that was all.

After staring for some time, Jimmy decided that the only thing that made sense about the arrangement was for the floor down there to be an elevator. But *what* it elevated he was never likely to know; he could only guess that it was quite large, and possibly quite dangerous.

During the next few hours, he walked more than ten kilometres along the edge of the Sea, and the checkerboard squares had begun to blur together in his memory. He had seen some that were totally enclosed in tent-like structures of wire mesh, as if they were giant bird-cages. There were others which seemed to be pools of congealed liquid, full of swirl-patterns; however, when he tested them gingerly, they were quite solid. And there was one so utterly black that he could not even see it clearly; only the sense of touch told him that anything was there.

Yet now there was a subtle modulation into something he could understand. Ranging one after the other towards the south was a series of – no other word would do – *fields*. He might have been walking past an experimental farm on Earth; each square was a smooth expanse of carefully levelled earth, the first he had ever seen in the metallic landscapes of Rama.

The great fields were virgin, lifeless – waiting for crops that had never been planted. Jimmy wondered what their purpose could be, since it was incredible that creatures as advanced as the Ramans would engage in any form of agriculture; even on Earth, farming was no more than a popular hobby and a source of exotic luxury foods. But he could swear that these were potential farms, immaculately prepared. He had never seen earth that looked so clean; each square was covered with a great sheet of tough, transparent plastic. He tried to cut through it to obtain a sample, but his knife would barely scratch the surface.

Further inland were other fields, and on many of them were complicated constructions of rods and wires, presumably intended for the support of climbing plants. They looked very bleak and desolate, like leafless trees in the depths of winter. The winter they had known must have been long and terrible indeed, and these few weeks of light and warmth might be only a brief interlude before it came again.

Jimmy never knew what made him stop and look more closely into the metal maze to the south. Unconsciously, his mind must have been checking every detail around him; it had noticed, in this fantastically alien landscape, something even more anomalous.

About a quarter of a kilometre away, in the middle of a trellis of wires and rods, glowed a single speck of colour. It was so small and inconspicuous that it was almost at the limit of visibility; on Earth, no one would have looked at it twice. Yet undoubtedly one of the reasons he had noticed it now was because it reminded him of Earth ...

He did not report to Hub Control until he was sure that there was no mistake, and that wishful thinking had not deluded him. Not until he was only a few metres away could he be completely sure that life as he knew it had intruded into the sterile, aseptic world of Rama. For blooming here in lonely splendour at the edge of the southern continent was a flower.

As he came closer, it was obvious to Jimmy that something had gone wrong. There was a hole in the sheathing that, presumably, protected this layer of earth from contamination by unwanted life-forms. Through this break extended a green stem, about as thick as a man's little finger, which twined its way up through the trellis-work. A metre from the ground it burst into an efflorescence of bluish leaves, shaped more like feathers than the foliage of any plant known to Jimmy. The stem ended, at eye-level, in what he had first taken to be a single flower. Now he saw, with no surprise at all, that it was actually three flowers tightly packed together.

The petals were brightly coloured tubes about five centimetres long; there were at least fifty in each bloom, and they glittered with such metallic blues, violets and greens, that they seemed more like the wings of a butterfly than anything in the vegetable kingdom. Jimmy knew practically nothing about botany, but he was puzzled to see no trace of any structures resembling petals or stamens. He wondered if the likeness to terrestrial flowers might be a pure coincidence; perhaps this was something more akin to a coral polyp. In either case, it would seem to imply the existence of small, airborne creatures to serve either as fertiliz-ing agents – or as food.

It did not really matter. Whatever the scientific definition, to Jimmy this was a flower. The strange miracle, the un-Raman-like accident of its existence here reminded him of all that he would never see again; and he was determined to possess it.

That would not be easy. It was more than ten metres away, separated from him by a lattice-work made of thin rods. They formed a cubic pattern, repeated over and over again, less than forty centimetres on either side. Jimmy would not have been flying sky-bikes unless he had been slim and wiry, so he knew he could crawl through the interstices of the grid. But getting out again might be quite a different matter; it would certainly be impossible for him to turn around, so he would have to retreat backwards.

Hub Control was delighted with his discovery, when he had described the flower and scanned it from every available angle. There was no objection when he said: 'I'm going after it.' Nor did he expect there to be; his life was now his own, to do with as he pleased.

He stripped off all his clothes, grasped the smooth metal rods, and started to wriggle into the framework. It was a tight fit; he felt like a prisoner escaping through the bars of his cell. When he had inserted himself completely into the lattice he tried backing out again, just to see if there were any problems. It was considerably more difficult, since he now had to use his outstretched arms for pushing instead of pulling, but he saw no reason why he should get helplessly trapped.

Jimmy was a man of action and impulse, not of introspec-tion. As he squirmed uncomfortably along the narrow corridor of rods, he wasted no time asking himself just why he was performing so quixotic a feat. He had never been interested in flowers in his whole life, yet now he was gambling his last ener-gies to collect one.

It was true that this specimen was unique, and of enormous scientific value. But he really wanted it because it was his last link with the world of life and the planet of his birth.

Yet when the flower was in his grasp, he had sudden qualms. Perhaps it was the only flower that grew in the whole of Rama; was he justified in picking it?

If he needed any excuse, he could console himself with the thought that the Ramans themselves had not included it in their plans. It was obviously a freak, growing ages too late – or too soon. But he did not really require an excuse, and his hesitation was only momentary. He reached out, grasped the stem, and gave a sharp jerk.

The flower came away easily enough; he also collected two of the leaves, then started to back slowly through the lattice. Now that he had only one free hand, progress was extremely difficult, even painful, and he soon had to pause to regain his breath. It was then that he noticed that the feathery leaves were closing, and the headless stem was slowly unwinding itself from its supports. As he watched with a mixture of fascination and dismay, he saw that the whole plant was steadily retreating into the ground, like a mortally injured snake crawling back into its hole.

I've murdered something beautiful, Jimmy told himself. But then Rama had killed him. He was only collecting what was his rightful due.

31
Terminal Velocity

Commander Norton had never yet lost a man, and he had no intention of starting now. Even before Jimmy had set off for the South Pole, he had been considering ways of rescuing him in the event of accident; the problem, however, had turned out to be so difficult that he had found no answer. All that he had managed to do was to eliminate every obvious solution.

How does one climb a half-kilometre vertical cliff; even in reduced gravity? With the right equipment – and training – it would be easy enough. But there were no piton-guns aboard *Endeavour*, and no one could think of any other practical way of driving the necessary hundreds of spikes into that hard, mirror surface.

He had glanced briefly at more exotic solutions, some frankly crazy. Perhaps a simp, fitted with suction pads, could make the ascent. But even if this scheme was practical, how long would it take to manufacture and text such equipment – and to train a simp to use it? He doubted if a man would have the necessary strength to perform the feat.

Then there was more advanced technology. The EVA propulsion units were tempting, but their thrust was too small, since they were designed for zero-gee operation. They could not possibly lift the weight of a man, even against Rama's modest gravity.

Could an EVA thrust be sent up on automatic control, carrying only a rescue line? He had tried out this idea on Sergeant

Myron, who had promptly shot it down in flames. There were, the engineer pointed out, severe stability problems; they might be solved, but it would take a long time – much longer than they could afford.

What about balloons? There seemed a faint possibility here, if they could devise an envelope and a sufficiently compact source of heat. This was the only approach that Norton had not dismissed, when the problem suddenly ceased to be one of theory, and became a matter of life and death, dominating the news in all the inhabited worlds.

While Jimmy was making his trek along the edge of the Sea, half the crackpots in the solar system were trying to save him. At Fleet Headquarters, all the suggestions were considered, and about one in a thousand was forwarded to *Endeavour*. Dr Carlisle Perera's arrived twice – once via the Survey's own network, and once by PLANETCOM, RAMA PRIORITY. It had taken the scientist approximately five minutes of thought and one millisecond of computer time.

At first, Commander Norton thought it was a joke in very poor taste. Then he saw the sender's name and the attached calculations, and did a quick double-take.

He handed the message to Karl Mercer.

'What do you think of this?' he asked, in as non-committal a tone of voice as he could manage.

Karl read it swiftly, then said, 'Well I'm damned! He's right, of course.'

'Are you *sure*?'

'He was right about the storm, wasn't he? We should have thought of this; it makes me feel a fool.'

'You have company. The next problem is – how do we break it to Jimmy?'

'I don't think we should ... until the last possible minute. That's how I'd prefer it, if I was in his place. Just tell him we're on the way.'

Though he could look across the full width of the Cylindrical Sea, and knew the general direction from which *Resolution* was coming. Jimmy did not spot the tiny craft until it had already passed New York. It seemed incredible that it could carry six men – and whatever equipment they had brought to rescue him.

When it was only a kilometre away, he recognised Commander Norton, and started waving. A little later the skipper spotted him, and waved back.

'Glad to see you're in good shape, Jimmy,' he radioed. 'I promised we wouldn't leave you behind. Now do you believe me?'

Not quite, Jimmy thought; until this moment he had still wondered if this was all a kindly plot to keep up his morale. But the Commander would not have crossed the Sea just to say goodbye; he must have worked out *something*.

'I'll believe you, Skipper,' he said, 'when I'm down there on the deck. *Now* will you tell me how I'm going to make it?'

Resolution was now slowing down, a hundred metres from the base of the cliff; as far as Jimmy could tell, she carried no unusual equipment – though he was not sure what he had expected to see.

'Sorry about that, Jimmy – but we didn't want you to have too many things to worry about.'

Now *that* sounded ominous; what the devil did he mean?

Resolution came to a halt, fifty metres out and five hundred below; Jimmy had almost a bird's-eye view of the Commander as he spoke into his microphone.

'This is it, Jimmy. You'll be perfectly safe, but it will require nerve. We know you've got plenty of that. *You're going to jump.*'

'Five hundred metres!'

'Yes, but at only half a gee.'

'So – have you ever fallen two hundred and fifty on Earth?'

'Shut up, or I'll cancel your next leave. You should have worked this out for yourself ... it's just a question of terminal velocity. In this atmosphere, you can't reach more than ninety kilometres an hour – whether you fall two hundred or two thousand metres. Ninety's a little high for comfort, but we can trim it some more. This is what you'll have to do, so listen carefully ...'

'I will,' said Jimmy. 'It had better be good.'

He did not interrupt the Commander again, and made no comment when Norton had finished. Yes, it made sense, and was so absurdly simple that it would take a genius to think of it. And, perhaps, someone who did not expect to do it himself ...

Jimmy had never tried high-diving, or made a delayed parachute drop, which would have given him some psychological preparation for this feat. One could tell a man that it was perfectly safe to walk a plank across an abyss – yet even if the structural calculations were impeccable, he might still be unable to do it. Now Jimmy understood why the Commander had been so evasive about the details of the rescue. He had been given no time to brood, or to think of objections.

'I don't want to hurry you,' said Norton's persuasive voice from half a kilometre below. 'But the sooner the better.'

Jimmy looked at his precious souvenir, the only flower in Rama. He wrapped it very carefully in his grimy handkerchief, knotted the fabric, and tossed it over the edge of the cliff.

It fluttered down with reassuring slowness, but it also took a very long time getting smaller, and smaller, and smaller, until he could no longer see it. But then *Resolution* surged forward, and he knew that it had been spotted.

'Beautiful!' exclaimed the Commander enthusiastically. 'I'm sure they'll name it after you. OK – we're waiting ...

Jimmy stripped off his shirt – the only upper garment anyone ever wore in this now tropical climate – and stretched it thoughtfully. Several times on his trek he had almost discarded it; now it might help to save his life.

For the last time, he looked back at the hollow world he alone had explored, and the distant, ominous pinnacles of the Big and Little Horns. Then, grasping the shirt firmly with his right hand, he took a running jump as far out over the cliff as he could.

Now there was no particular hurry; he had a full twenty seconds in which to enjoy the experience. But he did not waste any time, as the wind strengthened around him and *Resolution* slowly expanded in his field of view. Holding his shirt with both hands, he stretched his arms above his head, so that the rushing air filled the garment and blew it into a hollow tube.

As a parachute, it was hardly a success; the few kilometres an hour it subtracted from his speed was useful, but not vital. It was doing a much more important job – keeping his body vertical, so that he would arrow straight into the sea.

He still had the impression that he was not moving at all, but that the water below was rushing up towards him. Once he had committed himself, he had no sense of fear; indeed, he felt a certain indignation against the skipper for keeping him in the dark. Did he *really* think that he would be scared to jump, if he had to brood over it too long?

At the very last moment, he let go of his shirt, took a deep breath, and grabbed his mouth and nose with his hands. As he had been instructed, he stiffened his body into a rigid bar, and locked his feet together. He would enter the water as cleanly as a falling spear ...

'It will be just the same,' the Commander had promised, 'as stepping off a diving board on Earth. Nothing to it – *if* you make a good entry.'

'And if I don't?' he had asked.

'Then you'll have to go back and try again.'

Something slapped him across the feet – hard, but not viciously. A million slimy hands were tearing at his body; there was a roaring in his ears, a mounting pressure – and even though his eyes were tightly closed, he could tell that darkness was falling as he arrowed down into the depths of the Cylindrical Sea.

With all his strength, he started to swim upwards towards the fading light. He could not open his eyes for more than a single blink; the poisonous water felt like acid when he did so. He seemed to have been struggling for ages, and more than once he had a nightmare fear that he had lost his orientation and was really swimming downwards. Then he would risk another quick glimpse, and every time the light was stronger.

His eyes were still clenched tightly shut when he broke water. He gulped a precious mouthful of air, rolled over on his back, and looked around.

Resolution was heading towards him at top speed; within seconds, eager hands had grabbed him and dragged him aboard.

'Did you swallow any water?' was the Commander's anxious question.

'I don't think so.'

'Rinse out with this, anyway. That's fine. How do you feel?'

'I'm not really sure. I'll let you know in a minute. Oh … thanks, everybody.' The minute was barely up when Jimmy was only too sure how he felt.

'I'm going to be sick,' he confessed miserably. His rescuers were incredulous.

'In a dead calm – on a flat sea?' protested Sergeant Barnes, who seemed to regard Jimmy's plight as a direct reflection on her skill.

'I'd hardly call it *flat*,' said the Commander, waving his arm around the band of water that circled the sky. 'But don't be ashamed – you may have swallowed some of that stuff. Get rid of it as quickly as you can.'

Jimmy was still straining, unheroically and unsuccessfully, when there was a sudden flicker of light in the sky behind them. All eyes turned towards the South Pole, and Jimmy instantly forgot his sickness. The Horns had started their firework display again.

There were the kilometre-long streamers of fire, dancing from the central spike to its smaller companions. Once again they began their stately rotation, as if invisible dancers were winding their ribbons around an electric maypole. But now they began to accelerate, moving faster and faster until they blurred into a flickering cone of light.

It was a spectacle more awe-inspiring than any they had yet seen here, and it brought with it a distant crackling roar which added to the impression of overwhelming power. The display lasted for about five minutes; then it stopped as abruptly as if someone had turned a switch.

'I'd like to know what the Rama Committee make of *that*.' Norton muttered to no one in particular. 'Has anyone here got any theories?'

There was no time for an answer, because at that moment Hub Control called in great excitement.

'*Resolution!* Are you OK? Did you feel that?'

'Feel *what*?'

'We think it was an earthquake – it must have happened the minute those fireworks stopped.'

'Any damage?'

'I don't think so. It wasn't really violent – but it shook us up a bit.'

'We felt nothing at all. But we wouldn't, out here in the Sea,'

'Of course, silly of me. Anyway, everything seems quiet now ... until next time.'

'Yes, until the next time,' Norton echoed. The mystery of Rama was steadily growing; the more they discovered about it, the less they understood.

There was a sudden shout from the helm.

'Skipper – look – up there in the sky!'

Norton lifted his eyes, swiftly scanning the circuit of the Sea.

He saw nothing, until his gaze had almost reached the zenith, and he was staring at the other side of the world.

'My God,' he whispered slowly, as he realised that the 'next time' was already almost here.

A tidal wave was racing towards them, down the eternal curve of the Cylindrical Sea.

32
The Wave

Yet even in that moment of shock, Norton's first concern was for his ship.

'*Endeavour!*' he called. 'Situation report!'

'All OK, Skipper,' was the reassuring answer from the Exec. 'We felt a slight tremor, but nothing that could cause any damage. There's been a small change of attitude – the bridge says about point two degrees. They also think the spin rate has altered slightly – we'll have an accurate reading on that in a couple of minutes.'

So it's beginning to happen, Norton told himself, and a lot earlier than we expected; we're still a long way from perihelion, and the logical time for an orbit change. But some kind of trim was undoubtedly taking place – and there might be more shocks to come.

Meanwhile, the effects of this first one were all too obvious, up there on the curving sheet of water which seemed perpetually falling from the sky. The wave was still about ten kilometres away, and stretched the full width of the Sea from northern to southern shore. Near the land, it was a foaming wall of white, but in deeper water it was a barely visible blue line, moving much faster than the breakers on either flank. The drag of the shoreward shallows was already bending it into a bow, with the central portion getting further and further ahead.

'Sergeant,' said Norton urgently. 'This is *your* job. What can we do?'

Sergeant Barnes had brought the raft completely to rest and was studying the situation intently. Her expression, Norton was relieved to see, showed no trace of alarm – rather a certain zestful excitement, like a skilled athlete about to accept a challenge.

'I wish we had some soundings,' she said. 'If we're in deep water, there's nothing to worry about.'

'Then we're all right. We're still four kilometres from shore.'

'I hope so, but I want to study the situation.'

She applied power again, and swung *Resolution* around until it was just under way, heading directly towards the approaching wave. Norton judged that the swiftly moving central portion would reach them in less than five minutes, but he could also see that it presented no serious danger. It was only a racing ripple a fraction of a metre high, and would scarcely rock the boat. The walls of foam lagging far behind it were the real menace.

Suddenly, in the very centre of the Sea, a line of breakers appeared. The wave had clearly hit a submerged wall, several kilometres in length, not far below the surface. At the same time, the breakers on the two flanks collapsed, as they ran into deeper water.

Anti-slosh plates, Norton told himself. Exactly the same as in *Endeavour*'s own propellant tanks – but on a thousand-fold greater scale. There must be a complex pattern of them all around the Sea, to damp out any waves as quickly as possible. The only thing that matters now is: are we right on top of one?

Sergeant Barnes was one jump ahead of him. She brought *Resolution* to a full stop and threw out the anchor. It hit bottom at only five metres.

'Haul it up!' she called to her crewmates. 'We've got to get away from here!'

Norton agreed heartily; but in which direction? The Sergeant was headed full speed *towards* the wave, which was now only five kilometres away. For the first time, he could hear the sound of its approach – a distant, unmistakable roar which he had never expected to hear inside Rama. Then it changed in intensity; the central portion was collapsing once more – and the flanks were building up again.

He tried to estimate the distance between the submerged baffles, assuming that they were spaced at equal intervals. If he was right, there should be one more to come; if they could station the raft in the deep water between them, they would be perfectly safe.

Sergeant Barnes cut the motor, and threw out the anchor again. It went down thirty metres without hitting bottom.

'We're OK,' she said, with a sigh of relief. 'But I'll keep the motor running.'

Now there were only the lagging walls of foam along the coast; out here in the central Sea it was calm again, apart from the inconspicuous blue ripple still speeding towards them. The Sergeant was just holding *Resolution* on course towards the disturbance, ready to pour on full power at a moment's notice.

Then, only two kilometres ahead of them, the Sea started to foam once more. It humped up in white-maned fury, and now its roaring seemed to fill the world. Upon the sixteen-kilometre-high wave of the Cylindrical Sea, a smaller ripple was superimposed, like an avalanche thundering down a mountain slope. And that ripple was quite large enough to kill them.

Sergeant Barnes must have seen the expressions on the faces of her crewmates. She shouted above the roar: 'What are you scared about? I've ridden bigger ones than this.' That was not quite true; nor did she add that her earlier experience had been in a well-built surf-boat, not an improvised raft. 'But if we *have* to jump, wait until I tell you. Check your life-jackets.'

She's magnificent, thought the Commander – obviously enjoying every minute, like a Viking warrior going into battle. And she's probably right – unless we've miscalculated badly.

The wave continued to rise, curving upwards and over. The slope above them probably exaggerated its height, but it looked enormous – an irresistible force of nature that would overwhelm everything in its path.

Then, within seconds, it collapsed, as if its foundations had been pulled out from underneath it. It was over the submerged barrier, in deep water again. When it reached them a minute later *Resolution* merely bounced up and down a few times before Sergeant Barnes swung the raft around and set off at top speed towards the north.

'Thanks, Ruby – that was splendid. But will we get home before it comes round for the second time?'

'Probably not; it will be back in about twenty minutes. But it will have lost all its strength then; we'll scarcely notice it.'

Now that the wave had passed, they could relax and enjoy the voyage – though no one would be completely at ease until they were back on land. The disturbance had left the water swirling round in random eddies, and had also stirred up a most peculiar acidic smell – 'like crushed ants', as Jimmy aptly put it. Though unpleasant, the odour caused none of the attacks of sea-sickness that might have been expected; it was something so alien that human physiology could not respond to it.

A minute later, the wave front hit the next underwater barrier, as it climbed away from them and up the sky. This time, seen from the rear, the spectacle was unimpressive and the voyagers felt ashamed of their previous fears. They began to feel themselves masters of the Cylindrical Sea.

The shock was therefore all the greater when, not more than a hundred metres away, something like a slowly rotating wheel began to rear up out of the water. Glittering metallic spokes, five metres long, emerged dripping from the sea, spun for a moment in the fierce Raman glare, and splashed back into the water. It was as if a giant starfish with tubular arms had broken the surface.

At first sight, it was impossible to tell whether it was an animal or a machine. Then it flopped over and lay half-awash, bobbing up and down in the gentle aftermath of the wave.

Now they could see that there were nine arms, apparently jointed, radiating from a central disc. Two of the arms were broken, snapped off at the outer joint. The others ended at a complicated collection of manipulators that reminded Jimmy very strongly of the crab he had encountered. The two creatures came from the same line of evolution – or the same drawing-board.

At the middle of the disc was a small turret, bearing three large eyes. Two were closed, one open – and even that appeared to be blank and unseeing. No one doubted that they were watching the death-throes of some strange monster, tossed up to the surface by the submarine disturbance that had just passed.

Then they saw that it was not alone. Swimming round it, and snapping at its feebly moving limbs, were two small beasts like overgrown lobsters. They were efficiently chopping up the monster, and it did nothing to resist, though its own claws seemed quite capable of dealing with the attackers.

Once again, Jimmy was reminded of the crab that had demolished *Dragonfly*. He watched intently as the one-sided conflict continued, and quickly confirmed his impression.

'Look, Skipper,' he whispered. 'Do you see – they're not eating it. They don't even have any mouths. *They're simply chopping it to pieces.* That's exactly what happened to *Dragonfly*.'

'You're right. They're dismantling it – like – like a broken machine.' Norton wrinkled his nose. 'But no dead machine ever smelled like that!'

Then another thought struck him.

'My God – suppose they start on us! Ruby, get us back to shore as quickly as you can!'

Resolution surged forward with reckless disregard for the life of her power cells. Behind them, the nine spokes of the great starfish – they could think of no better name for it – were clipped steadily shorter, and presently the weird tableau sank back into the depths of the Sea.

There was no pursuit, but they did not breathe comfortably again until *Resolution* had drawn up to the landing stage and they had stepped thankfully ashore. As he looked back across that mysterious and now suddenly sinister band of water, Commander Norton grimly determined that no one would ever sail it again. There were too many unknowns, too many dangers ...

He looked back upon the towers and ramparts of New York, and the dark cliff of the continent beyond. They were safe now from inquisitive man.

He would not tempt the gods of Rama again.

33
Spider

From now on, Norton had decreed, there would always be at least three people at Camp Alpha, and one of them would always be awake. In addition, all exploring parties would follow the same routine. Potentially dangerous creatures were on the move inside Rama, and though none had shown active hostility, a prudent commander would take no chances.

As an extra safeguard, there was always an observer up on the Hub, keeping watch through a powerful telescope. From this vantage point, the whole interior of Rama could be surveyed, and even the South Pole appeared only a few hundred metres away. The territory round any group of explorers was to be kept under regular observation; in this way, it was hoped to eliminate any possibility of surprise. It was a good plan – and it failed completely.

After the last meal of the day, and just before the 22.00 hour sleep period, Norton, Rodrigo, Calvert and Laura Ernst were watching the regular evening news telecast specially beamed to them from the transmitter at Inferno, Mercury. They had been particularly interested in seeing Jimmy's film of the Southern continent, and the return across the Cylindrical Sea – an episode which had excited all viewers. Scientists, news commentators, and members of the Rama Committee had given their opinions, most of them contradictory. No one could agree whether the crab-like creature Jimmy had encountered was an animal, a machine, a genuine Raman – or something that fitted none of these categories.

They had just watched, with a distinctly queasy feeling, the giant starfish being demolished by its predators when they discovered that they were no longer alone. There was an intruder in the camp.

Laura Ernst noticed it first. She froze in sudden shock, then said: 'Don't move, Bill. Now look slowly to the right.'

Norton turned his head. Ten metres away was a slender-legged tripod surmounted by a spherical body no larger than a football. Set around the body were three large, expressionless eyes, apparently giving 360 degrees of vision, and trailing beneath it were three whiplike tendrils. The creature was not quite as tall as a man, and looked far too fragile to be dangerous, but that did not excuse their carelessness in letting it sneak up on them unawares. It reminded Norton of nothing so much as a three-legged spider, or daddy-long-legs, and he wondered how it had solved the problem – never challenged by any creature on Earth – of tripedal locomotion.

'What do you make of it, Doc?' he whispered, turning off the voice of the TV newscaster.

'Usual Raman three-fold symmetry. I don't see how it could hurt us, though those whips might be unpleasant – and they could be poisonous, like a coelenterate's. Sit tight and see what it does.'

After regarding them impassively for several minutes, the creature suddenly moved – and now they could understand why they had failed to observe its arrival. It was *fast*, and it covered the ground with such an extraordinary spinning motion that the human eye and mind had real difficulty in following it.

As far as Norton could judge – and only a high-speed camera could settle the matter – each leg in turn acted as a pivot around which the creature whirled its body. And he was not sure, but it also seemed to him that every few 'steps' it reversed its direction of spin, while the three whips flickered over the ground like lightning as it moved. Its top speed – though this also was very hard to estimate – was at least thirty kilometres an hour.

It swept swiftly round the camp, examining every item of equipment, delicately touching the improvised beds and chairs and tables, communication gear, food containers, Electrosans, cameras, water tanks, tools – there seemed to be nothing that it ignored, except the four watchers. Clearly, it was intelligent enough to draw a distinction between humans and their inanimate property; its actions gave the unmistakable impression of an extremely methodical curiosity or inquisitiveness.

'I wish I could examine it!' Laura exclaimed in frustration, as the creature continued its swift pirouette. 'Shall we try to catch it?'

'How?' Calvert asked, reasonably enough.

'You know – the way primitive hunters bring down fast-moving animals with a couple of weights whirling around at the end of a rope. It doesn't even hurt them.'

'That I doubt,' said Norton. 'But even if it worked, we can't risk it. We don't know how intelligent this creature is – and a trick like that could easily break its legs. Then we would be in real trouble – from Rama, Earth and everyone else.'

'But I've got to have a specimen!'

'You may have to be content with Jimmy's flower – unless one of these creatures cooperates with you. Force is out. How would you like it if something landed on Earth and decided that *you* would make a nice specimen for dissection?'

'I don't want to dissect it,' said Laura, not at all convincingly. 'I only want to examine it.'

'Well, alien visitors might have the same attitude towards you, but you could have a very uncomfortable time before you believed them. We must make no move that could possibly be regarded as threatening.'

He was quoting from Ship's Orders, of course, and Laura

knew it. The claims of science had a lower priority than those of space-diplomacy.

In fact, there was no need to bring in such elevated considerations; it was merely a matter of good manners. They were all visitors here, and had never even asked permission to come inside ...

The creature seemed to have finished its inspection. It made one more high-speed circuit of the camp, then shot off at a tangent – towards the stairway.

'I wonder how it's going to manage the steps?' Laura mused. Her question was quickly answered; the spider ignored them completely, and headed up the gently sloping curve of the ramp without slackening its speed.

'Hub Control,' said Norton. 'You may have a visitor shortly; take a look at the Alpha Stairway Section Six. And incidentally, thanks a lot for keeping such a good watch on us.'

It took a minute for the sarcasm to sink in; then the Hub observer started to make apologetic noises.

'Er – I can just see *something*, Skipper, now you tell me it's there. But what is it?'

'Your guess is as good as mine,' Norton answered, as he pressed the *General Alert* button. 'Camp Alpha calling all stations. We've just been visited by a creature like a three-legged spider, with very thin legs, about two metres high, small spherical body, travels very fast with a spinning motion. Appears harmless but inquisitive. It may sneak up on you before you notice it. Please acknowledge.'

The first reply came from London, fifteen kilometres to the east.

'Nothing unusual here, Skipper.'

The same distance to the west, Rome answered, sounding suspiciously sleepy.

'Same here, Skipper. Uh, just a moment ...'

'What is it?'

'I put my pen down a minute ago – it's gone! What – oh!'

'Talk sense!'

'You won't believe this, Skipper. I was making some notes – you know I like writing, and it doesn't disturb anybody – I was using my favourite ball-point, it's nearly two hundred years old – well, now it's lying on the ground, about five metres away! I've got it – thank goodness – it isn't damaged.'

'And how do you suppose it got there?'

'Er – I may have dozed off for a minute. It's been a hard day.'

Norton sighed, but refrained from comment; there were so few of them, and they had so little time in which to explore a world. Enthusiasm could not always overcome exhaustion, and he wondered if they were taking unnecessary risks. Perhaps he should not split his men up into such small groups, and try to cover so much territory. But he was always conscious of the swiftly passing days, and the unsolved mysteries around them. He was becoming more and more certain that something was about to happen, and that they would have to abandon Rama even before it reached perihelion – the moment of truth when any orbit change must surely take place.

'Now listen, Hub, Rome, London – everyone,' he said. 'I want a report at every half-hour through the night. We must assume that from now on we may expect visitors at any time. Some of them may be dangerous, but at all costs we have to avoid incidents. You all know the directives on this subject.'

That was true enough; it was part of their training – yet perhaps none of them had ever really believed that the long-theorised 'physical contact with intelligent aliens' would occur in their lifetimes – still less that they would experience it themselves.

Training was one thing, reality another; and no one could be sure that the ancient, human instincts of self-preservation would not take over in an emergency. Yet it was essential to give every entity they encountered in Rama the benefit of the doubt, up to the last possible minute – and even beyond.

Commander Norton did not want to be remembered by history as the man who started the first interplanetary war.

Within a few hours there were hundreds of the spiders, and they were all over the plain. Through the telescope, it could be seen that the southern continent was also infested with them – but not, it seemed, the island of New York.

They took no further notice of the explorers, and after a while the explorers took little notice of them – though from time to time Norton still detected a predatory gleam in his Surgeon-Commander's eye. Nothing would please her better, he was sure, than for one of the spiders to have an unfortunate accident, and he would not put it past her to arrange such a thing in the interests of science.

It seemed virtually certain that the spiders could not be intelligent; their bodies were far too small to contain much in the way of brains, and indeed it was hard to see where they stored all the energy to move. Yet their behaviour was curiously purposeful and coordinated; they seemed to be everywhere, but they never visited the same place twice. Norton frequently had the impression that they were *searching* for something. Whatever it was, they did not seem to have discovered it.

They went all the way up to the central Hub, still scorning the three great stair ways. How they managed to ascend the vertical sections, even under almost zero gravity, was not clear; Laura theorised that they were equipped with suction pads.

And then, to her obvious delight, she got her eagerly desired specimen. Hub Control reported that a spider had fallen down the vertical face and was lying, dead or incapacitated, on the first platform. Laura's time up from the plain was a record that would never be beaten.

When she arrived at the platform, she found that, despite the low velocity of impact, the creature had broken all its legs. Its eyes were still open, but it showed no reactions to any external tests. Even a fresh human corpse would have been livelier, Laura decided; as soon as she got her prize back to *Endeavour*, she started to work with her dissecting kit.

The spider was so fragile that it almost came to pieces without her assistance. She disarticulated the legs, then started on the delicate carapace, which split along three great circles and opened up like a peeled orange.

After some moments of blank incredulity – for there was nothing that she could recognise or identify – she took a series of careful photographs. Then she picked up her scalpel.

Where to start cutting? She felt like closing her eyes, and stabbing at random, but that would not have been very scientific.

The blade went in with practically no resistance. A second later, Surgeon-Commander Ernst's most unlady-like yell echoed the length and breadth of *Endeavour*.

It took an annoyed Sergeant McAndrews a good twenty minutes to calm down the startled simps.

34
His Excellency Regrets

'As you are all aware, gentlemen,' said the Martian Ambassador, 'a great deal has happened since our last meeting. We have much to discuss – and to decide. I'm therefore particularly sorry that our distinguished colleague from Mercury is not here.'

That last statement was not altogether accurate. Dr Bose was not particularly sorry that HE the Hermian Ambassador was absent. It would have been much more truthful to say that he was worried. All his diplomatic instincts told him that something was happening, and though his sources of information were excellent, he could gather no hints as to what it might be.

The Ambassador's letter of apology had been courteous and entirely uncommunicative. His Excellency had regretted that urgent and unavoidable business had kept him from attending the meeting, either in person or by video. Dr Bose found it very hard to think of anything more urgent – or more important – than Rama.

'Two of our members have statements to make. I would first like to call on Professor Davidson.'

There was a rustle of excitement among the other scientists on the Committee. Most of them had felt that the astronomer, with his well-known cosmic viewpoint, was not the right man to be Chairman of the Space Advisory Council. He sometimes gave the impression that the activities of intelligent life were an unfortunate irrelevance in the majestic universe of stars and galaxies, and that it was bad manners to pay too much attention to it. This had not endeared him to exobiologists such as Dr Perera, who took exactly the opposite view. To them, the only purpose of the Universe was the production of intelligence, and they were apt to talk sneeringly about purely astronomical phenomena. 'Mere dead matter' was one of their favourite phrases.

'Mr Ambassador,' the scientist began, 'I have been analysing the curious behaviour of Rama during the last few days, and would like to present my conclusions. Some of them are rather startling.'

Dr Perera looked surprised, then rather smug. He strongly approved of anything that startled Professor Davidson.

'First of all, there was the remarkable series of events when that young lieutenant flew over to the Southern hemisphere. The electrical discharges themselves, though spectacular, are not important; it is easy to show that they contained relatively little energy. But they coincided with a change in Rama's rate of spin, and its attitude – that is, its orientation in space. *This* must have involved an enormous amount of energy; the discharges which nearly cost Mr – er Pak his life were merely a minor by-product – perhaps a nuisance that had to be minimised by those giant lightning conductors at the South Pole.

'I draw two conclusions from this. When a spacecraft – and we must call Rama a spacecraft, despite its fantastic size – makes a change of attitude, that usually means it is about to make a change of orbit. We must therefore take seriously the views of those who believe that Rama may be preparing to become another planet of our sun, instead of going back to the stars.

'If this is the case. *Endeavour* must obviously be prepared to cast off – is that what spaceships do? – at a moment's notice. She may be in very serious danger while she is still physically attached to Rama. I imagine that Commander Norton is already well aware of this possibility, but I think we should send him an additional warning.'

'Thank you very much, Professor Davidson. Yes – Dr Solomons?'

'I'd like to comment on that,' said the science historian. 'Rama seems to have made a change of spin *without* using any jets or reaction devices. This leaves only two possibilities, it seems to me.

'The first one is that it has internal gyroscopes, or their equivalent. They must be enormous; where are they?

'The second possibility – which would turn all our physics upside down – is that it has a reactionless propulsion system. The so-called Space Drive, which Professor Davidson doesn't believe in. If this is the case, Rama may be able to do almost anything. We will be quite unable to anticipate its behaviour, even on the gross physical level.'

The diplomats were obviously somewhat baffled by this exchange, and the astronomer refused to be drawn. He had gone out on enough limbs for one day.

'I'll stick to the laws of physics, if you don't mind, until I'm forced to give them up. If we've not found any gyroscopes in Rama, we may not have looked hard enough, or in the right place.'

Ambassador Bose could see that Dr Perera was getting impatient. Normally, the exobiologist was as happy as anyone else to engage in speculation; but now, for the first time, he had some solid facts. His long-impoverished science had become wealthy overnight.

'Very well – if there are no other comments – I know that Dr Perera has some important information.'

'Thank you, Mr Ambassador. As you've all seen, we have at last obtained a specimen of a Raman life-form, and have observed several others at close quarters. Surgeon-Commander Ernst, *Endeavour*'s medical officer, has sent a full report on the spider-like creature she dissected.

'I must say at once that some of her results are baffling, and in any other circumstances I would have refused to believe them.

'The spider is definitely organic, though its chemistry differs from ours in many respects – it contains considerable quantities of light metals. Yet I hesitate to call it an animal, for several fundamental reasons.

'In the first place, it seems to have no mouth, no stomach, no gut – no method of ingesting food! Also no air intakes, no lungs, no blood, no reproductive system ...

'You may wonder what it *has* got. Well, there's a simple musculature, controlling its three legs and the three whip-like tendrils or feelers. There's a brain – fairly complex, mostly concerned with the creature's remarkably developed triocular vision. But eighty per cent of the body consists of a honeycomb of large cells, and this is what gave Dr Ernst such an unpleasant surprise when she started her dissection. If she'd been luckier she might have recognised it in time, because it's the one Raman structure that *does* exist on Earth – though only in a handful of marine animals.

'Most of the spider is simply a battery, very much like that found in electric cells and rays. But in this case, it's apparently not used for defence. *It's the creatures source of energy.* And that is why it has no provisions for eating and breathing; it doesn't need such primitive arrangements. And incidentally, this means that it would be perfectly at home in a vacuum ...

'So we have a creature which, to all intents and purposes, is nothing more than a mobile eye. It has no organs of manipulation; those tendrils are much too feeble. If I had been given its specifications, I would have said it was merely a reconnaissance device.

'Its behaviour certainly fits that description. All the spiders ever do is to run around and look at things. That's all they *can* do ...

'But the other animals are different. The crab, the starfish, the sharks – for want of better words – can obviously manipulate their environment and appear to be specialised for various functions. I assume that they are also electrically powered since, like the spider, they appear to have no mouths.

'I'm sure you'll appreciate the biological problems raised by all this. Could such creatures evolve naturally? I really don't think so. They appear to be *designed* like machines, for specific jobs. If I had to describe them, I would say that they are robots – biological robots – something that has no analogy on Earth.

'If Rama is a spaceship, perhaps they are part of its crew. As to how they are born – or created – that's something I can't tell you. But I can guess that the answer's over there in New York. If Commander Norton and his men can wait long enough, they may encounter increasingly more complex creatures, with unpredictable behaviour. Somewhere along the line they may meet the Ramans themselves – the real makers of this world.

'And when *that* happens, gentlemen, there will be no doubt about it all ...'

35
Special Delivery

Commander Norton was sleeping soundly when his personal communicator dragged him away from happy dreams. He had been holidaying with his family on Mars, flying past the awesome, snow-capped peak of Nix Olympica – mightiest volcano in the solar system. Little Billie had started to say something to him; now he would never know what it was.

The dream faded; the reality was his executive officer, up on the ship.

'Sorry to wake you, Skipper,' said Lieutenant-Commander Kirchoff. 'Triple A priority from Headquarters.'

'Let me have it,' Norton answered sleepily.

'I can't. It's in code – Commander's Eyes Only.'

Norton was instantly awake. He had received such a message only three times in his whole career, and on each occasion it had meant trouble.

'Damn!' he said. 'What do we do now?'

His Exec did not bother to answer. Each understood the problem perfectly; it was one that Ship's Orders had never anticipated. Normally, a commander was never more than a few minutes away from his office and the code book in his personal safe. If he started now, Norton might get back to the ship – exhausted – in four or five hours. That was not the way to handle a Class AAA Priority.

'Jerry,' he said at length. 'Who's on the switchboard?'

'No one; I'm making the call myself.'

'Recorder off?'

'By an odd breach of regulations, yes.'

Norton smiled. Jerry was the best Exec he had ever worked with. He thought of everything.

'OK. You know where my key is. Call me back.'

He waited as patiently as he could for the next ten minutes, trying – without much success – to think of other problems. He hated wasting mental effort; it was very unlikely that he could out-guess the message that was coming, and he would know its contents soon enough. *Then* he would start worrying effectively.

When the Exec called back, he was obviously speaking under considerable strain.

'It's not really *urgent* Skipper – an hour won't make any difference. But I prefer to avoid radio. I'll send it down by messenger.'

'But *why*— Oh, very well – I trust your judgement. Who will carry it through the airlocks?'

'I'm going myself; I'll call you when I reach the Hub.'

'Which leaves Laura in charge.'

'For one hour, at the most. I'll get right back to the ship.'

A medical officer did not have the specialised training to be acting commander, any more than a commander could be expected to do an operation. In emergencies, both jobs had sometimes been successfully switched; but it was not recommended. Well, one order had already been broken tonight ...

'For the record, you never leave the ship. Have you woken Laura?'

'Yes. She's delighted with the opportunity.'

'Lucky that doctors are used to keeping secrets. Oh – have you sent the acknowledgement?'

'Of course, in your name.'

'Then I'll be waiting.'

Now it was quite impossible to avoid anxious anticipations. 'Not *really* urgent – but I prefer to avoid radio ...'

One thing was certain. The Commander was not going to get much more sleep this night.

36
Biot Watcher

Sergeant Pieter Rousseau knew why he had volunteered for this job; in many ways, it was a realisation of a childhood dream. He had become fascinated by telescopes when he was only six or seven years old, and much of his youth had been spent collecting lenses of all shapes and sizes. These he had mounted in cardboard tubes, making instruments of ever-increasing power until he was familiar with the moon and planets, the nearer space-stations, and the entire landscape within thirty kilometres of his home.

He had been lucky in his place of birth, among the mountains of Colorado; in almost every direction, the view was spectacular and inexhaustible. He had spent hours exploring, in perfect safety, the peaks which every year took their toll of careless climbers. Though he had seen much, he had imagined even more; he had liked to pretend that over each crest of rock, beyond the reach of his telescope, were magic kingdoms full of wonderful creatures. And so for years he had avoided visiting the places his lenses brought to him, because he knew that the reality could not live up to the dream.

Now, on the central axis of Rama, he could survey marvels beyond the wildest fantasies of his youth. A whole world lay spread out before him – a small one, it was true, yet a man could spend an entire lifetime exploring four thousand square kilometres, even when it was dead and changeless.

But now life, with all its infinite possibilities, had come to

Rama. If the biological robots were not living creatures, they were certainly very good imitations.

No one knew who invented the word 'biot'; it seemed to come into instant use, by a kind of spontaneous generation. From his vantage point on the Hub, Pieter was Biot-Watcher-in-Chief, and he was beginning – so he believed – to understand some of their behaviour patterns.

The Spiders were mobile sensors, using vision – and probably touch – to examine the whole interior of Rama. At one time there had been hundreds of them rushing around at high speed, but after less than two days they had disappeared; now it was quite unusual to see even one.

They had been replaced by a whole menagerie of much more impressive creatures; it had been no minor task, thinking of suitable names for them. There were the Window Cleaners, with large padded feet, who were apparently polishing their way the whole length of Rama's six artificial suns. Their enormous shadows, cast right across the diameter of the world, sometimes caused temporary eclipses on the far side.

The crab that had demolished *Dragonfly* seemed to be a Scavenger. A relay chain of identical creatures had approached Camp Alpha and carried off all the debris that had been neatly stacked on the outskirts; they would have carried off everything else if Norton and Mercer had not stood firm and defied them. The confrontation had been anxious but brief; thereafter, the Scavengers seemed to understand what they were allowed to touch, and arrived at regular intervals to see if their services were required. It was a most convenient arrangement, and indicated a high degree of intelligence – either on the part of the Scavengers themselves, or some controlling entity elsewhere.

Garbage disposal on Rama was very simple; everything was thrown into the Sea, where it was, presumably, broken down into forms that could be used again. The process was rapid; *Resolution* had disappeared overnight, to the great annoyance of Ruby Barnes. Norton had consoled her by pointing out that it had done its job magnificently – and he would never have allowed anyone to use it again. The Sharks might not be as discriminating as the Scavengers.

No astronomer discovering an unknown planet could have been happier than Pieter when he spotted a new type of biot and secured a good photo of it through his telescope. Unfortunately, it seemed that all the interesting species were over at the South Pole, where they were performing mysterious tasks round the Horns. Something that looked like a centipede with suction pads could be seen from time to time exploring Big Horn itself, while round the lower peaks Pieter had caught a glimpse of a burly creature that could have been a cross between a hippopotamus and a bulldozer. And there was even a double-necked giraffe, which apparently acted as a mobile crane.

Presumably, Rama, like any ship, required testing, checking and repairing after its immense voyage. The crew was already hard at work; when would the passengers appear?

Biot classifying was not Pieter's main job; his orders were to keep watch on the two or three exploring parties that were always out, to see that they did not get into trouble, and to warn them if anything approached. He alternated every six hours with anyone else who could be spared, though more than once he had been on duty for twelve hours at a stretch. As a result, he now knew the geography of Rama better than any man who would ever live. It was as familiar to him as the Colorado mountains of his youth.

When Jerry Kirchoff emerged from Airlock Alpha, Pieter knew at once that something unusual was happening. Personnel transfers never occurred during the sleeping period, and it was now past midnight by Mission Time. Then Pieter remembered how short-handed they were, and was shocked by a much more startling irregularity.

'Jerry – who's in charge of the ship?'

'*I* am,' said the Exec coldly, as he flipped open his helmet. 'You don't think I'd leave the bridge while I'm on watch, do you?'

He reached into his suit carry-all, and pulled out a small can still bearing the label: CONCENTRATED ORANGE JUICE: TO MAKE FIVE LITRES.

'You're good at this Pieter. The skipper is waiting for it.'

Pieter hefted the can, then said, 'I hope you've put enough mass inside it – sometimes they get stuck on the first terrace.'

'Well, you're the expert.'

That was true enough. The Hub observers had had plenty of practice, sending down small items that had been forgotten or were needed in a hurry. The trick was to get them safely past the low-gravity region, and then to see that the Coriolis effect did not carry them too far away from the Camp during the eight-kilometre roll downhill.

Pieter anchored himself firmly, grasped the can, and hurled it down the face of the cliff. He did not aim directly towards Camp Alpha, but almost thirty degrees away from it.

Almost immediately, air resistance robbed the can of its initial speed, but then the pseudo-gravity of Rama took over and it started to move downwards at a constant velocity. It hit once near the base of the ladder, and did a slow-motion bounce which took it clear of the first terrace.

'It's OK now,' said Pieter. 'Like to make a bet?'

'No,' was the prompt reply. 'You know the odds.'

'You're no sportsman. But I'll tell you now – it will stop within three hundred metres of the Camp.'

'That doesn't sound very close.'

'You might try it some time. I once saw Joe miss by a couple of kilometres.'

The can was no longer bouncing; gravity had become strong enough to glue it to the curving face of the North Dome. By the time it had reached the second terrace it was rolling along at twenty or thirty kilometres an hour, and had reached very nearly the maximum speed that friction would allow.

'Now we'll have to wait,' said Pieter, seating himself at the telescope, so that he could keep track of the messenger. 'It will be there in ten minutes. Ah, here comes the skipper – I've got used to recognising people from this angle – now he's looking up at us.'

'I believe that telescope gives you a sense of power.'

'Oh, it does. I'm the only person who knows everything that's happening in Rama. At least, I *thought* I did,' he added plaintively, giving Kirchoff a reproachful look.

'If it will keep you happy, the skipper found he'd run out of toothpaste.'

After that, conversation languished; but at last Pieter said: 'Wish you'd taken that bet ... he's only got to walk fifty metres ... now he sees it ... mission complete.'

'Thanks, Pieter – a very good job. Now you can go back to sleep.'

'Sleep! I'm on watch until 0400.'

'Sorry – you *must* have been sleeping. Or how else could you have dreamed all this?'

SPACE SURVEY HQ TO COMMANDER SSV ENDEAVOUR.
PRIORITY AAA. CLASSIFICATION YOUR EYES ONLY.
NO PERMANENT RECORD.
SPACE GUARD REPORTS ULTRA HIGH SPEED VEHICLE
APPARENTLY LAUNCHED MERCURY TEN TO TWELVE
DAYS AGO ON RAMA INTERCEPT. IF NO ORBIT
CHANGE ARRIVAL PREDICTED DATE 322 DAYS 15
HOURS. MAY BE NECESSARY YOU EVACUATE BEFORE
THEN. WILL ADVISE FURTHER.

C IN C

Norton read the message half a dozen times to memorise the

date. It was hard to keep track of time inside Rama; he had to look at his calendar watch to see that it was now Day 315. That might leave them only one week ...

The message was chilling, not only for what it said, but for what it implied. The Hermians had made a clandestine launch – that in itself a breach of Space Law. The conclusion was obvious; their 'vehicle' could only be a missile.

But *why*? It was inconceivable – well, almost inconceivable – that they would risk endangering *Endeavour*, so presumably he would receive ample warning from the Hermians themselves. In an emergency, he could leave at a few hours' notice, though he would do so only under extreme protest, at the direct orders of the Commander-in-Chief.

Slowly, and very thoughtfully, he walked across to the improvised life-support complex and dropped the message into an electrosan. The brilliant flare of laser light bursting out through the crack beneath the seat-cover told him that the demands of security were satisfied. It was too bad, he told himself, that all problems could not be disposed of so swiftly and hygienically.

37
Missile

The missile was still five million kilometres away when the glare of its plasma braking jets became clearly visible in *Endeavour*'s main telescope. By that time the secret was already out, and Norton had reluctantly ordered the second and perhaps final evacuation of Rama; but he had no intention of leaving until events gave him no alternative.

When it had completed its braking manoeuvre, the unwelcome guest from Mercury was only fifty kilometres from Rama, and apparently carrying out a survey through its TV cameras. These were clearly visible – one fore and one aft – as were several small omni-antennas and one large directional dish, aimed steadily at the distant star of Mercury. Norton wondered what instructions were coming down that beam, and what information was going back.

Yet the Hermians could learn nothing that they did not already know; all that *Endeavour* had discovered had been broadcast throughout the solar system. This spacecraft – which had broken all speed records to get here – could only be an extension of its makers' will, an instrument of their purpose. That purpose would soon be known, for in three hours the Hermian Ambassador to the United Planets would be addressing the General Assembly.

Officially, the missile did not yet exist. It bore no identification marks, and was not radiating on any standard beacon frequency. This was a serious breach of law, but even SPACEGUARD had not yet issued a formal protest. Everyone was waiting, with nervous impatience, to see what Mercury would do next.

It had been three days since the missile's existence – and origin – had been announced; all that time, the Hermians had remained stubbornly silent. They could be very good at that, when it suited them.

Some psychologists had claimed that it was almost impossible to understand fully the mentality of anyone born and bred on Mercury. Forever exiled from Earth by its three-times-more-powerful gravity, Hermians could stand on the Moon and look across the narrow gap to the planet of their ancestors – even of their own parents – but they could never visit it. And so, inevitably, they claimed that they did not want to.

They pretended to despise the soft rains, the rolling fields, the lakes and seas, the blue skies – all the things that they could know only through recordings. Because their planet was drenched with such solar energy that the day time temperature often reached six hundred degrees, they affected a rather swaggering roughness that did not bear a moment's serious examination. In fact, they tended to be physically weak, since they could only survive if they were totally insulated from their environment. Even if he could have tolerated the gravity, a Hermian would have been quickly incapacitated by a hot day in any equatorial country on Earth.

Yet in matters that really counted, they *were* tough. The psychological pressures of that ravening star so close at hand, the engineering problems of tearing into a stubborn planet and wrenching from it all the necessities of life – these had produced a Spartan and in many ways highly admirable culture. You could rely on the Hermians; if they promised something, they would do it – though the bill might be considerable. It was their own joke that, if the sun ever showed signs of going nova, they would contract to get it under control – once the fee had been settled. It was a non-Hermian joke that any child who showed signs of interest in art, philosophy or abstact mathematics was ploughed straight back into the hydroponic farms. As far as criminals and psychopaths were concerned, this was not a joke at all. Crime was one of the luxuries that Mercury could not afford.

Commander Norton had been to Mercury once, had been enormously impressed – like most visitors – and had acquired many Hermian friends. He had fallen in love with a girl in Port Lucifer, and had even contemplated signing a three-year contract, but parental disapproval of anyone from outside the orbit of Venus had been too strong. It was just as well.

'Triple A message from Earth, Skipper,' said the bridge. 'Voice and back-up text from Commander-in-Chief. Ready to accept?'

'Check and file text; let me have the voice.'

'Here it comes.'

Admiral Hendrix sounded calm and matter-of-fact, as if he was issuing a routine fleet order, instead of handling a situation unique in the history of space. But then, he was not ten kilometres from the bomb.

'C-in-C to Commander, *Endeavour*. This is a quick summary of the situation as we see it now. You know that the General Assembly meets at fourteen hundred hours and you'll be listening to the proceedings. It is possible that you may then have to take action immediately, without consultation; hence this briefing.

'We've analysed the photos you have sent us; the vehicle is a standard space-probe, modified for high-impulse and probably laser-riding for initial boost. Size and mass are consistent with fusion bomb in the five hundred to one thousand megaton range; the Hermians use up to one hundred megatons routinely in their mining operations, so they would have had no difficulty in assembling such a warhead.

'Our experts also estimate that this would be the minimum size necessary to assure destruction of Rama. If it was detonated against the thinnest part of the shell – underneath the Cylindrical Sea – the hull would be ruptured and the spin of the body would complete its disintegration.

'We assume that the Hermians, if they are planning such an act, will give you ample time to get clear. For your information, the gamma-ray flash from such a bomb could be dangerous to you up to a range of a thousand kilometres.

'But that is not the most serious danger. The fragments of Rama, weighing tons and spinning off at almost a thousand kilometres an hour, could destroy you at an *unlimited* distance. We therefore recommend that you proceed along the spin axis, since no fragments will be thrown off in that direction. Ten thousand kilometres should give an adequate safety margin.

'This message cannot be intercepted; it is going by multiple-pseudo-random routing, so I can talk in clear English. Your reply may not be secure, so speak with discretion and use code when necessary. I will call you immediately after the General Assembly discussion. Message concluded. C-in-C, out.'

38
General Assembly

According to the history books – though no one could really believe it – there had been a time when the old United Nations had 172 members. The United planets had only seven; and that was sometimes bad enough. In order of distance from the Sun, they were Mercury, Earth, Luna, Mars, Ganymede, Titan and Triton.

The list contained numerous omissions and ambiguities which presumably the future would rectify. Critics never tired of pointing out that most of the United Planets were not planets at all, but satellites. And how ridiculous that the four giants, Jupiter, Saturn, Uranus and Neptune were not included ...

But no one lived on the Gas Giants, and quite possibly no one ever would. The same might be true of the other major absentee, Venus. Even the most enthusiastic of planetary engineers agreed that it would take centuries to tame Venus; meanwhile the Hermians kept their eyes on her, and doubtless brooded over long-range plans.

Separate representation for Earth and Luna had also been a bone of contention; the other members argued that it put too much power in one corner of the solar system. But there were more people on the Moon than all the other worlds except Earth itself – and it *was* the meeting place of the UP. Moreover, Earth and Moon hardly every agreed on anything, so they were not likely to constitute a dangerous bloc.

Mars held the asteroids in trust – except for the Icarian group (supervised by Mercury) and a handful with perihelions beyond Saturn – and thus claimed by Titan. One day the larger asteroids, such as Pallas, Vesta, Juno and Ceres, would be important enough to have their own ambassadors, and membership of the UP would then reach two figures.

Ganymede represented not only Jupiter – and therefore more mass than all the rest of the solar system put together – but also the remaining fifty or so Jovian satellites, if one included temporary captures from the asteroid belt (the lawyers were still arguing over this). In the same way, Titan took care of Saturn, its rings and the other thirty-plus satellites.

The situation for Triton was even more complicated. The large moon of Neptune was the outermost body in the solar system under permanent habitation; as a result, its ambassador wore a considerable number of hats. He represented Uranus and its eight moons (none yet occupied); Neptune and its other three satellites; Pluto and its solitary moon; and lonely, moonless Persephone. If there were planets beyond Persephone, they too would be Triton's responsibility. And as if that was not enough, the Ambassador for the Outer Darkness, as he was sometimes called, had been heard to ask plaintively: 'What about comets?' It was generally felt that this problem could be left for the future to solve.

And yet, in a very real sense, that future was already here. By some definitions, Rama *was* a comet; they were the only other visitors from the interstellar deeps, and many had travelled on hyperbolic orbits even closer to the Sun than Rama's. Any space-lawyer could make a very good case out of that – and the Hermian Ambassador was one of the best.

'We recognise His Excellency the Ambassador for Mercury.'

As the delegates were arranged counter-clockwise in order of distance from the sun, the Hermian was on the President's extreme right. Up to the very last minute, he had been interfacing with his computer; now he removed the synchronizing spectacles which allowed no one else to read the message on the display screen. He picked up his sheaf of notes, and rose briskly to his feet.

'Mr President, distinguished fellow delegates, I would like to begin with a brief summary of the situation which now confronts us.'

From some delegates, that phrase 'a brief summary' would have evoked silent groans among all listeners; but everyone knew that Hermians meant exactly what they said.

'The giant spaceship, or artificial asteroid, which has been christened Rama was detected over a year ago, in the region beyond Jupiter. At first it was believed to be a natural body, moving on a hyperbolic orbit which would take it round the sun and on to the stars.

'When its true nature was discovered, the Solar Survey Vessel *Endeavour* was ordered to rendezvous with it. I am sure we will all congratulate Commander Norton and his crew for the efficient way in which they have carried out their unique assignment.

'At first, it was believed that Rama was dead – frozen for so many hundreds of thousands of years that there was no possibility of revival. This may still be true, in a strictly biological sense. There seems general agreement, among those who have studied the matter, that no living organism of any complexity can survive more than a very few centuries of suspended animation. Even at absolute zero, residual quantum effects eventually erase too much cellular information to make revival possible. It therefore appeared that, although Rama was of enormous archaeological importance, it did not present any major astro-political problems.

'It is now obvious that this was a very naïve attitude, though even from the first there were some who pointed out that Rama was too precisely aimed at the Sun for pure chance to be involved.

'Even so, it might have been argued – indeed, it was argued – that here was an experiment that had failed. Rama had reached the intended target, but the controlling intelligence had not survived. This view also seems very simple-minded; it surely underestimates the entities we are dealing with.

'What we failed to take into account was the possibility of *non*-biological survival. If we accept Dr Perera's very plausible theory, which certainly fits all the facts, the creatures who have been observed inside Rama did not exist until a short time ago. Their patterns, or templates, were stored in some central information bank, and when the time was ripe they were manufactured from available raw materials – presumably the metallo-organic soup of the Cylindrical Sea. Such a feat is still somewhat beyond our own ability, but does not present any theoretical problems. We know that solid state circuits, unlike living matter, can store information without loss, for indefinite periods of time.

'So Rama is now in full operating condition, serving the purpose of its builders – whoever they may be. From our point of view, it does not matter if the Ramans themselves have all been dead for a million years, or whether they too will be re-created, to join their servants, at any moment. With or without them, their will is being done – and will continue to be done.

'Rama has now given proof that its propulsion system is still operating. In a few days, it will be at perihelion, where it would logically make any major orbit change. We may therefore soon have a new planet – moving through the solar space over which my government has jurisdiction. Or it may, of course, make additional changes and occupy a final orbit at any distance from the sun. It could even become a satellite of a major planet – such as Earth ...

'We are therefore, fellow delegates, faced with a whole spectrum of possibilities, some of them very serious indeed. It is foolish to pretend that these creatures *must* be benevolent and will not interfere with us in any way. If they come to our solar system, they need something from it. Even if it is only scientific knowledge – consider how that knowledge may be used ...

'What confronts us now is a technology hundreds – perhaps thousands – of years in advance of ours, and a *culture* which may have no points of contact whatsoever. We have been studying the behaviour of the biological robots – the biots – inside Rama, as shown on the films that Commander Norton has relayed, and we have arrived at certain conclusions which we wish to pass on to you.

'On Mercury we are perhaps unlucky in having no indigenous life-forms to observe. But, of course, we have a complete record of terrestrial zoology, and we find in it one striking parallel with Rama.

'This is the termite colony. Like Rama, it is an artificial world with a controlled environment. Like Rama, its functioning depends upon a whole series of specialised biological machines – workers, builders, farmers – *warriors*. And although we do not know if Rama has a queen, I suggest that the island known as New York serves a similar function.

'Now, it would obviously be absurd to press this analogy too far; it breaks down at many points. But I put it to you for this reason.

'What degree of cooperation or understanding would ever be possible between human beings and termites? When there is no conflict of interest, we tolerate each other. But when either needs the other's territory or resources, no quarter is given.

'Thanks to our technology and our intelligence, we can always win, if we are sufficiently determined. But sometimes it is not easy, and there are those who believe that, in the long run, final victory may yet go to the termites ...

'With this in mind, consider now the appalling threat that Rama may – I do not say *must* – present to human civilisation. What steps have we taken to counter it, if the worst eventuality should occur? None whatsoever; we have merely talked and speculated and written learned papers.

'Well, my fellow delegates, Mercury has done more than this. Acting under the provisions of Clause 34 of the Space Treaty of 2057, which entitled us to take any steps necessary to protect the integrity of our solar space, we have dispatched a high-energy nuclear device to Rama. We will indeed be happy if we never have to utilise it. But now, at least, we are not helpless – as we were before.

'It may be argued that we have acted unilaterally, without prior consultation. We admit that. But does anyone here imagine – with all respect, Mister President – that we could have secured any such agreement in the time available? We consider that we are acting not only for ourselves, but for the whole human race. All future generations may one day thank us for our foresight.

'We recognised that it would be a tragedy – even a crime – to destroy an artifact as wonderful as Rama. If there is any way in which this can be avoided, *without risk to humanity*, we will be very happy to hear of it. We have not found one, and time is running out.

'Within the next few days, before Rama reaches perihelion, the choice will have to be made. We will, of course, give ample warning to *Endeavour* – but we would advise Commander Norton always to be ready to leave at an hour's notice. It is conceivable that Rama may undergo further dramatic transformations at any moment.

'That is all, Mister President, fellow delegates. I thank you for your attention. I look forward to your cooperation.'

39
Command Decision

'Well, Rod, how do the Hermians fit into your theology?'

'Only too well, Commander,' replied Rodrigo with a humourless smile. 'It's the age-old conflict between the forces of good and the forces of evil. And there are times when men have to take sides in such a conflict.'

I thought it would be something like that, Norton told himself. This situation must have been a shock to Boris, but he would not have resigned himself to passive acquiescence. The Cosmo-Christers were very energetic, competent people. Indeed, in some ways they were remarkably like the Hermians.

'I take it you have a plan, Rod.'

'Yes, Commander. It's really quite simple. We merely have to disable the bomb.'

'Oh, And how do you propose to do that?'

'With a small pair of wire-cutters.'

If this had been anyone else, Norton would have assumed that they were joking. But not Boris Rodrigo.

'Now just a minute! It's bristling with cameras. Do you suppose the Hermians will just sit and watch you?'

'Of course; that's all they *can* do. When the signal reaches them, it will be far too late. I can easily finish the job in ten minutes.'

'I see. They certainly *will* be mad. But suppose the bomb is booby-trapped so that interference sets it off?'

'That seems very unlikely; what would be the purpose? This

bomb was built for a specific deep-space mission, and it will be fitted with all sorts of safety devices to prevent detonation *except* on a positive command. But that's a risk I'm prepared to take – and it can be done without endangering the ship. I've worked everything out.'

'I'm sure you have,' said Norton. The idea was fascinating – almost seductive in its appeal; he particularly liked the idea of the frustrated Hermians, and would give a good deal to see their reactions when they realised – too late – what was happening to their deadly toy.

But there were other complications, and they seemed to multiply as Norton surveyed the problem. He was facing by far the most difficult, and the most crucial, decision in his entire career.

And that was a ridiculous understatement. He was faced with the most difficult decision *any* commander had ever had to make; the future of the entire human race might well depend upon it. For just suppose the Hermians were right?

When Rodrigo had left, he switched on the DO NOT DISTURB sign; he could not remember when he had last used it, and was mildly surprised that it was working. Now, in the heart of his crowded, busy ship, he was completely alone – except for the portrait of Captain James Cook, gazing at him down the corridors of time.

It was impossible to consult with Earth; he had already been warned that any messages might be tapped – perhaps by relay devices on the bomb itself. That left the whole responsibility in his hands.

There was a story he had heard somewhere about a President of the United States – was it Roosevelt or Perez? – who had a sign on his desk saying 'The buck stops here'. Norton was not quite certain what a buck was, but he knew when one had stopped at his desk.

He could do nothing, and wait until the Hermians advised him to leave. How would that look in the histories of the future? Norton was not greatly concerned with posthumous fame or infamy, yet he would not care to be remembered for ever as the accessory to a cosmic crime – which it had been in his power to prevent.

And the plan was flawless. As he had expected, Rodrigo had worked out every detail, anticipated every possibility, even the remote danger that the bomb might be triggered when tampered with. If that happened, *Endeavour* could still be safe, behind the shield of Rama. As for Lieutenant Rodrigo himself, he seemed to regard the possibility of instant apotheosis with complete equanimity.

Yet, even if the bomb was successfully disabled, that would be far from the end of the matter. The Hermians might try again – unless some way could be found of stopping them. But at least weeks of time would have been bought; Rama would be far past perihelion before another missile could possibly reach it. By then, hopefully, the worst fears of the alarmists might have been disproved. Or the reverse ...

To act, or not to act – that was the question. Never before had Commander Norton felt such a close kinship with the Prince of Denmark. Whatever he did, the possibilities for good and evil seemed in perfect balance. He was faced with the most morally difficult of all decisions. If his choice was wrong, he would know very quickly. But if he was correct – he might never be able to prove it ...

It was no use relying any further on logical arguments and the endless mapping of alternative futures. That way, one could go round and round in circles for ever. The time had come to listen to his inner voices.

He returned the calm, steady gaze across the centuries.

'I agree with you, Captain,' he whispered. 'The human race

has to live with its conscience. Whatever the Hermians argue, survival is not everything.'

He pressed the call button for the bridge circuit and said slowly, 'Lieutenant Rodrigo – I'd like to see you.'

Then he closed his eyes, hooked his thumbs in the restraining straps of his chair, and prepared to enjoy a few moments of total relaxation.

It might be some time before he would experience it again.

40
Saboteur

The scooter had been stripped of all unnecessary equipment; it was now merely an open framework holding together propulsion, guidance and life-support systems. Even the seat for the second pilot had been removed, for every kilogramme of extra mass had to be paid for in mission time.

That was one of the reasons, though not the most important, why Rodrigo had insisted on going alone. It was such a simple job that there was no need for any extra hands, and the mass of a passenger would cost several minutes of flight time. Now the stripped-down scooter could accelerate at over a third of a gravity; it could make the trip from *Endeavour* to the bomb in four minutes. That left six to spare; it would be sufficient.

Rodrigo looked back only once when he had left the ship; he saw that, as planned, it had lifted from the central axis and was thrusting gently away across the spinning disc of the North Face. By the time he reached the bomb, it would have placed the thickness of Rama between them.

He took his time, flying over the polar plain. There was no hurry here, because the bomb's cameras could not yet see him, and he could therefore conserve fuel. Then he drifted over the curving rim of the world – and there was the missile, glittering in sunlight fiercer even than that shining on the planet of its birth.

Rodrigo had already punched in the guidance instructions. He initiated the sequence; the scooter spun on its gyros, and came up to full thrust in a matter of seconds. At first the sensation of weight seemed crushing; then Rodrigo adjusted to it. He had, after all, comfortably endured twice as much inside Rama – and had been born under three times as much on Earth.

The huge, curving exterior wall of the fifty-kilometre cylinder was slowly falling away beneath him as the scooter aimed itself directly at the bomb. Yet it was impossible to judge Rama's size, since it was completely smooth and featureless – so featureless, indeed, that it was difficult to tell that it was spinning.

One hundred seconds into the mission; he was approaching the halfway point. The bomb was still too far away to show any details, but it was much brighter against the jet-black sky. It was strange to see no stars – not even brilliant Earth or dazzling Venus; the dark filters which protected his eyes against the deadly glare made that impossible. Rodrigo guessed that he was breaking a record; probably no other man had ever engaged in extra-vehicular work so close to the sun. It was lucky for him that solar activity was low.

At two minutes ten seconds the flip-over light started flashing, thrust dropped to zero, and the scooter spun through a hundred and eighty degrees. Full thrust was back in an instant, but now he was decelerating at the same mad rate of three metres per second squared – rather better than that, in fact, since he had lost almost half his propellent mass. The bomb was twenty-five kilometres away; he would be there in another two minutes. He had hit a top speed of fifteen hundred kilometres an hour – which, for a space-scooter, was utter insanity, and probably another record. But this was hardly a routine EVA, and he knew precisely what he was doing.

The bomb was growing; and now he could see the main antenna, holding steady on the invisible star of Mercury. Along that beam, the image of his approaching scooter had been flashing at the speed of light for the last three minutes. There were still two to go, before it reached Mercury.

What would the Hermians do, when they saw him? There would be consternation, of course; they would realise instantly that he had made a rendezvous with the bomb several minutes before they even knew he was on the way. Probably some stand-by observer would call higher authority – that would take more time. But even in the worst possible case – even if the officer on duty had authority to detonate the bomb, and pressed the button immediately – it would take another five minute for the signal to arrive.

Though Rodrigo was not gambling on it – Cosmo-Christers *never* gambled – he was quite sure that there would be no such instantaneous reaction. The Hermians would hesitate to destroy a reconnaissance vehicle from *Endeavour*, even if they suspected its motives. They would certainly attempt some form of communication first – and that would mean *more* delay.

And there was an even better reason; they would not waste a gigaton bomb on a mere scooter. Wasted it would be, if it was detonated twenty kilometres from its target. They would have to move it first. Oh, he had plenty of time ... but he would still assume the very worst.

He would act as if the triggering impulse would arrive in the shortest possible time – just five minutes.

As the scooter closed in across the last few hundred metres, Rodrigo quickly matched the details he could now see with those he had studied in the photographs taken at long range. What had been only a collection of pictures became hard metal and smooth plastic – no longer abstract, but a deadly reality.

The bomb was a cylinder about ten metres long and three in diameter – by a strange coincidence, almost the same proportions as Rama itself. It was attached to the framework of the carrier vehicle by an open lattice-work of short I-beams. For some reason, probably to do with the location of the centre of mass, it was supported at *right angles* to the axis of the carrier, so that it conveyed an appropriately sinister hammer-head impression. It was indeed a hammer, one powerful enough to smash a world.

From each end of the bomb, a bundle of braided cables ran along the cylindrical side and disappeared through the lattice-work into the interior of the vehicle. All communication and control was here; there was no antenna of any kind on the bomb itself. Rodrigo had only to cut those two sets of cables and there would be nothing here but harmless, inert metal.

Although this was exactly what he had expected, it still seemed a little too easy. He glanced at his watch; it would be another thirty seconds before the Hermians, even if they had been watching when he rounded the edge of Rama, could know of his existence. He had an absolutely certain five minutes for uninterrupted work – and a ninety-nine per cent probability of much longer than that.

As soon as the scooter had drifted to a complete halt, Rodrigo grappled it to the missile framework so that the two formed a rigid structure. That took only seconds; he had already chosen his tools, and was out of the pilot's seat at once, only slightly hampered by the stiffness of his heavy-insulation suit.

The first thing he found himself inspecting was a small metal plate bearing the inscription:

DEPARTMENT OF POWER ENGINEERING
Section D,
47, Sunset Boulevard,
Vulcanopolis, 17464
For information apply to Mr Henry K. Jones

Rodrigo suspected that, in a very few minutes, Mr Jones might be rather busy.

The heavy wire-cutters made short work of the cable. As the first strands parted, Rodrigo gave scarcely a thought to the fires of hell that were pent up only centimetres away; if his actions triggered them, he would never know.

He glanced again at his watch; this had taken less than a minute, which meant that he was on schedule. Now for the back-up cable – and then he could head for home, in full view of the furious and frustrated Hermians.

He was just beginning to work on the second cable assembly when he felt a faint vibration in the metal he was touching. Startled, he looked back along the body of the missile.

The characteristic blue-violet glow of a plasma thruster in action was hovering round one of the attitude control jets. The bomb was preparing to move.

The message from Mercury was brief, and devastating. It arrived two minutes after Rodrigo had disappeared around the edge of Rama.

COMMANDER ENDEAVOUR FROM MERCURY SPACE CONTROL, INFERNO WEST. YOU HAVE ONE HOUR FROM RECEIPT OF THIS MESSAGE TO LEAVE VICINITY OF RAMA. SUGGEST YOU PROCEED MAXIMUM ACCELERATION ALONG SPIN AXIS. REQUEST ACKNOWLEDGEMENT. MESSAGE ENDS.

Norton read it with sheer disbelief, then anger. He felt a childish impulse to radio back that all his crew were inside Rama, and it would take hours to get everyone out. But that would achieve nothing – except perhaps to test the will and nerve of the Hermians.

And why, several days before perihelion, had they decided to act? He wondered if the mounting pressure of public opinion was becoming too great, and they decided to present the rest of the human race with a *fait accompli*. It seemed an unlikely explanation; such sensitivity would have been uncharacteristic.

There was no way in which he could recall Rodrigo, for the scooter was now in the radio shadow of Rama and would be out of contact until they were in line of sight again. That would not be until the mission was completed – or had failed.

He would have to wait it out; there was still plenty of time – a full fifty minutes. Meanwhile, he had decided on the most effective answer to Mercury.

He would ignore the message completely, and see what the Hermians did next.

Rodrigo's first sensation, when the bomb started to move, was not one of physical fear; it was something much more devastating. He believed that the universe operated according to strict laws, which not even God Himself could disobey – much less the Hermians. No message could travel faster than light; he was five minutes ahead of anything that Mercury could do.

This could only be a coincidence – fantastic, and perhaps deadly, but no more than that. By chance, a control signal must have been sent to the bomb at about the time he was leaving *Endeavour*; while he was travelling fifty kilometres, it had covered eighty million.

Or perhaps this was only an automatic change of attitude, to counter over-heating somewhere in the vehicle. There were places where the skin temperature approached fifteen hundred degrees, and Rodrigo had been very careful to keep in the shadows as far as possible.

A second thrusters started to fire, checking the spin given by the first. No, this was *not* a mere thermal adjustment. The bomb was re-orientating itself, to point towards Rama ...

Useless to wonder *why* this was happening at this precise moment in time. There was one thing in his favour; the missile was a low acceleration device. A tenth of a gee was the most that it could manage. He could hang on.

He checked the grapples attaching the scooter to the bomb

framework, and re-checked the safety line on his own suit. A cold anger was growing in his mind, adding to his determination. Did this manoeuvre mean that the Hermians were going to explode the bomb without warning, giving *Endeavour* no chance to escape? That seemed incredible – an act not only of brutality but of folly, calculated to turn the rest of the solar system against them. And what would have made them ignore the solemn promise of their own Ambassador?

Whatever their plan, they would not get away with it.

The second message from Mercury was identical with the first, and arrived ten minues later. So they had extended the deadline – Norton still had one hour. And they had obviously waited until a reply from *Endeavour* could have reached them before calling him again.

Now there was another factor; by this time they must have seen Rodrigo, and would have had several minutes in which to take action. Their instructions could already be on the way. They could arrive at any second.

He should be preparing to leave. At any moment, the sky-filling bulk of Rama might become incandescent along the edges, blazing with a transient glory that would far outshine the sun.

When the main thrust came on, Rodrigo was securely anchored. Only twenty seconds later, it cut off again. He did a quick mental calculation; the delta vee could not have been more than fifteen kilometres an hour. The bomb would take over an hour to reach Rama; perhaps it was only moving in close to get a quicker re-action. If so, that was a wise precaution; but the Hermians had left it too late.

Rodrigo glanced at his watch, though by now he was almost aware of the time without having to check. On Mercury, they would now be seeing him heading purposefully towards the bomb, and less than two kilometres away from it. They could have no doubt of his intentions, and would be wondering if he had already carried them out.

The second set of cables went as easily as the first; like any good workman, Rodrigo had chosen his tools well. The bomb was disarmed; or, to be more accurate, it could no longer be detonated by remote command.

Yet there was one other possibility, and he could not afford to ignore it. There were no external contact fuses, but there might be internal ones, armed by the shock of impact. The Hermians still had control over their vehicle's movements, and could crash it into Rama whenever they wished. Rodrigo's work was not yet completely finished.

Five minutes from now, in that control room somewhere on Mercury, they would see him crawling back along the exterior of the missile, carrying the modestly-sized wire-cutters that had neutralized the mightiest weapon ever built by man. He was almost tempted to wave at the camera, but decided that it would seem undignified; after all, he was making history, and millions would watch this scene in the years to come. Unless, of course, the Hermians destroyed the recording in a fit of pique; he would hardly blame them.

He reached the mounting of the long-range antenna, and drifted hand-over-hand along it to the big dish. His faithful cutters made short work of the multiplex feed system, chewing up cables and laser wave guides alike. When he made the last snip, the antenna started to swing slowly around; the unexpected movement took him by surprise, until he realised that he had destroyed its automatic lock on Mercury. Just five minutes from now, the Hermians would lose all contact with their servant. Not only was it impotent; now it was blind and deaf.

Rodrigo climbed slowly back to the scooter, released the shackles, and swung it round until the forward bumpers were pressing against the missile, as close as possible to its centre of mass. He brought thrust up to full power, and held it there for twenty seconds.

Pushing against many times its own mass, the scooter responded very sluggishly. When Rodrigo cut the thrust back to zero, he took a careful reading of the bomb's new velocity vector.

It would miss Rama by a wide margin– and it could be located again with precision at any future time. It was, after all, a very valuable piece of equipment.

Lieutenant Rodrigo was a man of almost pathological honesty. He would not like the Hermians to accuse him of losing their property.

41
Hero

'Darling,' began Norton, 'this nonsense has cost us more than a day, but at least it's given me a chance to talk to you.

'I'm still in the ship, and she's heading back to station at the polar axis. We picked Rod up an hour ago, looking as if he'd just come off duty after a quiet watch. I suppose neither of us will ever be able to visit Mercury again, and I'm wondering if we're going to be treated as heroes or villains when we get back to Earth. But *my* conscience is clear; I'm sure we did the right thing. I wonder if the Ramans will ever say "thank you".

'We can stay here only two more days; unlike Rama, we don't have a kilometre-thick skin to protect us from the sun. The hull's already developing dangerous hotspots and we've had to put out some local screening. I'm sorry – I didn't want to bore you with my problems ...

'So there's time for just one more trip into Rama, and I intend to make the most of it. But don't worry – I'm not taking any chances.'

He stopped the recording. That, to say the least, was stretching the truth. There was danger and uncertainty about every moment inside Rama; no man could ever feel really at home there, in the presence of forces beyond his understanding. And on this final trip, now that he knew they would never return and that no future operations would be jeopardized, he intended to press his luck just a little further.

'In forty-eight hours, then, we'll have completed this mission.

What happens then is still uncertain; as you know, we've used virtually all our fuel getting into this orbit. I'm still waiting to hear if a tanker can rendezvous with us in time to get back to Earth, or whether we'll have to make planet-fall at Mars. Anyway, I should be home by Christmas. Tell Junior I'm sorry I can't bring a baby biot; there's no such animal …

'We're all fine, but we're very tired. I've earned a long leave after all this, and we'll make up for lost time. Whatever they say about me, you can claim you're married to a hero. How many wives have a husband who saved a world?'

As always, he listened carefully to the tape before duping it, to make sure that it was applicable to both his families. It was strange to think that he did not know which of them he would see first; usually, his schedule was determined at least a year in advance, by the inexorable movements of the planets themselves.

But that was in the days before Rama; now nothing would ever be the same again.

42
Temple of Glass

'If we try it,' said Karl Mercer, 'do you think the biots will stop us?'

'They may; that's one of the things I want to find out. Why are you looking at me like that?'

Mercer gave his slow, secret grin, which was liable to be set off at any moment by a private joke he might or might not share with his shipmates.

'I was wondering, Skipper, if you think you own Rama. Until now, you've vetoed any attempt to cut into buildings. Why the switch? Have the Hermians given you ideas?'

Norton laughed, then suddenly checked himself. It was a shrewd question, and he was not sure if the obvious answers were the right ones.

'Perhaps I have been ultra-cautious – I've tried to avoid trouble. But this is our last chance; if we're forced to retreat we won't have lost much.'

'Assuming that we retreat in good order.'

'Of course. But the biots have never shown hostility; and except for the Spiders, I don't believe there's anything here that can catch us – if we do have to run for it.'

'*You* may run, Skipper, but I intend to leave with dignity. And incidentally, I've decided why the biots are so polite to us.'

'It's a little late for a new theory.'

'Here it is, anyway. They think we're Ramans. They can't tell the difference between one oxy-eater and another.'

'I don't believe they're *that* stupid.'

'It's not a matter of stupidity. They've been programmed for their particular jobs, and we simply don't come into their frame of reference.'

'Perhaps you're right. We may find out – as soon as we start to work on London.'

Joe Calvert had always enjoyed those old bank-robbery movies, but he had never expected to be involved in one. Yet this was, essentially, what he was doing now.

The deserted streets of 'London' seemed full of menace, though he knew that was only his guilty conscience. He did not *really* believe that the sealed and windowless structures ranged all around them were full of watchful inhabitants, waiting to emerge in angry hordes as soon as the invaders laid a hand on their property. In fact, he was quite certain that this whole complex – like all the other towns – was merely some kind of storage area.

Yet a second fear, also based on innumerable ancient crime dramas, could be better grounded. There might be no clanging alarm bells and screaming sirens, but it was reasonable to assume that Rama would have some kind of warning system. How otherwise did the biots know when and where their services were needed?

'Those without goggles, turn your backs,' ordered Sergeant Myron. There was a smell of nitric oxides as the air itself started to burn in the beam of the laser torch, and a steady sizzling as the fiery knife sliced towards secrets that had been hidden since the birth of man.

Nothing material could resist this concentration of power, and the cut proceeded smoothly at a rate of several metres a minute. In a remarkable short time, a section large enough to admit a man had been sliced out.

As the cut-away section showed no signs of moving, Myron

tapped it gently – then harder – then banged on it with all his strength. It fell inwards with a hollow, reverberating crash.

Once again, as he had done during that very first entrance into Rama, Norton remembered the archaeologist who had opened the old Egyptian tomb. He did not expect to see the glitter of gold; in fact, he had no preconceived ideas at all, as he crawled through the opening, his flashlight held in front of him.

A Greek temple made of glass – that was his first impression. The building was filled with row upon row of vertical crystalline columns, about a metre wide and stretching from floor to ceiling. There were hundreds of them, marching away into the darkness beyond the reach of his light.

Norton walked towards the nearest column and directed his beam into its interior. Refracted as through a cylindrical lens, the light fanned out on the far side to be focused and refocused, getting fainter with each repetition, in the array of pillars beyond. He felt that he was in the middle of some complicated demonstration in optics.

'Very pretty,' said the practical Mercer, 'but what does it mean? Who needs a forest of glass pillars?'

Norton rapped gently on one column. It sounded solid, though more metallic than crystalline. He was completely baffled, and so followed a piece of useful advice he had heard long ago: 'When in doubt, say nothing and move on.'

As he reached the next column, which looked exactly like the first, he heard an exclamation of surprise from Mercer.

'I could have sworn this pillar was empty – now there's something inside it.'

Norton glanced quickly back.

'Where?' he said. 'I don't see anything.'

He followed the direction of Mercer's pointing finger. It was aimed at nothing; the column was still completely transparent.

'You can't see it?' said Mercer incredulously. 'Come around this side. Damn – now I've lost it!'

'What's going on here?' demanded Calvert. It was several minutes before he got even the first approximation to an answer.

The columns were not transparent from every angle or under all illuminations. As one walked around them, objects would suddenly flash into view, apparently embedded in their depths like flies in amber – and would then disappear again. There were dozens of them, all different. They looked absolutely real and solid, yet many seemed to occupy the identical volume of space.

'Holograms,' said Calvert. 'Just like a museum on Earth.'

That was the obvious explanation, and therefore Norton viewed it with suspicion. His doubts grew as he examined the other columns, and conjured up the images stored in their interiors.

Hand-tools (though for huge and peculiar hands), containers, small machines with keyboards that appeared to have been made for more than five fingers, scientific instruments, startlingly conventional domestic utensils, including knives and plates which apart from their size would not have attracted a second glance on any terrestrial table ... they were all there, with hundreds of less identifiable objects, often jumbled up together in the same pillar. A museum, surely, would have some logical arrangement, some segregation of related items. This seemed to be a completely random collection of hardware.

They had photographed the elusive images inside a score of the crystal pillars when the sheer variety of items gave Norton a clue. Perhaps this was not a collection, but a *catalogue*, indexed according to some arbitrary but perfectly logical system. He thought of the wild juxtapositions that any dictionary or alphabetized list will give, and tried the idea on his companions.

'I see what you mean,' said Mercer. 'The Ramans might be equally surprised to find us putting – ah– camshafts next to cameras.'

'Or books beside boots', added Calvert, after several seconds' hard thinking. One could play this game for hours, he decided, with increasing degrees of impropriety.

'That's the idea,' replied Norton. 'This may be an indexed catalogue for 3-D images – templates – solid blue-prints, if you like to call them that.'

'For what purpose?'

'Well, you know the theory about the biots ... the idea that they don't exist until they're needed and then they're created – synthesised – from patterns stored somewhere?'

'I see,' said Mercer slowly and thoughtfully. 'So when a Raman needs a left-handed blivet, he punches out the correct code number, and a copy is manufactured from the pattern in here.'

'Something like that. But please don't ask me about the practical details.'

The pillars through which they had been moving had been steadily growing in size, and were now more than two metres in diameter. The images were correspondingly larger; it was obvious that, for doubtless excellent reasons, the Ramans believed in sticking to a one-to-one scale. Norton wondered how they stored anything *really* big, if this was the case.

To increase their rate of coverage, the four explorers had now spread out through the crystal columns and were taking photographs as quickly as they could get their cameras focused on the fleeting images. This was an astonishing piece of luck, Norton told himself, though he felt that he had earned it; they could not possibly have made a better choice than this Illustrated Catalogue of Raman Artifacts. And yet, in another way, it could hardly have been more frustrating. There was nothing actually *here*, except impalpable patterns of light and darkness; these apparently solid objects did not really exist.

Even knowing this, more than once Norton felt an almost irresistible urge to laser his way into one of the pillars, so that he could have something material to take back to Earth. It was the same impulse, he told himself wryly, that would prompt a monkey to grab the reflection of a banana in a mirror.

He was photographing what seemed to be some kind of optical device when Calvert's shout started him running through the pillars.

'Skipper – Karl – Will – look at *this!*'

Joe was prone to sudden enthusiasms, but what he had found was enough to justify any amount of excitement.

Inside one of the two-metre columns was an elaborate harness, or uniform, obviously made for a vertically-standing creature, much taller than a man. A very narrow central metal band apparently surrounded the waist, thorax or some division unknown to terrestrial zoology. From this rose three slim columns, tapering outwards and ending in a perfectly circular belt, an impressive metre in diameter. Loops equally spaced along it could only be intended to go round upper limbs or arms. *Three* of them …

There were numerous pouches, buckles, bandoliers from which tools (or weapons?) protruded, pipes and electrical conductors, even small black boxes that would have looked perfectly at home in an electronics lab on Earth. The whole arrangement was almost as complex as a spacesuit, though it obviously provided only partial covering for the creature wearing it.

And was that creature a Raman? Norton asked himself. We'll probably never know; but it must have been intelligent – no mere animal could cope with all that sophisticated equipment.

'About two and a half metres high,' said Mercer thoughtfully, 'not counting the head – whatever *that* was like.'

'With three arms – and presumably three legs. The same plan as the Spiders, on a much more massive scale. Do you suppose that's a coincidence?'

'Probably not. We design robots in our own image; we might expect the Ramans to do the same.'

Joe Calvert, unusually subdued, was looking at the display with something like awe.

'Do you suppose they know we're here?' he half-whispered

'I doubt it,' said Mercer. 'We've not even reached their threshold of consciousness – though the Hermians certainly had a good try.'

They were still standing there, unable to drag themselves away, when Pieter called from the Hub, his voice full of urgent concern.

'Skipper – you'd better get outside.'

'What is it – biots heading this way?'

'No – something much more serious. *The lights are going out.*'

43
Retreat

When he hastily emerged from the hole they had lasered, it seemed to Norton that the six suns of Rama were as brilliant as ever. Surely, he thought, Pieter must have made a mistake ... that's not like him at all ...

But Pieter had anticipated just this reaction.

'It happened so slowly,' he explained apologetically, 'that it was a long time before I noticed any difference. But there's no doubt about it – I've taken a meter reading. The light level's down forty per cent.'

Now, as his eyes readjusted themselves after the gloom of the glass temple, Norton could believe him. The long day of Rama was drawing to it close.

It was still as warm as ever, yet Norton felt himself shivering. He had known this sensation once before, during a beautiful summer day on Earth. There had been an inexplicable weakening of light as if darkness was falling from the air, or the sun had lost its strength – though there was not a cloud in the sky. Then he remembered; a partial eclipse was in progress.

'This is it,' he said grimly. 'We're going home. Leave all the equipment behind – we won't need it again.'

Now, he hoped, one piece of planning was about to prove its worth. He had selected London for this raid because no other town was so close to a stairway; the foot of Beta was only four kilometers away.

They set off at the steady, loping trot which was the most

comfortable mode of travelling at half a gravity. Norton set a pace which, he estimated, would get them to the edge of the plain without exhaustion, and in the minimum of time. He was acutely aware of the eight kilometers they would still have to climb when they had reached Beta, but he would feel much safer when they had actually started the ascent.

The first tremor came when they had almost reached the stairway. It was very slight, and instinctively Norton turned towards the south, expecting to see another display of fireworks around the Horns. But Rama never seemed to repeat itself exactly; if there were any electrical discharges above those needle-sharp mountains, they were too faint to be seen.

'Bridge,' he called, 'did you notice that?'

'Yes, Skipper – very small shock. Could be another attitude change. We're watching the rate gyro – nothing yet. Just a minute! Positive reading! Can just detect it – less than a microradian per second, but holding.'

So Rama was beginning to turn, though with almost imperceptible slowness. Those earlier shocks might have been a false alarm – but this, surely, was the real thing.

'Rate increasing – five microrad. Hello, did you feel *that* shock?'

'We certainly did. Get all the ship's systems operational. We may have to leave in a hurry.'

'Do you expect an orbit change already? We're still a long way from perihelion.'

'I don't think Rama works by our textbooks. Nearly at Beta. We'll rest there for five minutes.'

Five minutes was utterly inadequate, yet it seemed an age. For there was now no doubt that the light was failing, and failing fast.

Though they were all equipped with flashlights, the thought of darkness here was now intolerable; they had grown so psychologically accustomed to the endless day that it was hard to remember the conditions under which they had first explored this world. They felt an overwhelming urge to escape – to get out into the light of the Sun, a kilometre away on the other side of these cylindrical walls.

'Hub Control!' called Norton. 'Is the searchlight operating? We may need it in a hurry.'

'Yes, Skipper. Here it comes.'

A reassuring spark of light started to shine eight kilometers above their heads. Even against the now fading day of Rama, it looked surprisingly feeble; but it had served them before, and would guide them once again if they needed it.

This, Norton was grimly aware, would be the longest and most nerve-wracking climb they had ever done. Whatever happened, it would be impossible to hurry; if they over-exerted themselves, they would simply collapse somewhere on that vertiginous slope, and would have to wait until their protesting muscles permitted them to continue. By this time, they must be one of the fittest crews that had ever carried out a space mission; but there were limits to what flesh and blood could do.

After an hour's steady plodding they had reached the fourth section of the stairway, about three kilometres from the plain. From now on, it would be much easier; gravity was already down to a third of Earth value. Although there had been minor shocks from time to time, no other unusual phenomena had occurred, and there was still plenty of light. They began to feel more optimistic, and even to wonder if they had left too soon. One thing was certain, however; there was no going back. They had all walked for the last time on the plain of Rama.

It was while they were taking a ten-minute rest on the fourth platform that Joe Calvert suddenly exclaimed:

'What's that noise, Skipper?'

'Noise! – I don't hear anything.'

'High-pitched whistle – dropping in frequency, you *must* hear it.'

'Your ears are younger than mine – oh, now I do.'

The whistle seemed to come from everywhere. Soon it was loud, even piercing, and falling swiftly in pitch. Then it suddenly stopped.

A few seconds later it came again, repeating the same sequence. It had all the mournful, compelling quality of a lighthouse siren sending out its warnings into the fog-shrouded night. There was a message here, and an urgent one. It was not designed for their ears, but they understood it. Then, as if to make doubly sure, it was reinforced by the lights themselves.

They dimmed almost to extinction, then started to flash. Brilliant beads, like ball lightning, raced along the six narrow valleys that had once illuminated this world. They moved from both Poles towards the Sea in a synchronized, hypnotic rhythm which could have only one meaning. 'To the Sea!' the lights were calling. 'To the Sea!' And the summons was hard to resist; there was not a man who did not feel a compulsion to turn back, and to seek oblivion in the water of Rama.

'Hub Control!' Norton called urgently. 'Can you see what's happening?'

The voice of Pieter came back to him; he sounded awed, and more than a little frightened.

'Yes, Skipper. I'm looking across at the Southern continent. There are still scores of biots over there – including some big ones. Cranes, Bulldozers – lots of Scavengers. And they're all rushing back to the Sea faster than I've ever seen them move before. There goes a Crane – right over the edge! Just like Jimmy, but going down a lot quicker ... it smashed to pieces when it hit ... and here come the Sharks – they're tearing into it ... ugh; it's not a pleasant sight ...

'Now I'm looking at the plain. Here's a Bulldozer that seems to have broken down ... it's going round and round in circles. Now a couple of Crabs are tearing into it, pulling it to pieces ... Skipper, I think you'd better get back right away.'

'Believe me,' Norton said with deep feeling, 'we're coming just as quickly as we can.'

Rama was battening down the hatches, like a ship preparing for a storm. That was Norton's overwhelming impression, though he could not have put it on a logical basis. He no longer felt completely rational; two compulsions were warring in his mind – the need to escape, and the desire to obey those bolts of lightning that still flashed across the sky, ordering him to join the biots in their march to the sea.

One more section of stairway – another ten-minute pause, to let the fatigue poisons drain from his muscles. Then on again – another two kilometres to go, but let's try not to think about that—

The maddening sequence of descending whistles abruptly ceased. At the same moment, the fireballs racing along the slots of the Straight Valleys stopped their seaward strobing; Rama's six linear suns were once more continuous bands of light.

But they were fading fast, and sometimes they flickered, as if tremendous jolts of energy were being drained from waning power sources. From time to time, there were slight tremors underfoot; the bridge reported that Rama was still swinging with imperceptible slowness, like a compass needle responding to a weak magnetic field. This was perhaps reassuring; it was when Rama *stopped* its swing that Norton would really begin to worry.

All the biots had gone, so Pieter reported. In the whole interior of Rama, the only movement was that of human beings, crawling with painful slowness up the curving face of the north dome.

Norton had long since overcome the vertigo he had felt on that first ascent, but now a new fear was beginning to creep into his mind. They were so vulnerable here, on this endless climb from plain to Hub. Suppose that, when it had completed its attitude change, Rama started to accelerate?

Presumably its thrust would be along the axis. If it was in the northward direction, that would be no problem; they would be held a little more firmly against the slope which they were ascending. But if it was towards the south, they might be swept off into space, to fall back eventually on the plain far below.

He tried to reassure himself with the thought that any possible acceleration would be very feeble. Dr Perera's calculations had been most convincing; Rama could not possibly accelerate at more than a fiftieth of a gravity, or the Cylindrical Sea would climb the southern cliff and flood an entire continent. But Perera had been in a comfortable study back on Earth, not with kilometres of overhanging metal apparently about to crash down upon his head. And perhaps Rama was designed for periodic flooding—

No, that was ridiculous. It was absurd to imagine that all these trillions of tons could suddenly start moving with sufficient acceleration to shake him loose. Nevertheless, for all the remainder of the ascent, Norton never let himself get far from the security of the handrail.

Lifetimes later, the stairway ended; only a few hundred metres of vertical, recessed ladder were left. It was no longer necessary to climb this section since one man at the Hub, hauling on a cable, could easily hoist another against the rapidly diminishing gravity. Even at the bottom of the ladder a man weighed less than five kilos; at the top, practically zero.

So Norton relaxed in the sling, grasping a rung from time to time to counter the feeble Coriolis force still trying to push him off the ladder. He almost forgot his knotted muscles, as he had his last view of Rama.

It was about as bright now as a full moon on Earth; the overall scene was perfectly clear, but he could no longer make out the finer details. The South Pole was now partially obscured by a glowing mist; only the peak of Big Horn protruded through it – a small, black dot, seen exactly head-on.

The carefully-mapped but still unknown continent beyond the Sea was the same apparently random patchwork that it had always been. It was too foreshortened, and too full of complex detail, to reward visual examination, and Norton scanned it only briefly.

He swept his eyes round the encircling band of the Sea, and noticed for the first time a regular pattern of disturbed water, as if waves were breaking over reefs set at geometrically precise intervals. Rama's manoeuvring was having some effect, but a very slight one. He was sure that Sergeant Barnes would have sailed forth happily under these conditions, had he asked her to cross the Sea in her lost *Resolution*.

New York, London, Paris, Moscow, Rome ... he said farewell to all the cities of the northern continent, and hoped the Ramans would forgive him for any damage he had done. Perhaps they would understand that it was all in the cause of science.

Then, suddenly, he was at the Hub, and eager hands reached out to grab him, and to hurry him through the airlocks. His overstrained legs and arms were trembling so uncontrollably that he was almost unable to help himself, and he was content to be handled like a half-paralysed invalid.

The sky of Rama contracted above him, as he descended into the central crater of the Hub. As the door of the inner airlock shut off the view for ever, he found himself thinking: 'How strange that night should be falling, now that Rama is closest to the sun!'

44
Space Drive

A hundred kilometres was an adequate safety margin, Norton had decided. Rama was now a huge black rectangle, exactly broadside-on, eclipsing the sun. He had used this opportunity to fly *Endeavour* completely into shadow, so that load could be taken off the ship's cooling systems and some overdue maintenance could be carried out. Rama's protective cone of darkness might disappear at any moment, and he intended to make as much use of it as he could.

Rama was still turning; it had now swung through almost fifteen degrees, and it was impossible to believe that some major orbit change was not imminent. On the United Planets, excitement had now reached a pitch of hysteria, but only a faint echo of this came to *Endeavour*. Physically and emotionally, her crew was exhausted; apart from a skeleton watch, everyone had slept for twelve hours after take-off from the North Polar Base. On doctor's orders, Norton himself had used electro-sedation; even so, he had dreamed that he was climbing an infinite stairway.

The second day back on ship, everything had almost returned to normal; the exploration of Rama already seemed part of another life. Norton started to deal with the accumulated office work and to make plans for the future; but he refused the requests for interviews that had somehow managed to insinuate themselves into the Survey and even SPACEGUARD radio circuits. There were no messages from Mercury, and the

UP General Assembly had adjourned its session, though it was ready to meet again at an hour's notice.

Norton was having his first good night's sleep, thirty hours after leaving Rama, when he was rudely shaken back to consciousness. He cursed groggily, opened a bleary eye at Karl Mercer – and then, like any good commander, was instantly wide awake.

'It's stopped turning?'

'Yes. Steady as a rock.'

'Let's go to the bridge.'

The whole ship was awake; even the simps knew that something was afoot, and made anxious, meeping noises until Sergeant McAndrews reassured them with swift hand-signals. Yet as Norton slipped into his chair and fastened the restraints round his waist, he wondered if this might be yet another false alarm.

Rama was now foreshortened into a stubby cylinder, and the searing rim of the sun had peeked over one edge. Norton jockeyed *Endeavour* gently back into the umbra of the artificial eclipse, and saw the pearly splendour of the corona reappear across a background of the brighter stars. There was one huge prominence, at least half a million kilometres high, that had climbed so far from the sun that its upper branches looked like a tree of crimson fire.

So now we have to wait, Norton told himself. The important thing is not to get bored, to be ready to react at a moment's notice, to keep all the instruments aligned and recording, no matter how long it takes ...

That was strange. The star field was shifting, almost as if he had actuated the Roll thrusters. But he had touched no controls, and if there had been any real movement, he would have sensed it at once.

'Skipper!' said Calvert urgently from the Nav position, 'we're rolling – look at the stars! *But I'm getting no instrument readings!*'

'Rate gyros operating?'

'Perfectly normal – I can see the zero jitter. But we're rolling several degrees a second!'

'That's impossible!'

'Of course it is – but look for yourself ...'

When all else failed, a man had to rely on eyeball instrumentation. Norton could not doubt that the star field was indeed slowly rotating – there went Sirius, across the rim of the port. Either the universe, in a reversion of pre-Copernican cosmology, had suddenly decided to revolve around *Endeavour*; or the stars were standing still, and the ship was turning.

The second explanation seemed rather more likely, yet it involved apparently insoluble paradoxes. If the ship was really turning at this rate, he would have *felt* it – literally by the seat of his pants, as the old saying went. And the gyros could not all have failed, simultaneously and independently.

Only one answer remained. Every atom of *Endeavour* must be in the grip of some force – and only a powerful gravitational field could produce this effect. At least, no other *known* field ...

Suddenly, the stars vanished. The blazing disc of the sun had emerged from behind the shield of Rama, and its glare had driven them from the sky.

'Can you get a radar reading? What's the Doppler?'

Norton was fully prepared to find that this too was inoperative, but he was wrong.

Rama was under way at last, accelerating at the modest rate of 0.015 gravities. Dr Perera, Norton told himself, would be pleased; he had predicted a maximum of 0.02. And *Endeavour* was somehow caught in its wake like a piece of flotsam, whirling round and round behind a speeding ship ...

Hour after hour, that acceleration held constant; Rama was falling away from *Endeavour* at steadily increasing speed. As its distance grew, the anomalous behaviour of the ship slowly ceased; the normal laws of inertia started to operate again. They could only guess at the energies in whose backlash they had been briefly caught, and Norton was thankful that he had stationed *Endeavour* at a safe distance before Rama had switched on its drive.

As to the nature of that drive, one thing was now certain, even though all else was mystery. There were no jets of gas, no beams of ions or plasma thrusting Rama into its new orbit. No one put it better than Sergeant-Professor Myron when he said, in shocked disbelief: 'There goes Newton's Third Law.'

It was Newton's Third law, however, upon which *Endeavour* had to depend the next day, when she used her very last reserves of propellent to bend her own orbit outwards from the sun. The change was slight, but it would increase her perihelion distance by ten million kilometres. That was the difference between running the ship's cooling system at ninety-five per cent capacity – and a certain fiery death.

When they had completed their own manoeuvre, Rama was two hundred thousand kilometres away, and difficult to see against the glare of the sun. But they could still obtain accurate radar measurements of its orbit; and the more they observed, the more puzzled they became.

They checked the figures over and over again, until there was no escaping from the unbelievable conclusion. It looked as if all the fears of the Hermians, the heroics of Rodrigo, and the rhetoric of the General Assembly, had been utterly in vain.

What a cosmic irony, said Norton as he looked at his final figures, if after a million years of safe guidance Rama's computers had made one trifling error – perhaps changing the sign of an equation from plus to minus.

Everyone had been so certain that Rama would lose speed, so that it could be captured by the sun's gravity and thus become a new planet of the solar system. It was doing just the opposite.

It was gaining speed – and in the worst possible direction.

Rama was falling ever more swiftly into the sun.

45
Phoenix

As the details of its new orbit became more and more clearly defined, it was hard to see how Rama could possibly escape disaster. Only a handful of comets had ever passed as close to the sun; at perihelion, it would be less than half a million kilometres above that inferno of fusing hydrogen. No solid material could withstand the temperature of such an approach; the tough alloy that comprised Rama's hull would start to melt at ten times that distance.

Endeavour had now passed its own perihelion, to everyone's relief, and was slowly increasing its distance from the sun. Rama was far ahead on its closer, swifter orbit, and already appeared well inside the outermost fringes of the corona. The ship would have a grandstand view of the drama's final stage.

Then, five million kilometres from the sun, and still accelerating, Rama started to spin its cocoon. Until now, it had been visible under the maximum power of *Endeavour*'s telescopes as a tiny bright bar; suddenly it began to scintillate, like a star seen through horizon mists. It almost seemed as if it was disintegrating; when he saw the image breaking up, Norton felt a poignant sense of grief at the loss of so much wonder. Then he realised that Rama was still there, but that it was surrounded by a shimmering haze.

And then it was gone. In its place was a brilliant, star-like object, showing no visible disc – as if Rama had suddenly contracted into a tiny ball.

It was some time before they realised what had happened. Rama had indeed disappeared: it was now surrounded by a perfectly reflecting sphere, about a hundred kilometres in diameter. All that they could now see was the reflection of the sun itself, on the curved portion that was closest to them. Behind this protective bubble, Rama was presumably safe from the solar inferno.

As the hours passed, the bubble changed its shape. The image of the sun became elongated, distorted. The sphere was turning into an ellipsoid, its long axis pointed in the direction of Rama's flight. It was then that the first anomalous reports started coming in from the robot observatories, which, for almost two hundred years, had been keeping a permanent watch on the sun.

Something was happening to the solar magnetic field, in the region around Rama. The million-kilometre-long lines of force that threaded the corona, and drove its wisps of fiercely ionized gas at speeds which sometimes defied even the crushing gravity of the sun, were shaping themselves around that glittering ellipsoid. Nothing was yet visible to the eye, but the orbiting instruments reported every change in magnetic flux and ultraviolet radiation.

And presently, even the eye could see the changes in the corona. A faintly-glowing tube or tunnel, a hundred thousand kilometres long, had appeared high in the outer atmosphere of the sun. It was slightly curved, bending along the orbit which Rama was tracing, and Rama itself – or the protective cocoon around it – was visible as a glittering head racing faster and faster down that ghostly tube through the corona.

For it was still gaining speed; now it was moving at more than two thousand kilometres a second, and there was no question of it ever remaining a captive of the sun. Now, at last, the Raman strategy was obvious; they had come so close to the sun merely to tap its energy at the source, and to speed themselves even faster on the way to their ultimate unknown goal ...

And presently it seemed that they were tapping more than

energy. No one could ever be certain of this, because the nearest observing instruments were thirty million kilometres away, but there were definite indications that matter was flowing from the sun *into Rama itself*, as if it was replacing the leakages and losses of ten thousand centuries in space.

Faster and faster Rama swept around the sun moving now more swiftly than any object that had ever travelled through the solar system. In less than two hours, its direction of motion had swung through more than ninety degrees, and it had given a final, almost contemptuous proof of its total lack of interest in all the worlds whose peace of mind it had so rudely disturbed.

It was dropping out of the Ecliptic, down into the southern sky, far below the plane in which all the planets move. Though that, surely, could not be its ultimate goal, it was aimed squarely at the Greater Magellanic Cloud, and the lonely gulfs beyond the Milky Way.

46
Interlude

'Come in,' said Commander Norton absentmindedly at the quiet knock on his door.

'Some news for you, Bill. I wanted to give it first, before the crew gets into the act. And anyway, it's my department.'

Norton still seemed far away. He was lying with his hands clasped under his head, eyes half shut, cabin light low – not really drowsing, but lost in some reverie or private dream.

He blinked once or twice, and was suddenly back in his body.

'Sorry Laura – I don't understand. What's it all about?'

'Don't say you've forgotten!'

'Stop teasing, you wretched woman. I've had a few things on my mind recently.'

Surgeon-Commander Ernst slid a captive chair across in its slots and sat down beside him.

'Though interplanetary crises come and go, the wheels of Martian bureaucracy grind steadily away. But I suppose Rama helped. Good thing you didn't have to get permission from the Hermians as well.'

Light was dawning.

'Oh – Port Lowell has issued the permit!'

'Better than that – it's already being acted on.' Laura glanced at the slip of paper in her hand. 'Immediate,' she read. 'Probably right now, your new son is being conceived. Congratulations.'

'Thank you. I hope he hasn't minded the wait.'

Like every astronaut, Norton had been sterilized when he entered the service; for a man who would spend years in space, radiation-induced mutation was not a risk – it was a certainty. The spermatozoon that had just delivered its cargo of genes on Mars, two hundred million kilometres away, had been frozen for thirty years, awaiting its moment of destiny.

Norton wondered if he would be home in time for the birth. He had earned rest, relaxation – such normal family life as an astronaut could ever know. Now that the mission was essentially over, he was beginning to unwind, and to think once more about his own future, and that of both his families. Yes, it would be good to be home for a while, and to make up for lost time – in many ways ...

'This visit,' protested Laura rather feebly, 'was purely in a professional capacity.'

'After all these years,' replied Norton, 'we know each other better than that. Anyway, you're off duty now.'

'*Now* what are you thinking?' demanded Surgeon-Commander Ernst, very much later. 'You're not becoming sentimental, I hope.'

'Not about us. About Rama. I'm beginning to miss it.'

'Thanks very much for the compliment.'

Norton tightened his arms around her. One of the nicest things about weightlessness, he often thought, was that you could really hold someone all night, without cutting off the circulation. There were those who claimed that love at one gee was so ponderous that they could no longer enjoy it.

'It's a well-known fact, Laura, than men, unlike women, have *two*-track minds. But seriously – well, *more* seriously – I do feel a sense of loss.'

'I can understand that.'

'Don't be so clinical; that's not the only reason. Oh, never mind.' He gave up. It was not easy to explain, even to himself.

He had succeeded beyond all reasonable expectation; what his men had discovered in Rama would keep scientists busy for decades. And, above all, he had done it without a single casualty.

But he had also failed. One might speculate endlessly, but the nature and the purpose of the Ramans was still utterly unkown. They had used the solar system as a refueling stop – as a booster station – call it what you will, and had then spurned it completely, on their way to more important business. They would probably never even know that the human race existed; such monumental indifference was worse than any deliberate insult.

When Norton had glimpsed Rama for the last time, a tiny star hurtling outwards beyond Venus, he knew that part of his life was over. He was only fifty-five, but he felt he had left his youth down there on the curving plain, among mysteries and wonders now receding inexorably beyond the reach of man. Whatever honours and achievements the future brought him, for the rest of his life he would be haunted by a sense of anticlimax, and the knowledge of opportunities missed.

So he told himself; but even then, he should have known better.

And on far-off Earth, Dr Carlisle Perera had as yet told no one how he had woken from a restless sleep with the message from his subconscious still echoing in his brain:

The Ramans do everything in threes.

ABOUT THE AUTHOR

ARTHUR C. CLARKE was born in Minehead in 1917. During the Second World War he served as an RAF radar instructor, rising to the rank of Flight-Lieutenant. After the war he won a B.Sc. in physics and mathematics with first class honours from King's College, London. One of the most respected of all science fiction writers, he also won the Kalinga Prize, the Aviation Space-Writers' Prize and the Westinghouse Science Writing Prize. He also shared an Oscar nomination with Stanley Kubrick for the screenplay of *2001: A Space Odyssey*, which was based on his story 'The Sentinel'. He lived in Sri Lanka from 1956 until his death in 2008.

ABOUT GOLLANCZ

Gollancz is the oldest SF publishing imprint in the world. Since being founded in 1927 Gollancz has continued to publish a focused selection of bestselling and award-winning authors. The front-list includes **Ben Aaronovitch**, **Joe Abercrombie**, **Charlaine Harris**, **Joanne Harris**, **Joe Hill**, **Alastair Reynolds**, **Patrick Rothfuss**, **Nalini Singh** and **Brandon Sanderson**.

As one of the largest Science Fiction and Fantasy imprints in the UK it is no surprise we have one of the most extensive backlists in the world. Find high-quality SF on Gateway written by such authors as **Philip K. Dick**, **Ursula Le Guin**, **Connie Willis**, **Sir Arthur C. Clarke**, **Pat Cadigan**, **Michael Moorcock** and **George R.R. Martin**.

We also have a strand of publishing in translation, which includes French, Polish and Russian authors. Gollancz is home to more award-winning authors than any other imprint, with names including **Aliette de Bodard**, **M. John Harrison**, **Paul McAuley**, **Sarah Pinborough**, **Pierre Pevel**, **Justina Robson** and many more.

The SF Gateway
More than 3,000 classic, rare and previously out-of-print SF novels at your fingertips.
www.sfgateway.com

The Gollancz Blog
Bringing you news from our worlds to yours. Stories, interviews, articles and exclusive extracts just for you!
www.gollancz.co.uk

GOLLANCZ
LONDON